BEST
GAY EROTICA
OF THE YEAR

VOLUME THREE

BEST
GAY EROTICA
OF THE YEAR
VOLUME THREE

BEST
GAY EROTICA
OF THE YEAR

VOLUME THREE

Edited by
ROB ROSEN

CLEiS
PRESS

Copyright © 2017 by Rob Rosen.

All rights reserved. Except for brief passages quoted in newspaper, magazine, radio, television or online reviews, no part of this book may be reproduced in any form or by any means, electronic or mechanical, including photocopying, recording, or information storage or retrieval system, without permission in writing from the Publisher.

Published in the United States by Cleis Press, an imprint of Start Midnight, LLC, 101 Hudson St, Suite 3705, Jersey City, NJ 07302.

Printed in the United States.
Cover design: Scott Idleman/Blink
Cover photograph: iStock
Text design: Frank Wiedemann
First Edition.
10 9 8 7 6 5 4 3 2 1

Trade paper ISBN: 978-1-62778-220-3
E-book ISBN: 978-1-62778-221-0

For Kenny, forever and always

CONTENTS

INTRODUCTION

Nerdy particle-physicists and hunky actors, nasty private detectives and even nastier stranded motorists, thieves, alien emissaries, horny songwriters, hornier husbands and fathers, bartenders and models, and ancient vampires . . . these are the men who fill the ensuing pages to the brim with stories both tender and rough, touching and tantalizing. Whether it's one-night stands or sensual encounters between longtime lovers, twosomes, threeways, some ways you'll probably never see, um, *coming*, the stories that follow will surely surprise and entertain you as only a *Best Gay Erotica* collection can.

Rhidian Brenig Jones temptingly starts us off with "Shame the Devil," a stunningly told coming-out story of friends who become lovers. T. R. Verten follows with the tale of two closeted Hollywood stars who steal a moment in a bathroom stall, while the paparazzi waits just outside, in "Red Carpet Jitters." In "Collider," M. McFerren introduces us to two college buddies and erstwhile lovers who reconnect via a phone call that finally brings to light their past relationship. Noted erotica writer Landon Dixon offers up a blackmailing private dick in "Hard Case," while Richard Michaels gives us "Whiteout," which reinforces the notion that helping out a stranded stranger can sometimes lead to dire, unexpected consequences. Jonathan Asche gives us the haunting tale of "The Last Time I Saw Him"; I present a late-night hookup in "Love on the Rocks"; Richard May delivers an epic vampire story in "Hemoglobin"; and Michael Roberts wonderfully finishes us off with "Conference Call," a phone-sex yarn with a hilarious twist. On the soon-to-be sticky pages in between, you'll find fabulous accounts of deep-space aliens, frat boys and college studs, ghosts, cowboys, and classical musicians, just to name a few.

With settings as diverse as bars and bathrooms, deserts and alien worlds, frat houses and dorm rooms, and countries both near and far, the stories within are, as always, of the highest literary quality. In short, this is why we deservedly call this anthology *Best Gay Erotica of the Year, Volume 3*.

Because twice might be nice, but three times is the charm, baby!

Enjoy and happy reading.

Rob Rosen
San Francisco

SHAME THE DEVIL

Rhidian Brenig Jones

"James?"

At the far end of the table we were all sitting at, Katie's boyfriend was bending a beer mat into quarters. Hands have always done it for me, and his were as well shaped as the rest of him, strong and tan, edged with dark hair. I watched him reduce the mat to confetti, and visualized those long fingers gripping my cock, others moving in my ass as he lowered his head to suck. I wondered whether his stubble would prickle; I've had guys who've rasped my balls, cheese-grater chins leaving my perineum abraded and sore. Happy days.

"James!"

I dragged my attention back to her. "What?"

"I was just saying, have you heard about the cameras in hotel rooms?"

"What cameras in hotel rooms?"

"You know when the smoking ban came in and they installed smoke detectors? Well, some of them have hidden cameras. They film people having sex and sell the films on the Dark Web."

"Not on eBay? Damn."

"I'm serious. This girl in the gym was telling us. It happened to someone she knew. She was a Jehovah's Witness."

This lovely non sequitur merited a respectful silence. We all reached for our drinks.

She looked around. "It's true. And *I'll* never have sex in a hotel room again, I can tell you."

Patrick snorted. "Hear that, pal?"

A muscle jumped in Adam's jaw. He shoved his chair back and eyebrows rose all around as he crossed the bar to the gents. I'd have followed him—no harm in copping a look—but Katie clutched my arm.

She whispered, "James, d'you think Adam's acting strange?"

"No more than usual." This wasn't entirely true. Adam wasn't keen on small talk and was generally a serious kind of guy, which was a thoughtful, reserved contrast to his ditzy girlfriend, but he had seemed a bit out of it all night. Katie's latest bollocks had obviously pissed him off, but he should've been used to it by then; Katie, it should be noted, frequently talked bollocks. She'd been panicking a few weeks earlier because she'd swallowed the thing about charging a phone in a microwave. The sharpest knife in the drawer she was not, but she'd provided a sturdy little shoulder to cry on after I'd walked in on my ex buried to the root in an electrician. I liked her a lot.

She leaned toward me. "Can I ask you something?"

"Sure."

"D'you think I'm sexy? Be honest."

As if there was the remotest chance. "You're asking the wrong man, Kate."

"No, I'm not. Tell me. Am I sexy?"

"Well, you've got knockout tits."

"James, *please.*"

I couldn't judge through straight eyes, but I was versed in the theory, if not the practice. Katie wasn't sexy. She had a soft, milkmaid prettiness, and I think that was the problem. There was a naïveté about her, a kittenish innocence that evoked a desire to protect, not fuck. Naomi, three seats along, older, skinny, and flat chested, nevertheless gave off a kind of indefinable hotness that even I recognized. "Of course you are. Why d'you ask?"

She'd colored, hectic blotches spreading from cleavage to cheeks. "Adam doesn't want to have sex. We haven't for ages."

Sex with Adam. My insides constricted at the thought of him on his knees, cock in hand, shuffling forward to slide it in. I cleared my throat.

"He doesn't even want to cuddle. I mean, that's not normal, is it? We've only been together since March."

A mismatch of such epic proportions, I was surprised they'd lasted three hours, let alone three months. Airheadedness might seem cute at first, but it quickly loses its charm, no matter the E-cup attractions on offer. Adam was, what, twenty-eight, twenty-nine, and reluctant to fuck? Usually, only one reason: someone else was dropping her drawers behind the scene. I recalled the pain of finding Stephen with his dick in the sparky, and girded metaphorical loins for the misery to come. "Have you talked to him about it?"

"Not really."

"No, in other words."

"I've been thinking he might be stressed or something, you know how hard he works. I thought he could do with some vitamins, but then I saw this thing on the Internet and—"

"Forget the Internet. Just talk to him."

"I can't."

"You're going to have to."

"*I can't*. I'd die if he said he didn't fancy me. James, d'you think I'm fat?"

"Fuck's sake, Kate." I flicked a glance at Adam, who had since returned from the loo. He was watching us expressionlessly and I stared until he dropped his eyes. "Does he make you happy?"

The hesitation said it all. "Of course he does."

"You don't seem all that sure."

She fiddled with her bracelet, turning it on her wrist, link by link. "I really like him. He's so bloody gorgeous, isn't he? I thought this one would last."

"It won't if it's not meant to. You asked me to be honest? Okay. I don't think you're right for each other. But if you don't want to kick him into touch, you'll have to talk. Only thing you can do."

"Would you?"

"No point. I caught Stephen bang to rights. Not much to be said after that."

It took her a few seconds to process this. "No, I mean would you talk to Adam? Ask him what's wrong?"

"Are you fucking *nuts*?"

"You're going to Ben's stag do, aren't you? You could ask him then. If he's had a few drinks he might . . . well, you know. You could bring it up, kind of . . . *casually*."

Twelve guys out on the lash, followed by a strip club.

The only things going to be brought up Friday were eleven straight dicks and one yawn.

"Not a chance, Katie. Forget it."

She looked at me sulkily. "I'd have done it for you."

"Well, I won't do it for you. Your relationship; you sort it."

There he was, along with the rest of the guys, watching as they roared and hooted under the jaundiced eyes of the bouncers. A bony chick with hair extensions and immobile breasts gyrated on the stage, sliding purple talons into her G-string and bending double to wobble her ass at the punters. The tackiness of it, the synthetic pouts and lip-licks bored me, and my thoughts drifted to a performance I'd once watched in Berlin. Orange tan, waxed pecs, and glow-white porcelain veneers maybe, but you can't fake an erection. He'd sauntered between the tables, oiled torso gleaming, laughing and jerking his hips away when some desperate fool made a grab for his dick.

Miss Bambi had finally shed the G-string and was giving its crotch an ecstatic lick. Probably dry as a nun's fanny. I checked my watch and wondered how much more of this farce I could take.

"Right, boys, get 'em in." Ben fumbled at the kitty glass and blinked as he knocked it over.

"I'll get them." Adam gathered up a handful of notes and shoved them into his pocket.

I stood as well. Anything to relieve the tedium. And be near him.

We squeezed into a relatively quiet corner at the bar, and he waved tenners at the harassed bar staff.

"Probably not your thing," he remarked.

Well, well, it speaks. "Might be, if dicks were involved."

He leaned back on one elbow and I sneaked a sideways glance as we watched a policewoman in fishnets clamp a handcuff on a giggling Japanese guy's wrist. It struck me again that the brooding Heathcliff thing was all well and good, but if Adam ever managed a genuine smile I'd elevate him from *pretty damn hot, all things considered* and file him under *drop-dead fucking gorgeous*. Nothing to do with his orientation—I have no tragic fantasies about seducing straight guys—or even his looks, although I've always been powerfully attracted to dark-haired men. Cool eyed, slender, tight bodied, charged with the irresistible magnetism of bone-deep masculinity. But there was something more, something indefinable about him that resonated in me. I'd been trying to figure it out since Kate introduced him to us, but it was beyond definition. Perhaps de Montaigne had it right and it was no more than he was he and I was I.

"Not my thing, either," he said.

"Sorry?"

"Strippers. Not my thing."

"No?"

"No."

Because I wasn't sure how to respond to this, I asked, "Katie get off okay at the airport?" The hens were being turned loose on Newcastle: party central of the northeast.

"Yeah, seems like."

"Great girl. I was in a bad place once, and she was there for me."

"So she said."

Rattled by his offhand tone, I added pointedly, "She's a good friend."

"If that's all she is to you."

Where had that come from? Christ, was he *jealous*? Did he have some kind of weird dog in the manger thing going on? He'd finally managed to collar a barmaid, and I was left staring at the back of his beautiful, perplexing head.

A week later, I was trying to decide whether to watch porn or lurk in Grindr, when my phone rang. I ignored it. I'd trained my friends to follow up with an immediate text if anyone was bleeding from the eyes or facing a murder charge.

Laptop on my chest, I lay back on the couch and dipped into a few of my favorite sites. I loved watching a man masturbate, whether onscreen or on my bed. I got off on watching the tension build in the abdomen, the quivering and clench of muscles, thighs falling open to give a glimpse of a sweet hole. A man on his own, lost in what he was doing to himself. Doing it as only he could. There was a particular French guy with a fractional turn in one eye which, god knows why, I found deeply sexy. Suddenly, my phone chimed a text and my burgeoning erection wilted.

The message was brief:

James, could you give me a ring tomorrow.
Thanks,
Adam

By midday, I reckoned I'd put it off long enough. I stuck my head round the door and told my PA he could go to lunch.

He played his tongue over the stud in his lip. "Want anything from Prêt?"

"I'm okay, thanks."

"You should eat, James. Got to keep that big body fed."

"I might be eating out."

"*Ooh.* Anywhere nice? Anyone nice? Do I know him?"

Despite the piercings, Mohawk, and eyeliner, Paul was a brilliant PA. I just wished sometimes that his interest in my nonexistent love life was less avid. I shut the door on his smirk and picked up my phone. I didn't sit—always make a difficult call standing, I say. One thing I was sure of: I had no intention of helping to broker a split between Katie and the Dark Lord. If I had to soothe a bruised heart, my hands would need to be squeaky clean.

"Adam? It's James."

"James." There was silence, and then, "Thanks for calling."

"No problem."

I waited out another pause and scowled at a pigeon hunched on the window ledge outside. It had some horrible red growth on its toes. I bloody hate pigeons.

"I was wondering . . . fancy a drink tonight? I, uh, need a word."

I hesitated for a couple of seconds, wariness feebly battling curiosity, but who was I kidding? "I suppose it's about Katie."

"It is, yes, but could we leave it till later?"

"Okay. Where?"

"I was thinking the Ferryman? About eight?"

"Right."

"James, I'd appreciate it if you didn't mention this to her."

"Any particular reason why not?"

"It's complicated."

Bet it isn't. I agreed to keep my disloyal mouth shut, and smacked the window at the pigeon.

I got there on the dot of eight; call me old-fashioned, but I like to be punctual. Monday night, and customers were sparse. He was standing at the bar, one foot on the rail, staring into his beer. I walked slowly, the better to appreciate the stretch of his shoulders and the inviting curve of his ass. He might have been a cheating sod, but he was a hot cheating sod, and I had to fight the temptation to blow on the back of his neck.

"All right?" I leaned an elbow on the bar. He smelled good. Always did. Clean. Be good to have him clean in my bed, to breathe in the underlying musk of a warm male body caught in bush and crack, to feel his asshole opening to the probe of my tongue.

"James. Thanks for coming. Pint?"

"Stella. Thanks." I nodded at the Red Dragon draped on the wall, an unheard-of English tribute to Wales, who'd reached the semifinals of Euro 16. England had been kicked out after playing like donkeys. "How d'you think it's going to go?"

"Don't know. Wales might do it. They've got Bale."

"You think he's up to Ronaldo?"

"Doubtful." He smiled, and I felt a quick slithering in my guts. "Want to go outside?"

The pub stood on the site of an old ferryman's hut. A penny to cross until a Victorian bridge put him out of business. I followed him to a table at the farthest end of the beer garden, and we looked out over the river to the far bank, where a gang of kids was messing around in the pebbly shallows. It was safe enough when the water was low.

He asked abruptly, "Have you heard of homeopathic crystals?" He ran a finger up the condensation on his glass. "Crystals that have homeopathic traces in their structure so you get the power of homeopathy harnessed to the energy of the crystal. Goes without saying they're a con. Some psychologist set up a site. Huge success, till he revealed it was just an experiment to test the sucker potential of the public. He refunded their money, but people refused to believe they didn't exist. There's this theory out there that big pharma's conspired to keep them off the market."

He sipped his pint, and I guessed what was coming next.

"Katie's been trying to get hold of them for me."

"She means well. She reckons you're stressed. Work or something."

"Work doesn't stress me." He steepled his fingers over his mouth and blew slowly through them. "I'm going to finish with her, James."

Spy cameras and magic crystals. Poor Katie. "Another girl?"

"No." He must have seen the scepticism on my face. "There isn't."

"Okay. But why tell me? I'd have thought she should hear it first."

As if I hadn't spoken, he said, "Kate's a lovely person. Kind, warm. Pretty. I like her, but we're not right. I thought we could be, but we aren't. We see the world differently. We want different things. Need different things. I wanted . . . I tried to make it work."

We sat in silence, until I asked again, "Why are you telling me this?"

He turned to face me full on. There are only two reasons adult men lock eyes, and I didn't think he was preparing to throw a punch. Understanding dawned, and my heart began to bang against my chest wall.

"Don't you know?" he asked.

I shook my head and kept shaking it, as if this would stop the pieces falling into place. I'd thought the stares, the way I'd often caught him looking at me, were down to jealousy, or the simple fact that he didn't like me. I'm not usually slow in picking up signals, but it had never entered my head.

"I'm not sure what you're saying here." I jerked my hand away as he reached for it.

"What I'm saying is, I've been trying to be something I'm not. Someone as gorgeous as Katie, and I have to think about dicks to get hard? One particular dick. Doesn't that tell you something?"

The treacherous bolt of excitement I felt was instantly superseded by an image of my friend, eyes huge with hurt. I got to my feet so fast that my chair fell over. "It tells me there's a shit storm coming and you're trying to get me involved." I stabbed a finger. "Don't. You and Katie, it's nothing to do with me. You do what you have to, but *keep me out of it.*"

I kicked the chair away and left him to his beer.

I'd been prepared for tears, and they came, but not as many as I expected. I kissed Katie's boiling cheek and pulled her to lie against me. She blew into a fresh tissue. "I'm glad in a way," she said, mopping. "You know, that it's not my fault. Can't compete with a man, can I?"

"Probably not."

"I just wish . . . I mean, if he is, he is, but . . . oh, James."

"He's a tosser. Forget him. Come on, drown your sorrows."

"This won't help," she said, poking an ice cube.

"Course it will. Numbs the pain." I'd been half-cut on Grey Goose for a week after Stephen.

"I'll be over the limit."

"Stay, then."

"Can I sleep with you?"

We often shared a bed. I liked sleeping with her. I found her comforting, as I used to find a little woolly dinosaur I'd had when I was four. I still had him, worn and grubby, tucked away at the top of the wardrobe.

"He said he was going to come out. D'you think he will? Oh god, can you imagine what they'll say? I hope people won't be horrible to him. Matthew told me he always thought Adam was a bender."

"Matthew's a homophobic twat who talks through his ass. He didn't suspect fuck. Christ, *I* didn't, and I should know. If Adam's decided to come out, that's up to him. Things'll be said, that's for sure. No way round that."

"You could help him."

"Katie, Katie . . . " I rested my chin on her sweet, silly, generous head.

"You could help him with . . . well, with gay stuff."

"What gay stuff? He can find out everything he needs on the net, probably already has. He'll work things out soon enough, once he meets someone. Come on. Bed."

I couldn't sleep, though, partly because Katie was a little furnace, pouring out heat in one of my T-shirts. I'd already shifted as far from her as I could without falling out on my butt, so I hung on to the edge of the mattress and stared into the dark, replaying the scene at the Ferryman. Adam wanted me, and the fuck of it was, I wanted him, and not just for sex, although the thought of him writhing under me made my cock tighten. He intrigued me. I was curious about what lay behind the detachment, the impenetrable facade. What might be released once he faced the world as an out gay man? He'd be himself, but what was *himself*? And why had he felt compelled to live a lie? Had he fucked men on the quiet? Must have done.

Katie gave a snuffling snore and reached out an arm. I got out of bed and slid back in on the other side. I slapped the pillow over and buried my face in cool cotton. Sleep took a long time coming.

A week later, Ben married his Marie.

"Another good man down," Patrick said. He sniffed suspiciously at his drink. "What is this anyhow?"

"Elderflower champagne. Marie's father makes it."

"Tastes like piss."

"And you'd know that how?"

"Fuck off."

I grinned and leaned back on the hideously uncomfortable gilt chair, watching him scan the crowded marquee. "God's sake, ask her to dance or something."

"I don't know . . . you reckon she's still got a thing for *Queer as Folk*? Shit, sorry James."

As to Adam, who was also old friends with Ben, hence his presence there, I hadn't encountered him again until I'd joined the rest of the groomsmen at the church that morning. My focus should have been on Ben, who'd been sick with nerves—it had taken some straight talking and a hip flask to calm him down—but half my attention had been on Adam, heart-stoppingly handsome in morning dress. We'd exchanged a few stilted words, and that had been that. Neither of us had known what to say, and it had been easier to spend the rest of the day avoiding each other.

"I don't know if I can," said Patrick.

"Can what?"

"Katie. Really punching above my weight there."

"Come on. Be a big boy, a brave soldier. Just bloody ask her. Rescue her from the aunties."

He stared at me, then took a decisive breath. "Right."

The first piano notes, signalling the beginning of the end of the party, had brought most people to their aching feet. Patrick murmured in Katie's ear, and she nodded, smiling, and continued to smile as he took her hand and they threaded their way on to the minuscule dance floor. Katie and Patrick. Yes, that was more like it.

Someone tapped my shoulder. I looked up. "Dance?" Adam asked.

I'd be exaggerating if I said that a shock wave felled the wedding guests, but there were a few glares from the Colonel Blimps and a few dowager hands clutched pearls. I winked at the wolf whistles from our corner as Adam rested his hands on my biceps and I held his waist. We kept our lower bodies from touching, and even when the crush of dancers threatened to force us together, we maintained a crucial couple of inches between zipper and crotch. We were both trembling.

"Haven't seen you here before," I said, dry mouthed. "Come here often?"

He drew his head back so he could see my face. "This feels so weird."

"You'll get used to it." I moved closer. "You smell nice. What is it?"

"John Varvatos."

A few heads away, Katie caught my eye. We exchanged a glance, asking and answering, until she nodded and gave me a tremulous smile. I was glad of it. I didn't want to lose her friendship, but Adam was dancing with me. Adam, in my arms. It might have felt strange to him, but it was blowing my mind.

"James?" The brush of his beard on my ear thrilled through me.

"*Mmm?*"

"Come back to my flat later?"

I raised my arms and linked my hands at the back of his neck. "Sure."

I'd been as nervous as hell the first time I ventured into a guy's bed, scared that he wouldn't want me when push came to shove, and even more scared that he would. Staring out of the window at the harbor lights, Adam seemed as strung up as I'd been.

"Hey." I patted the couch. He sat alongside me, ramrod straight. "We don't have to do anything you don't want. We don't have to do anything at all. There's no rush."

He threw me a look. "I'm thirty-one, James, and I've never even kissed a man."

Fuuuck. "Want to tell me?"

"I'm a Catholic . . . well, I was. Don't know about now. You're brought up in the faith, you're taught that homosexuality is wrong. Sinful. I've heard that my whole life. What do they call it . . . *intrinsically disordered.*"

It occurred to me to point out that there was nothing

more intrinsically disordered than priests raping altar boys, but I kept it to myself. "So, what's changed?"

"Ben getting married. Did you see him? So bloody happy, like a dog with two dicks. I was watching him with Marie, and something clicked in my head. Why was it okay for him but not for me? Why could I never be with someone I love, never love in the way that's right for me?"

"Adam, it's—"

"I'll tell you what's sinful. Lying is sinful. Leading a person on, like I was leading Katie on. Don't get me wrong; I like her, I like women. Christ knows I've fucked enough. But that's all it's ever been. Fucking. Physical release. I've never felt any connection. Most of the time, I'd have preferred a wank." He hunched forward and clasped his hands between his knees. "I did try to make it good for them, though. I wasn't that cold-blooded."

"And was it?"

"I know where a woman's on-switch is, and that always helps. What about you? Have you ever . . . ?"

I shook my head. "Thoroughbred. So, Katie . . . ?"

"She's so sweet. Yeah, I know she can be off the wall, but . . . she made no demands. I thought that we could make a go of it, that I could make myself . . . that I could *will* myself straight. What a fucking idiot. And then I realized she was beginning to have feelings for me. I was stringing her along, and it was cruel. I'd see her with you, and the only thing in my head was how much I wanted you." He extended his fingers, then curled them back into fists. "I had to be honest with her. With myself. She was lovely about it, when I told her."

"You didn't tell her you had the hots for me, did you?"

"Rub salt in the wound? Do me a favor."

"And do you? Have the hots for me?"

"I'd have thought that's obvious."

My erection was upright against my belly. Hunched forward as he was, his groin was hidden, but even under the shadow of scruff, I could see the pulse tripping crazily in his throat. "So what d'you think we should do about it?" I asked.

"Depends on how you feel about me."

"High time you found out, isn't it?"

Dotting kisses on his eyelids, his nose, the angle of his jaw, I slipped each button free and pushed his shirt off his shoulders. Dark hair hazed his pecs, glossy and fine. I mouthed each nipple, then trailed my lips to his armpit. Cupping his face, I kissed his musk into him, loving the first, tentative touch of his tongue in my mouth, his feverish response when kissing became hard and deep and wet. His zipper was pushed out in a curve, tricky to maneuver over the bulge, but I finally got it open. One quick tug, and I followed his trousers and boxers to the floor.

Not the nine-inch monster beloved of porn writers, but a beautiful prick, nonetheless. Thick and smooth, angled high from a dense bush, the foreskin almost fully retracted by the force of his arousal. His glans was wet, and when I gripped the base of his shaft, a glimmering bead formed and trickled from the slit. His balls cupped in my palm, I extended my forefinger to his asshole and took his cock in, all the way in to the back of my throat. He began to pant as his hands tightened in my hair. He wouldn't last, couldn't last, not the way he was thrusting. I felt the warning swell and drew back to mouth his glans, sucking, sucking, my finger gently massaging his hole. He gave a groan, and a shuddering spasm twisted his body. His semen was thick, almost jellied, and I kept it in my mouth, letting it bathe his cock for a while before I let it slip down my throat.

"I'm sorry, James, I couldn't . . . "

"Hey." I got to my feet and pulled him against me, pressing my erection against the hard bone of his hip. "Told you. No rush."

"Adam?"

"*Ngh?*"

"I don't want to come like this."

He seemed reluctant to stop. Understandable: there's nothing as good as having a cock in your mouth, unless it's having one in your ass, and he'd been starved for years.

He licked up the side of my shaft and flickered his tongue over the tie. "How, then?"

"Fucking."

"You want to fuck me?" he asked.

I hauled him up to lie on my chest. He was erect again, his shaft solid and warm next to mine. I ran my hands down satiny skin to his buttocks, separating them and squeezing them together. I hadn't caught sight of his asshole by this point, but my future plans involved more than looking at it. "Other way round."

He bit gently at the curve of my shoulder. "Okay."

"Need my wallet."

"I've got some. In the drawer." He hid his face against my neck, shy suddenly. "And lube. I knew I'd need them at some point. I wanted to practice. I bought a dildo from Prowler when I was in London."

I nearly came at the thought. How would he have done it? On his back, arm curled under his thigh to stick it in?

Squatting to lower himself? On all fours, reaching back? Lube glistening as he positioned its head. The push and the gradual distension. The enormous stretch of his hole around the plastic girth of the toy. Adam. Fucking himself.

"But I couldn't do it. I don't know what I was doing wrong, but it hurt like buggery. Gave it up as a bad job."

Amused, I kissed him. "Buggery doesn't hurt, not if it's done right. I won't hurt you, Adam."

He felt around in the drawer, and brought out a pack of condoms and a bottle of Liquid Silk. I rolled one on him as he knelt between my thighs. His fingers were shaking as he smeared the lube. I closed my eyes and waited, but when things seemed to have ground to a halt, I raised my head from the pillow.

The mask was gone, all guard down. Here was the truth of him, revealed in the hard, bright stare. My hole clenched with wanting and he let out a breathy whine of lust.

Just his middle finger in, in to the palm, exploring unfamiliar terrain. A slither out and the slide in of a second finger, circling the pliant walls, not sure, testing, pressing . . .

"Is that it? There?"

"Not so hard. Just kind of . . . stroke it. Stroke around. Oh, fuck . . . "

You know what it's like. The feel of a man's fingers playing with your prostate. Waves of pleasure radiating through your cock, your balls, and the dark glory of sensation in your ass. For me, it's as if I'm being held on the brink of an orgasm that never comes. Until it does.

"Adam."

He was careful and slow, pushing, pausing, and pushing in a little farther. I hadn't been fucked since Stephen, and despite the copious grease, I felt the burn. I loved the brief pain. I loved the responsiveness of my body. I loved that it was Adam's cock penetrating me.

"What does it feel like?" His mouth was against my neck, each breath a hitching gasp.

"Full. Pressure inside. Adam, oh *Christ,* fuck me!"

Hips rocking, he began to thrust in earnest. I felt the thud on my buttocks and that luscious, pulling drag, the intensity of pleasure you get when a cock withdraws, as if your guts are going to follow it out. Faster, in and out, each slick glide, each wet slap of his balls getting me closer. I wrapped my legs around his waist, and the press of his belly gave me the exquisite friction I needed to come. I lifted my face for his kiss. He took my cry into his mouth and hammered his prick into me, over and over, until his rhythm faltered and broke. He stilled, then gave one last helpless thrust, all control gone. I heard his savage groan of release and felt the tiny spurts of his climax juddering high in my bowel. As he collapsed, his full weight hot and sweating on me, I wondered if maybe, one day, we wouldn't need to dam the flood. He pulled out, holding the condom in place like the fast learner he was, and once he'd tied it off, I took him in my arms. Maybe, one day, we wouldn't need protection. No need for latex when two men commit. When they make love.

"Work tomorrow, James. Better get some sleep."

"Call in sick. Spend the day with me."

"Can't do that. Lucky sod, we're not all self-employed."

"Swot."

"After work, though?" He picked a damp strand of hair off my temple.

"Don't know. I'll have to think about it."

He drew back, and I grinned at his expression of crestfallen dismay. "Right, I've thought about it. D'you like Chinese?"

"Yes. Prefer Thai, though."

"Thai it is. Okay, sex bomb, turn over."

He wriggled his ass into my lap and tucked my arm around his chest. I held his hand and spooned into him more closely, pressing a kiss to the top of his spine. He murmured something into the pillow and I shut my eyes. I slept well that night.

RED CARPET JITTERS

T. R. Verten

Actors are famously known for their weird rituals. Everyone in the industry knows this. Hell, the only people who are worse are pro athletes, who'll wear the same jersey if they're on a winning streak, or forgo sexual release of any kind, or eat only blueberry waffles for days on end. Whatever the fuck works, right?

You learn those rituals in high school plays. Words you won't say, good luck charms you'll wear. Pacing clockwise around the stage, crossing yourself. Praying. And then it gets drilled into you even harder in college or drama school, in summer stock and community theater. Or maybe your first crappy TV role, where you barely make the cut for Equity pay scale, a couple of pilots that go nowhere, Indie films, stage work. Perhaps Off -Broadway, maybe the West End, if you're lucky. And then the big one hits. A romantic comedy, usually, or, if you're really fortunate, a franchise gig where the studio supplies you with everything you need for superstardom: a trainer, a nutritionist, a publicist, and, to keep up the whole charade, a girlfriend-slash-beard. For the photo ops, of course.

Vincent has spent the last half hour talking up his *girlfriend* to the press line, while she poses for pictures in an off-white Zac Posen that's slit halfway up her thigh. She's not who he would have picked for himself—too tall, too pouty, and he's grossed out by her trashy tattoos. But she's in on the whole charade. Dating her publicist, in fact.

Her name is Maritza. They've been "dating" for eight months now, with a few prime photo ops, just as you'd expect. Holding hands in front of Moon Juice, antiquing in Silverlake. It's all carefully orchestrated and planned: an anonymous tip texted to one of their sympathetic sources from a burner phone. Untraceable. TMZ runs with it the next day, although not as the lead story. He's famous, all right, but not enough to be the lead. It's okay; he can live with that.

Famously private couple spotted canoodling on the beach. Is a proposal in their future?

Anyway, they've made it through the press line, and Vincent has a dumb actor ritual he has to complete before they head into the screening. Or rather, his costar does; he's just along for the ride. But he acts super casual, stops the whole junket and turns to his handler—and how did that happen, he finds himself wondering, that he has a bodyguard to watch his every move, and protect him from the insane groupies that come with being a teen idol—and says, with a jerk of his head as they pass the bathroom, "Hey, Frank, just gonna duck in here real quick, okay?"

Frank, a solid wall of muscle and beer fat clad in discreet black that does nothing to minimize his bulk, grunts his assent. Doesn't bat an eyelash when Joe follows him in there. *We're actors*, he repeats to himself. *We're known for stupid ritual.* In the limo, during the premiere, or later, in between interviews for the press junket. A mantra they chant or a line they have to snort before they can take the scrutiny that lies ahead. Joe is such an actor, just as Vincent is an actor, so if they tell their handlers or bodyguards or agents that they have to go to the bathroom together, any one of those people is going to assume it's simply another quirk that comes from being famous.

"Back in a second," Joe chirps to his own people. They smile and nod, which is what everyone does for the talent. Let everyone think it's drugs. A bump of something crystalline and sweet to carry them into the screening room, to bolster their spirits as they watch themselves projected to twenty times the usual size. It's less sensational than the truth, which is that they both have a ritual that has to be performed before press lines, and red carpets, and conventions, and photo shoots.

The bathroom has two stalls, one handicapped and roomier, with a sink built into the wall. It's all generic, standard-issue, white porcelain. The larger stall is the one that Joe will choose, with a movement born of long practice. They've worked together on three projects in the last half decade. Before every screening, they end up like this.

Even if he had any reservations about what they're about to do, Joe's ass in his tailored trousers is enticement enough. He flashes Vincent his flashbulb-bright smile—which, along with the perfect ass, is definitely what made him a star—and says, through downward-cast lashes, "Hey."

"Hey, yourself," Vincent says as Joe triple-checks that

the bathroom door is locked, then makes his way into the handicapped stall. He locks that door, too. Vincent swallows heavily. With their bodies this close together, he can smell Joe's spicy cologne, traces of the peppermint gum he was chewing in the limo, the fresh dry-cleaner scent wafting up from his tuxedo. He reaches out, squeezes Joe's arm, which is rock solid in his jacket. The muscles are less defined than they were during filming, now that he's not working out three hours a day, but they're still heavy in his grasp.

"You seem tense," Joe says, with a tone of reassurance. "It's just press; it'll be fine. Nothing you haven't done a thousand times before."

"Listen to you," Vincent grumbles, "you're, like, so Zen about the whole thing these days."

"I figured out how to relax." Joe grins, and, fuck, it's blinding. White teeth that manage to look real on him, not the Hollywood overbleached grin. Perfect blue eyes framed with sooty eyelashes. Dark hair and a beard to match. Handsome as hell in his suit, which is Tom Ford and classic in every sense of the word. Slim cut through the legs and managing to hug every line of his ass and the powerful thighs below it. That ass has been on countless movie posters, been the framing shot for establishing his character in at least two movies. Funny, Vincent thinks, how the public eats it up without question. Nobody wonders why his ass is his selling point, or thinks that he's anything less than perfect.

He looks fantastic in the suit. He's a mass of contradictions—all hard muscle and gracious charm—and maybe, if they ever got any time alone together that didn't end up with his cock down Joe's throat, he might have more time to ruminate on why Joe keeps coming back for it. Or why they both do.

But they have no time to call their own. That's the thing about being famous: your time no longer belongs to yourself. Anything you've got, you're stealing from the paying public. The press junket needs you, the fans need to consume you. There's the lineup, and the red carpet, and the conventions, and the photo ops. Rituals make these things bearable.

So they're quick. They've got to be that, and discreet as they can be. Joe wastes no time, palming Vincent through his black pants. Feeling him up under his button-down, dipping his fingers beneath his waistband. He kisses him once, square on the lips, with only the tiniest flash of tongue to keep it from being wholly chaste. That's another piece of this *thing* they have, whatever the fuck it is. It's all out in the open, done behind the backs of publicists and agents, masses of screeching fans. So Vincent can't walk the press line with swollen lips, certainly not with burns from Joe's finely trimmed beard on his jaw or face. So they kiss only the one time, firm and sweet. After applying a final, aching suck to Vincent's lower lip, Joe starts his preshow ritual and sinks to his knees.

"Fuck," Vincent breathes, because they must've done this two dozen times, and it will never cease to be amazing. Every time, every goddamn time, Joe will look up at Vincent and lick his fucking fat, pink, cock-sucking lips, and say something sweet or flirtatious, like, "What have we here? Oh, *hello*," as he undoes Vincent's flies, untucks his cock, and pulls him out. America's sweetheart, no fucking joke.

"Hey," Joe repeats, and unlike before, this time he's

not speaking to Vincent but to his dick, directly. He flicks his finger against the tip, and the motion startles Vincent's cock into paying attention. Vincent, for his part, has a lump thick in his throat as he stares vacantly off in any direction but where he wants to look.

There's the bathroom, which of course looks like any other moderately nice bathroom. There's a tiled corner, an industrial-sized toilet-paper roll, a railing that he's holding on to for dear life. He chances a glance down, and, okay, *bad idea*—what with Joe nuzzling his nose against Vincent's rapidly hardening dick and all.

If that's bad, then it's about to get much, much worse.

"Look, I know you don't buy into the self-help shit that I do," Joe says, "but you need some way to take your mind off things. God, I hate it when you're tense." The words are leveled right in front of his nose. Vincent's eyes squint. His vision blurs as Joe adjusts his hand so that Vincent's dick is pointing right at his face. He drops a tiny, sucking kiss onto the tip, trails a finger down the side. Vincent's cock twitches from the touch. Fuck, he's hard. He's hard, and in a minute there're going to be reporters asking him about their working relationship, about staying in shape, what did he eat, how was working with the trainer, did he go Method, how does his *girlfriend* feel about it—heaps upon heaps of bullshit—

"*Shh*," Joe says, those puffy pink lips mouthing around the crown of his cock. "Stop thinking."

"*Ung*," is the sound that makes its way out of Vincent's mouth, which is not attractive in the slightest. Joe chuckles and cups Vincent's balls with one big hand. Even his fingernails are perfect, buffed to a high sheen. His palms are smooth, their movements deliberate and assured.

He rubs the side of his face along Vincent's cock. His beard prickles the sensitive skin there. There's another large twitch from Vincent's dick. Joe smiles, chasing the pink burn with a finger. "Stop." Joe pops the head of the other actor's dick into his mouth, sucks once, hard, pops it out again. He grins, impishly, does it again. "Stop thinking."

"You're making it pretty difficult," Vincent manages to choke out. All the blood in his body has converged right at the tip of his dick, which tingles from the attention Joe has already paid it. The head is a bright, angry red. Fluid leads from the slit, which Joe slides the pad of his thumb over, digging very slightly into the hole, stretching it out. Another little sucking kiss; his tongue flicks out and laps softly at the head.

"God," Vincent can't help but say, "that's such a good look on you." And it is, too. What a fucking center-fold that would make. Cover of *Variety, People,* and all the rest. Forget boring staged pictures with picnics and puppies; this is the real deal.

Joe whines, pleased, and pops the warm head into his mouth again. He licks at the underside with his tongue, and then pulls back, thumb resting just below the crown. He sits back on his haunches expectantly. His color's up, his tuxedo still immaculate. How long that's gonna last, though—especially once Joe's hand flies up to wrap around Vincent's shaft, stroking firmly—is anyone's guess.

And then he focuses, gets to work. "Jesus," Vincent manages as Joe takes him in. That little wrinkle between his brows, so earnest, as he works his mouth down, slow, an inch at a time, until his pretty mouth is distended with the width of it. It's hot in there, burning like a furnace.

Vincent glances around the bathroom again: same tile, same fixtures, same floor.

A spit-filled gurgle comes from below his waist. He can't look. He can't.

Fuck it. He looks down, gasps at what he sees. Joe is down there on his knees like he's in heaven. Wide-mouthed, lips stretched as open as they can go, fucking his own throat on Vincent's dick. There's an obscene sound coming from down by Vincent's balls—wetness and cock and spit. The noise reverberates off the cold tile that surrounds them. It's so loud that, for a brief, horrible second, he's sure that everyone in that press line can hear.

With a drawn-out moan, Joe seals his lips over the head and returns to sucking the first few inches, down just below the crown. Vincent's dick is so hard, in the tight wet heat of Joe's reddened mouth. It's too much, all at once, and he shoves a knuckle in his mouth to muffle his own cry.

So this is Joe's thing, a thing he is wickedly talented at, and a thing that Vincent should really say no to when they're out in public like this. There's press right beyond that bathroom door. Fake girlfriends, former costars, producers past and potential. They might know he's not into women because, hell, a fair number of other A-listers prefer men themselves, but they expect high-profile talent to have some discretion: to fuck at home, in one of their million-dollar mansions on Malibu Drive, on vacation, if they must. Not for one of *People* magazine's sexiest men alive (Joe, 2014, the year he starred in a war biopic that showed his serious side and got himself a Best Supporting Actor nod) to be sucking off one of the 30-Under-30.

He should say no when Joe uses his hand to speed

things along, and say no when he takes Vincent's dick in one grip and smacks it across his lips, his cheek. But he's not a saint. He can take sixty more seconds of suction, tops. And then? "I need to come," he says, because it's making his stomach cramp something horrible. It's urgent.

"*Hmm*," Joe says, from beneath lowered eyelashes. He peeks up bashfully at Vincent and then smiles his movie-star smile. He gazes at Vincent with that fucking look, the one he pulls out in his photo shoots: teenaged girls hang the glossies up in their lockers; their boyfriends beat off to the grainy online scans of the same.

He tips his face up and purrs, "Go for it."

"I can't," Vincent protests, because they have to be photographed again at the end of the night, be seen getting into a limo and out at a restaurant, and then there's the stupid fucking after-party. He can't risk getting jizz on Joe's suit. It'll show up in the pictures, even once it's been wiped off, a barely noticeable shimmer on the collar, a shoulder.

Joe blinks, shows his lashes, and leans back a little farther. He parts his lips, licks them for good measure. "Sure you can," he says, huskily and demanding. "Come on, baby, I need it. Come on my face." *America's fucking sweetheart*, Vincent thinks, *and all he ever wants is a cock in his mouth and a hot load on his face.*

"Oh shit," Vincent gasps, working his hand on himself, trying to keep his eyes from screwing shut. He wants to see that first hot arc hit Joe's face—the second higher on his forehead than where he's aiming. Another, hot and painful, that nearly burns with the force of his ejaculation. His come hits the angle of Joe's perfect cheekbone, dripping down into his beard.

"Fuck, it just keeps coming," says Joe, and leans in to milk the final spurt out. He dips his nose like he's going to wipe it off on Vincent's pant leg, but pulls back at the last second. Probably for the best. There's a screening room waiting just outside these two swinging doors. Directors to appease, flesh to press. Once they leave this toilet stall and this bathroom, Vincent is going to have to smile and put his hand on the small of Maritza's back and guide her through the throng. He'll keep his arm around her until the theater lights dim, the two of them looking every inch the cozy couple.

From his position on the floor, Joe's breathing is ragged. His cheeks glow pink from beneath his beard and under their sheen of come. Vincent hates for him to wipe it off. He'd like to take his sweet time. Nuzzle that prickly beard, lick all traces of it away himself. But the ritual is over, and the screening will be starting soon. They have to get back and play their parts. He's the good boyfriend, the sure bet. Joe the all-American boyfriend every girl dreams about. God, if they could see him now.

"Help me up?" he asks, a second later, and Vincent pulls him to stand. Joe hovers over him, and even though he's covered in Vincent's come, Vincent's still the one who feels small. They make their way over to the little sink.

"Thanks," Vincent manages, after he's scrubbed at himself with some paper towels. Joe has rinsed his face and dried it, rather badly, under the hand dryer. Their publicists will be furious at their rumpled appearances. People think Vincent's a bad boy, so he can get away with it, but there will be gossip tomorrow about how disheveled he looks. Fuck it, let TMZ go to town.

"Thank you," Joe says, and flashes that bright smile

again. They're both buoyed by the experience. It's better than any drug could be, although it's so much less forgivable. "Now, let's go face this press line."

Yeah, there are rituals that actors have—Vincent shrugs to himself as the restroom door swings shut behind them—and they don't make all that much sense.

COLLIDER

M. McFerren

There's more paperwork involved in smashing together subatomic particles than one might imagine.

That's not to say it isn't exciting. Sent directly from my commencement ceremony in California to an internship with CERN in Switzerland, I'd be an idiot not to recognize how rare it is to be doing something so extraordinary at the meager age of twenty-four. It's a dream. Geneva is beautiful. I work alongside some of the strangest and most extraordinary minds in particle physics. On certain quiet nights, when those of us still here after hours are usually heads bowed over our desks, I like to wander through the halls and listen. Immense databases calculate without the rest that their human companions occasionally require. Colliders and synchrotrons, even powered down, seem to emit a resonant hum that carries through the floors.

This is the place where antimatter was made, the Higgs boson verified, and the World Wide Web created. This is where the core of the universe and everything within it could—potentially, theoretically—be quantified into comprehensible knowledge. Even the work required to make the tools needed for study overflows into new discoveries, in a constant outpouring of creation.

It's thrilling.

It's challenging.

And sometimes it's downright tedious.

When I return to my desk, there's a pile of paperwork that needs to be done before morning. Committing logs of check-ins and activities from paper to computer. Data entry, glorified. I refill my cup of coffee from the thermos, and consider California. Nine hours behind, though I hardly have to calculate it anymore. Every time I check the clock, I check his, too, and I know at this hour—when I first give thought to crashing out on one of the break-room couches—he's eating a late dinner at his desk.

It wouldn't hurt to check in, I justify to myself. See what Menlo Park is working on. It's research, right? Peer collaboration. It's definitely not because I'm putting off my work. It's definitely not because the loneliness at these hours is damn near painful.

I slide my phone closer and cradle it to my ear, speed-dialing SLAC. Press three. Press one. Press one again. Biting my lip, I rock back in my chair and listen to the ring. He catches me mid-sip, the coffee scalding as I choke on it.

"What's up, Raj." He always drags the *a* in my name out a little long.

"Hey, Chris. Hope I'm not interrupting."

There's a snort on the line, and I can hear his smile. "Of course you are. I just sat down with dinner, and I said to myself as soon as I picked up the fork, 'He's gonna call right now.' Like clockwork, man."

"We've got our own supersymmetry." I grin. "What's on the menu tonight?"

"Cup of dried ramen from my desk drawer, with a side of hot water from the kitchen, and a soupçon of hot sauce."

"Glad that the dietary standard of Stanford hasn't slipped in my absence."

Chris's laugh is as low and satisfying a sound as any of our machines warming to life. He's an accelerator in human form, a loop from which I can't seem to scatter free, cycling my personal particles with speeding pulses. We shared a room at university, then shared classes and a viciously competitive friendship. We shared more, too, on certain riotous nights of booze-soaked theorizing, as passion confused into colliding kisses and groping hands. I try not to think about it now, but I could no more do that than rewrite the fundamental laws of physics. He slurps up a noodle and I shiver.

"How's CERN?" he asks.

I resolutely avoid looking toward the stack of logs awaiting my attention. "Busy," I tell him, shoving a hand back through wiry black curls to clear them from my face, eyes on the ceiling. "There's a whole herd of Austrian engineers visiting."

"Is that the proper term for a group of engineers? A herd?"

"Maybe just for a group of Austrians."

"An assemblage of Austrians."

"An entourage of engineers."

When Chris laughs again, I lean back and rest my free hand on my chest. My heart beneath beats a swift staccato, clicking faster under my fingers. I spread them, but the attempt to rub that unwieldy muscle to peace again only stirs it more, spiraling pleasure tightly upward from the pit of my stomach. If I close my eyes, I can see him slouching with his pot noodles, deliberately dweeby glasses weighted heavy on his nose and a swath of pale hair peeking from under his ubiquitous black hoodie. He has the greenest eyes I've ever seen, though when we were shoved tightly together in one of our twin-size beds, they were nearly black.

Christ, a year apart and he's still going to be the goddamn death of me.

We talk about our work—the real work we're doing, not the administrative necessities. Our days off are spent meeting with scientists and professors, grinding out equations and fomenting theory in tiny offices piled high with reams of data. He's writing out algorithms that could have resonance on the study of dark matter. I tell him about doing mechanical checks on stretches of the Large Hadron Collider with an entourage of engineers. My cheeks heat when he laughs again.

We were a good fit, he and I, when our hyperspecific interests merged together rather than antagonized. His muttering, pensive focus on mathematics—fingers pressed to his eyes as his hand moved, as if possessed—harmonized in strange synchronicity with my fixation on tangible creations, turning his equations into physical tools. We were a good fit the first time we rutted hard against the other's hip and sucked marks against the other's skin, watching as they blossomed red where our lips had been. I was the dark matter to his light, our symmetry balanced, despite our differences. He preferred to lie against my back, his golden-haired chest pressed against my spine and his cock seeking entry in stiff stabs against my ass. I was all too willing to bend for him and push out my hips, and kiss him clumsily across my shoulder as he worked himself inside me and stretched me open until I ached.

Chris scrapes the empty Styrofoam cup with his fork and sets it back to the desk. I hear all this.

"I thought I might come visit soon," I say, like it's a passing thought.

"Why?"

We've never talked about it, never addressed at any point those many nights together, but it's all I can do not to call him an asshole and hang up from sheer reflex. We've danced around it for the whole time we were in school together. We dance around it now. Neither of us has ever acknowledged those nights once the moment ended. It's late. I'm exhausted and over-caffeinated, jittery nerves prickling. I'm behind on work that has to be done by morning, and rather than doing it, I'm on the phone with him again, talking about nothing, just to hear his voice.

I'm tired in a way that goes beyond the need for sleep. If he won't say it, I will.

"Don't you ever think about it?" The words tilt higher than intended, teetering on almost pathetic desperation. If he says no, then I won't ask again. Maybe I'll answer the flirty philosophical texts I get from the cute guy who works at the Prévessin site. Maybe I've just wasted years of my life on someone who saw me as an easy fling.

"Think about what?"

I know he groks what I'm saying, and my jaw aches, clenched tight. I want to groan. Instead, I answer tactfully. "University. The time we spent there. Together."

His pause lingers long, and I nearly crumple to my desk as he finally says, "Sometimes. Yeah."

"I think about it." It's still too vague. Scientists don't work in anything but absolute specificity, and that's what Chris is looking for now, too stubborn and too rational for anything less. Screw it. We've already started the accelerator, and there's nothing but wasted energy if we shut it down now. "I think about you," I tell him. "I think about us. Up late in the dorm, arguing and . . . "

"Raj," he sighs.

"And I wonder if coming here instead of staying there was a terrible idea."

He huffs a note of disbelief. "That's absurd."

"I know. I know it is, objectively. Rationally." I laugh, helpless. It sounds weak. "But I—"

He interrupts, taking the words out of my mouth. "I miss you."

Said words throw our yearslong acceleration into such a stop that my head spins. My lungs expand so quickly with the force of shock that my ribs feel as if they'll crack from the sudden collision. We've finally connected, the energy of thought and voice smashing together in a big bang of our own making, superseding our history of clumsy bodies crashing together, fueled by alcohol and youthful lust. He's missed me. He misses me. My throat clicks dry when I swallow.

"I miss you, too, man."

We both exhale in unison, connected despite the distance. For a few moments, we say nothing, giving ourselves pause enough that time starts to move again after its jump. I swear I can hear his heart through the phone. I swear I can feel his lips moving across my ear when he finally speaks again.

"I think about it," Chris says. "I think about all of it. All the studying we should have been doing, and how glad I am we didn't. How your hair always stood up wild when we were done, and you'd stumble around the room in just a sweatshirt, trying to find your clothes."

"I was a mess."

"You were beautiful." The energy in his voice creates a vacuum that pulls my pulse into a void. I'm dizzy. His words are bright moonlight through the starless dark behind my eyes. "I always wanted to tell you to stay. I almost did, every time. I think about that, too, every chance I had and every chance I didn't take. Why didn't you say anything?"

"Why didn't you?"

"I didn't know what to say. 'Hey, I know we're friends who like to fuck, but maybe you should stay and cuddle this time'? 'Hey, even though we have to face each other in class tomorrow, I really want to try a thousand different words to tell you how I feel about you'? I didn't know how you'd react. I'd rather have you as a friend than have you be weirded out by me," he says. I know he's smiling. I remember all too well how that crooked grin felt pressed against my bare shoulder as we lay together in the few quiet moments postcoitus, spent and sweaty and breathless. "I didn't even know if you liked dudes."

"I let you fuck me in the ass," I remind him, with a laugh, brows raising. "Frequently."

"Which probably should have been a sign, I guess." There's a pluck of tension that vibrates in Chris's voice, not at all displeased. When he sighs, it's a heavy sound, unlike the ones before. The strings that connect our particles sync in movement, and I slip my hand between my legs and squeeze gently to ease the rising ache there. "So, what do we do with this new data, Mr. CERN?"

"I wish I knew," I say, and I bite my bottom lip to hold back a sound that threatens to spill forth when I press my palm a little harder against my cock. "Same thing we always do when we discover something unexpected. Analyze it. Study it. Dissect and define it." I pause, and after a moment, add, "We repeat the experiment, to see if we reach the same conclusion."

The quick jerk of his breath confesses; his quiet moan declares. We're both alone, together, sparked by the newly stoked flames of memory that have never stopped simmering. Chris says my name as if it were an apology, and all I can do is laugh and lower my zipper.

"Are we really doing this?"

"I am." He laughs. "It's going to be weird if you're not, too."

I slide my hand beneath my underwear's elastic waistband. Dark curls spread coarse between my fingers as I squeeze the base of my cock, huffing a breath of pleasure. We really are doing this. Me and Chris, Chris and me, the way it should have been from the start. The way it was once, and might be again.

"You know you're the reason I didn't date anyone during college, right?" I said.

Chris snorts, a grin lightening his words. His chair creaks through the phone. "I just thought you were especially dedicated to studying. And being better than me in all our classes."

"That too."

"Are you doing it?"

"Yeah," I sigh, shoulders pressing back to the chair

as I slump comfortably, phone cradled in one hand, dick squeezed in the other. "Are you?"

He hums agreement, and I let myself imagine him as I have so many lonely late nights before. His stomach muscles defined with quivering pleasure, his erection proudly stiff and his expression soft. He likes to play with the head, thumbing across the slit and tugging in firm, slow squeezes from base to tip.

"I wish you were here," he says. I wish I were there, too. I would go to my knees for him, right under his desk. I would sit across his lap and let him slip stiffly inside me. I would kiss him.

God, I would kiss him. Suckling his bottom lip between my own and teasing it with teeth. Twining our tongues together until we couldn't breathe. Pressing my mouth to the corner of his, to his lightly freckled cheeks, to his brow, smelling his hair and rubbing my cheek against it.

"I'm here," I tell him, hips arching to push my cock into the tunnel of my hand. "I'm with you. I've always been with you."

"Sap." We laugh. We moan. We touch ourselves, and over the near-silent electric static of the phone line, over the quickening rush of our own pulse in our ears, we strain to hear the sounds of skin sliding against skin, clicking transmissions to the other as evidence of our desire.

Our excitation builds, creating heat beneath my skin and light behind my eyes. Fundamental forces of nature pull our gasps to matching rhythm. I stroke myself, fingers tightening beneath the corona of my cock, spreading along the thick veins that line it. I touch myself, but I think of him, his pupils wide and inky black, lips pink and parted, damp. It's not my own dick I'm touching, it's his, thick and hot and curved where mine is straight, circumcised where mine is not. It never looked imposing, but when he was inside me, I felt so full that there was hardly room in my body for breath. He always pressed his hand against my heart when he pulled me back against him. He always slowed when I set my hand to his hip, and sped when I dug my nails against his thigh.

Electricity ripples beneath my skin, tightening my muscles in spasms of broken symmetry that move my sounds, my masturbation, my heartbeat out of time with his. His moans are superconductive, prisms of sound formed from little whimpers and long groans, from him saying my name and peppering it with quiet curses. My balls tighten, twitching up against my body. My cock slicks with precome, beading copiously beneath my fingers as I pull my cock to the sound of my best friend's voice.

I want to taste him again. Suck him again. Lick him clean and watch as he bows his blond head over my cock and takes me between his lips in turn. I don't know what I'm telling him anymore, particles of sentences bursting forth half-formed on every breath. Fragments of feeling and fondness filter through declarations of desire. I want him inside me. On top of me. I want him to hold my face in his hands and make me feel in his kiss how much he's missed me.

And just as quickly as this formed, we disrupt. Sudden resistance slams hard through my body, and I whimper at the force of it, come spilling in thick ribbons of white against my fingers. I stroke myself through it and listen as he groans, long and low, imagining his shoulders hunched and his lashes fluttering against his cheeks. But unlike every other time we've shared a climax, I don't wonder how quickly he wants me gone. I don't want to be gone. I want to be here, right here, or there, or anywhere so long as he's there with me. He must hear my thoughts broadcast loud, because he laughs.

"I want you to stay, Raj," he whispers. "I should have told you a long time ago."

As our new formation cools and takes solid form, I think of the Higgs field. We've found our own equivalent quantum space, confirmed as reality by the other's presence in it. Call it friendship. Call it love. Whatever its name, it's ours, made manifest by the discovery of our matching particle.

"I think you're my boson, Chris."

"That shouldn't be so romantic." He laughs, a sleepy chuckle that sounds like a warm blanket feels on a cold day. "The Chris boson. I can't wait to see the proofs in that paper."

"You'll just find ways to poke holes in it," I say. "Egomaniac." I stretch to gather napkins from my desk to wipe my hand clean. "So, should I try to come?"

"I thought you just did."

"Shut up." I smile. "Should I come to California," I ask again, "or are we going to console ourselves with the idea of manifold realities, and accept that in some other iterative universe, we're already fucking each other senseless and telling each other embarrassing confessions about all the times we could have ended up apart?"

"You make string theory sound so desolate. Isn't it enough to know we're the other's cosmological constant?"

"Not when you could be inside me."

"Fair point," Chris says. "Don't come." I draw a breath, a joke perched on my tongue, and he interrupts, amused. "And don't tell me it's too late for that because you just did. You're so predictable."

"You don't want me to visit?" I ask instead, brow creasing. He doesn't give me enough time to analyze this error in function before he speaks again, and soothes my heart with words that feel like his hand pressed against my chest.

"You've been here before," he says, and I feel the smile, "and I've always wanted to visit Switzerland."

HARD CASE

Landon Dixon

"No! Please! You're hurting me! Stop!"

I grabbed the guy tighter around the neck and hammered my cock even harder into his ass. He, just barely in his early twenties, was playing the victim of the anal reaming I was dishing out, and we were both loving it.

I twisted his puffy pink nipples with one hand, choking him with the other, ramming my huge cock back and forth into his hot, tight, sucking chute. We were both standing naked, me behind fucking his ass, while he arched back against me and screamed out the open office window, his taut little buttcheeks shuddering as I slammed my thighs against them over and over, faster and faster, harder and harder. Let's call it a down payment on the dirty case he'd delivered to this dirty PI, namely me.

"Please! Please!" he cried out.

I pleased him, pumping quick and deep and brutal.

Tears ran down his pretty, anguished face, his boyish body bouncing on the end of my churning, sheathed cock in his sweet ass. I twisted his tender nipples, bit into his slender neck, spanked his mounded bottom with my corded thighs, driving his anus with my thundering cock all the while.

I hadn't had a young dude in a while, and I was getting his fucking money's worth.

"Oh my god! No! Please!" he shrieked, tugging frantically on his own jutting pink cock to the banging beat of my pile driver that was drilling his ass.

"Yeah! Yeah!" I sneered in his tender pink ear before almost biting his delicious lobe clean off.

He grabbed on to the sides of the open window and wailed out into the street ten stories below. His hole was like a punk's mouth, only tighter and hotter and more fit for punishment. His ass walls sucked on my cock as I pounded into his bowels.

Then his slim young body spasmed out of control in my arms. "Ooh!" he shrieked up at the wide blue sky, semen shooting out of his hand-jacked cock before sailing out of the window.

I grunted and gripped his quivering shoulders and pistoned his butt, savagely sawing his chute until I quickly caught fire.

"Fuck! Yeah!" I bellowed in his burning ear, hard-riding his gyrating bum.

I bucked and blasted, my ramming cock blowing off steaming semen into the guy's petulant portal. Jet after jet of white-hot jack jolted my body and soul, my head reeling with incredible bliss. Hell, I just about bumped the coming kid right out the window with the force of my own blistering orgasm as I creamed his ass.

"Think I got the 'tools' for the job now?" I hissed,

my spent cock packed in rubber and sperm inside his ruptured ass.

Jamie bobbed his head up and down, gasping for breath.

I confirmed the terms of our agreement, rutting my cock around in the warm, lubed-up mess of his asshole. "I seduce and fuck your ex's new husband, get it on video, give it to you to get your revenge on your ex; meanwhile, you give me one thousand dollars. Now."

He nodded, and I eased my still-hard hammer out of his manhole and wiped off. He padded over to his pants and pulled out his wallet, spilling one grand out of his recent divorce settlement onto my desk.

The guy apparently still "loved" his ex, and he didn't want his ex loving anyone else.

I was the hardcase PI he'd hired for this hard case.

The ex-husband was named Tom Jordan, a tall, distinguished-looking, older gent with plenty of money and personality, and a willingness to use both. Jamie had been married to the guy for two years, until Tom had laid hungry eyes on young Evan Andrews as he cleaned his pool one day. After that, Jamie's relationship with his wealthy Daddy had gone down the drain.

Evan wasn't skimming leaves and cleaning filters anymore; he was living the high life of toy-boy ease in Tom's spacious mansion now, right at home in a May-October marriage, just like Jamie had once been. I spotted Evan exiting the mansion and hopping into his sports car. I followed behind in my beater as the kid zipped to the gym. It was early yet, the place mostly empty.

By the time he'd gone through his workout routine, I

was already waiting for him in the shower room, ready, willing, and able to pull off the seduction I was getting paid to perform.

I'd kept the white-tiled room empty, steamed it up nice and sexy, and water-gilded and soaped my muscled body even steamier and sexier. Evan strolled in totally naked and naïvely unaware, his body just as boyishly buff as Jamie's, though tanned copper. His cock dangled down low between his lithe legs, his brown eyes scoping out the back of my big body through the clouds of steam. My cock was jutting out eleven inches hard and heavy in front of me, facing the wall, a grim grin on my thick, sensuous lips.

"Good workout?" Evan asked, all friendly-like as he scooped up a bar of soap from a wire basket built into the tiled wall. He then began to rub it over his body before twisting a tap on with his other hand.

I let him get wet, soapy, and warm, then turned to the side and slyly replied, "The *best* kind of workout."

He looked at my grinning, chiseled face. His eyes trailed down my thick neck, over my rugged smooth chest and jutting nipples, down my six-pack stomach to my long, hard cock that strained slippery between my stroking fingers. The kid gulped and gaped.

I slid my left hand up onto my damp, shining chest and rubbed my mounded pecs and strummed my pointed nipples, pumping slow and sultry and soapy along the swollen length of my jutting erection. I then stepped back into profile and slipped my left hand right in behind me, caressing my hard, wet, thrust-out buttcheeks, worming a pair of slick, strong fingers into my hole as I sawed back and forth, screwing my face into a lusty look of ecstasy.

Evan swallowed harder, openly ogling my dripping,

jacked cock and the fingers plundering my ass. He dropped his arms to his sides, the bar of soap sliding free, his cock rising up all on its own in the humid atmosphere of the shower room.

"Can . . . c-can I take a tug?" he stammered, stepping closer to me on the water-splashed tiles.

I grinned even broader. What man could resist the pull of my perfectly huge cock? Straight men had even gone gay on me just to feel my enormous erection, first in their widened hands, then in their unhinged mouths, and finally in their stretched-beyond-all-sensation anuses.

I nodded at Evan and dropped my hand away, stepping closer to him, my cock bobbing in greeting. He took a quick glance around, then grabbed on to my wrist-thick shaft and squeezed and pumped.

I shuddered and groaned, like *his* touch was really something special. Through slitted eyes I watched his pretty face light up as he felt the heavy throb and smooth shifting skin of my python, his own cock flooding with the power and the passion.

He poled out to an impressive length himself, his cock quivering and straining. I gazed down as he swirled his slick hand up and down on my dong, stepping in even closer now.

I let the kid get well and truly hooked on my cock, his face beaming and his body gleaming, his hard-on surging. Then, as he pumped me harder and faster, I suddenly grabbed his neck and mashed my wet lips against his drooling mouth.

He jerked back like a fish caught on the line, but he couldn't get away from me, didn't want to get away. He relaxed, let his pouty lips slacken against my moving ones, his hand churning my cock again. I knew I could reel him all the way in at my leisure.

We kissed, Frenching in the steam under the twin sprays of hot water. Our tongues swept together and entwined, moist and eager. I roughly grasped Evan's boyish pecs, coning them up to his engorged, dripping nipples. I pinched and rolled the rubbery protuberances. He moaned into my mouth, his hand flying on my cock. I pumped my hips, helping him jack my joyous length.

When I pulled my tongue out of his mouth, he blinked his glazed eyes and murmured, "Can I . . . suck your cock?"

I kissed him hard, twisting his nipples. "Not here. In the locker room."

I took his hand and led him out of the dripping, clouded shower and into the brightly lit locker room. I had my pinhole camera already set up in the head-level grating of locker fifty, which was all the way in the back, secluded, as private as we could get.

I stopped at that locker, then swept young Evan into my arms and pressed our wet, hot bodies and mouths together, our hard cocks squishing. Everything was in profile for the camera to record.

Evan moaned, slipped out of my arms, and went down to his knees on the rough green carpet, his pretty mouth aimed at my rigid cock. He gripped it again, a look of wonder and lust in his eyes. Then he stuck out his pink tongue and rimmed my huge hood.

I buckled and groaned, half acting, half reacting. Evan flowered his moist, red lips over my cap and mouthed as much of my mammoth shaft as he could, maybe one-third of it. I grunted and bucked.

He got a tight, sucking rhythm going, enthusiastically

blowing my cock and juggling my big, hanging balls. I grabbed on to his soft, damp brown hair and pumped into his suctioning mouth. First I went easy and not too deep, then hard and deep as I could drill. Evan gagged and drooled and grinned. He rolled his wide, watering eyes up at me as I fucked the back of his bulging throat and stretched mouth, all well within camera range. Fucker was wide-angle. With me, it needed to be.

Evan rocked back onto his butt with one of my heavy thrusts, my cock springing out of his mouth. "Fuck me!" he gasped, gulping air and grabbing onto my cock.

"Sure," I growled.

He jumped onto the lacquered wooden bench that split the green aisle between the two rows of gray lockers in half. He went up on his hands and knees, sticking his cute little bum up in the air. I crowded in at the end of that section of bench, behind his ass, in front of the camera. I grabbed the waiting rubber out of the locker, lubed my cock, then pulled one of Evan's buttcheeks back, shoving my cap up against his asshole.

"Yes, fuck me!" he cried, gripping the edges of the bench. "Fuck my ass with your huge cock!"

I gritted my teeth and pulled back, then rammed my cap against his pucker, applying pressure. Slowly, exquisitely, I expanded the guy's ass-ring and burst my hood into his hole. I then let go of his trembling cheek and gripped his narrow waist and slammed forward, plunging my entire cock into his chute.

"Oh! God!" he shrieked in a strangled voice.

My tremendous erection surged into his ass, stretching and straining his walls like they'd never been stretched and strained before, until my balls banged up against his shivering cheeks and I was sheathed in the gripping tight, hot tube of his ass. I pumped, fucking Evan's ass with gusto.

He gulped and groaned, his thin body rocking to my banging beat, his ass-ring gaping like a mouth around my shunting meat. My knuckles burned white on his skin as I sawed the kid's chute with my cock to the searing point.

Evan managed to grab his flapping cock so he could jack. He stifled a yell and jumped even higher onto the bench, semen shooting out of his prick. I fucked his spasming ass with a snarling fury, then jerked and spewed, blasting white-hot bursts of come against the rubber and his bowels.

Everything, of course, was explicitly captured on camera.

My client Jamie liked what he saw. He was eager to download the dirty deed I'd committed with Evan at the gym onto his handheld so he could email it to his ex. Revenge had never been served up hotter.

Still, I put a crimp in the guy's plans by demanding more cash. "I think another grand should do it," I informed him. "You've got the money." I held up my camera. "And I've got the goods."

"But . . . but you said it would only cost a thousand! I . . . I paid you already! And you fucked me!" His adorable boy-face almost burst into tears. "And now . . . you're trying to fuck me again!"

I shrugged, grinning wolfishly.

The door of my office suddenly busted open and Evan stood on the threshold, fuming.

"You're trying to blackmail me?" he yelled, and with good reason.

He stormed inside, his little fists balled at his sides and

his lean body shaking, his pretty face pouting. "You want me to pay you ten thousand dollars or you'll show my husband a video of you and me . . . "

He trailed off there when he saw Jamie.

I thought the pair of young gray-chasers were going to tear each other apart, but they somehow only had eyes, and rage, for me.

"He's trying to blackmail me for more money, too!" Jamie informed Evan.

They both glared at me.

"What kind of private detective are you, anyway!?" Evan demanded.

I backed up to the window. "A hard case," I said.

"How would *you* like a case of *hard?*" Jamie tossed at me.

They advanced, one on either side of my desk, their faces set and bodies rigid.

Sure, I could've thrown both of them out of my office, or the window, onto their pretty, young asses; I was that much bigger and badder than they were, after all. Still, I knew I had done wrong once too often and I deserved a comeuppance: a fittingly hard end to a hard case.

They rushed around my desk and each grabbed an arm. Jamie ripped off my shirt. Evan tore down my pants. My chest heaved, my nipples hummed. My cock swung up huge and hot and surging bigger, beating hard. Both kids grabbed on to my cock and pumped two-handed.

I didn't *have* to take it, but I sure as hell wanted to. The pair of punks were giving me the payoff, and I was willing to take what was coming.

Jamie twisted and bit my nipples as Evan dropped down and mouthed my cock, scraping my shaft and hood with his teeth. Jamie then went down and nibbled my nuts, raking his fingernails along my cock, while Evan rose up and stretched my nipples out with his teeth, going back and forth on them.

They both pushed me over my desk. Evan jumped in front of it, sticking his cock into my mouth until I sucked. Jamie rooted around my desk and found a rubber before shoving his cock into my ass, pumping away at it mercilessly.

They gave it to me good and hard at both ends. After fucking my face, mouth, and throat, Evan hopped around the desk and fucked my ass, Jamie making way and leaving some gape behind for Evan to fill. Jamie then sprang around the desk and crammed his cock into my mouth, fucking my face as I sucked him off.

I was bumped to and fro by the boyish banging, taking young, hung cock in my mouth and chute, getting churned to burning by the two barging erections. My own cock whacked the desktop like a slab of salami in rhythm to the two cocky guys as they got their flaming revenge.

Evan screamed out and shuddered behind me. His wildly humping cock jumped in my flaming hole and creamed the rubber full of hot, sticky come, just as Jamie shrieked and spasmed in front of me. His cock jerked and jetted into my mouth, spraying a torrent of heated spunk down my throat.

I gulped at both ends, my enormous erection leaping up and spouting hands-free, whitely striping my desk with my own forceful nut.

Jamie and Evan pulled out, zipped up, and confiscated my camera before sashaying out of my office, hand in hand, smiling and waving back at me. I sucked up semen in my mouth as I leaned over my desk, my eleven-inch length of meat still twitching and leaking atop the wood.

It was another hard case, with a twist-happy ending. Damn, I was turning into a regular softie.

WHITEOUT

Richard Michaels

It started to snow at two in the afternoon. Five minutes later, I couldn't see more than a foot in front of my car. Soon after that, I couldn't see even that far. The intensity or direction of the blizzard would change, the snow whirling over the hood and against the windshield, and I had to completely stop, hoping that any drivers behind me would see my taillights before they crashed into me and sent everybody skidding off the road into the all-encompassing whiteness.

Of course, most people had probably stayed home, knowing better than to venture out when the Wyoming weather bureau predicted a winter storm. But I had been sure that I could outdrive the frigid fury, so I set out from Riverton in the early afternoon, planning to finish the 120 miles to Casper before dark.

And here I was, just a bit out of town, and my foolishness was becoming more and more apparent. I had driven the slightly more than twenty miles between Riverton and Shoshoni on a multitude of occasions, and now I felt as if I were traveling it for the first time, inching along the highway, straining to see the asphalt, the gleam of a vehicle in front of me, the shining of a light at the side of the road to confirm that I had not left civilization.

But I might as well have been in the frozen Arctic tundra. There are so many areas in Wyoming where nothing prevents the wet winter snow from obliterating everything and transforming the world into a white blur.

It was luck, I suppose, that the dense curtain parted enough to reveal the car parked by the side of the road. Its lights were off, and it looked like some strange creature hulking in the dark, waiting to glide again toward its unimaginable lair.

I was ready to pass the car when I saw—when I thought I saw—something detach itself from the front of this lurking creature and move to the side nearer the road. I let up on the gas, reluctant even to touch the brake and perhaps precipitate my vehicle and me into a skid. I alternated my gaze between what little road was visible before me and the figure beside the snow-covered beast. Odds were that this was not some smaller creature that had separated from the much larger one, but was instead a person walking around the front of a car. Odds were.

I don't usually stop for people on the road. Even in Wyoming, sometimes especially in Wyoming, the stranded motorist is not who he seems to be, or the hitchhiker is not the helpless solitary individual. But under the circumstances, I thought, I could take a chance on a wintry afternoon when the rest of the world seemed to have vanished into a frozen landscape.

As the person (presumably a person) approached my

car, I lowered a window. The wind shifted, and I was stung in the face by an attack of white arrows. The figure leaned over.

Through the blowing snow, I could see little but a vague, formless blob, a hulking body with a shapeless head, a head that appeared to be an irregular circle of gray bisected by two pieces of fur. For a moment, I almost thought that I really was looking at some wild beast, some sort of woolly mammoth that prowled this extended, barely inhabited stretch of wasteland wilderness, hunting a foolish traveler for the main course of its afternoon repast. No such creature existed, of course. Well, it was highly doubtful that such a creature existed, but still—

Then, "Hi," said this creature. The wind went off at a new tangent, and the snow was not so blinding, and I was hearing and seeing a man covered by a heavy coat and the two ridges were the edges of a hood pulled tightly around his face so that only his eyes and nose were visible.

I was foolishly relieved, and I said to him, "Hi," added somewhat idiotically, "Is everything okay?"

"No, my car broke down. It just stopped, and I tell why, especially in this mess, so here I am."

"Can I do anything?" I asked. "Give you Shoshmar? My plan is to get a motel room there out the storm before going on to Calper."

He thought for a bit and said, "Yeah, that's a good idea. I can get somebody to bring car and see if we can get the damn thing go.

"You don't have a cell phone?"

"Cell phone. No, I don't—well, I left on my friend's house. I was storm; somehow forgotten to put it on and Shoshoni on a multitude of occasions, and now I felt as if I were traveling it for the first time, inching along the highway, straining to see the asphalt, the gleam of a vehicle in front of me, the shining of a light at the side of the road to confirm that I had not left civilization.

But I might as well have been in the frozen Arctic tundra. There are so many areas in Wyoming where nothing prevents the wet winter snow from obliterating everything and transforming the world into a white blur.

It was luck, I suppose, that the dense curtain parted enough to reveal the car parked by the side of the road. Its lights were off, and it looked like some strange creature hulking in the dark, waiting to glide again toward its unimaginable lair.

I was ready to pass the car when I saw—when I thought I saw—something detach itself from the front of this lurking creature and move to the side nearer the road. I let up on the gas, reluctant even to touch the brake and perhaps precipitate my vehicle and me into a skid. I alternated my gaze between what little road was visible before me and the figure beside the snow-covered beast. Odds were that this was not some smaller creature that had separated from the much larger one, but was instead a person walking around the front of a car. Odds were.

I don't usually stop for people on the road. Even in Wyoming, sometimes especially in Wyoming, the stranded motorist is not who he seems to be, or the hitchhiker is not the helpless solitary individual. But under the circumstances, I thought, I could take a chance on a wintry afternoon when the rest of the world seemed to have vanished into a frozen landscape.

As the person (presumably a person) approached my

car, I lowered a window. The wind shifted, and I was stung in the face by an attack of white arrows. The figure leaned over.

Through the blowing snow, I could see little but a vague, formless blob, a hulking body with a shapeless head, a head that appeared to be an irregular circle of gray bisected by two pieces of fur. For a moment, I almost thought that I really was looking at some wild beast, some sort of woolly mammoth that prowled this extended, barely inhabited stretch of western wilderness, hunting a foolish traveler for the main course of its afternoon repast. No such creature existed, of course. Well, it was highly doubtful that such a creature existed, but still—

Then, "Hi," said this creature. The wind went off at a new tangent, and the snow was not so blinding, and I was hearing and seeing a man covered by a heavy coat, and the two ridges were the edges of a hood pulled tightly around his face so that only his eyes and nose were visible.

I was foolishly relieved, and I said to him, "Hi," and added somewhat idiotically, "Is everything okay?"

"No, my car broke down. It just stopped, and I can't tell why, especially in this mess, so here I am."

"Can I do anything?" I asked. "Give you a ride to Shoshoni? My plan is to get a motel room there and wait out the storm before going on to Casper."

He thought for a bit and said, "Yeah, that seems to be a good idea. I can get somebody to bring me back to my car and see if we can get the damn thing moving again."

"You don't have a cell phone?"

"Cell phone. No, I don't—well, not with me. I think I left it at my friend's house. I was in a rush to beat the storm; must've forgotten to pocket it."

"Probably just as well. Even under the best of circumstances, the telephone reception out here isn't great," I told him. "I'll take you to Shoshoni, and in the morning, if they've cleared the roads, we can devise some plan to get your car. Then you can be on your way to—where were you going?"

"I was . . . I was going to Thermopolis."

"Well, climb in," I said. "I'll try to get us to Shoshoni in two pieces—you and I, I mean—and we'll go, I hope, from there."

"Thanks, buddy," he said, and he inched his way around my car to the passenger door. When he was in the car, he pushed back his hood and shook himself, unleashing a minor snowstorm.

"Sorry," he said.

"No problem," I assured him.

I shifted gears and tentatively pressed on the gas. After a few spins of the tires, we slowly moved forward.

As I tried to stay on the road—and as I tried to figure out where the road was—I glanced at him. His hair was in a sort of crew cut, and the vestige of sideburns had a tinge of gray. A scar ran down his jaw.

"I'm Hal," I said.

"I'm . . . Ernie," he answered, turning briefly toward me.

He was the sort of man I find appealing, not handsome but attractive in a rough-hewn way, probably in his forties, a few years older than I.

"So, why are you going to Casper?" he asked.

"Uh," I said. "I'm going to visit a friend."

"He must be a very good friend," commented Ernie, "if you're willing to travel all the way to Casper in this weather to see him."

"Uh," I said further, noticing that Ernie had presumed that my friend was male. "He is."

"*Hmm*," he said.

I was sure that Ernie was staring at me, but I didn't want to check and I did want to stay on the highway, so I didn't look at him.

I might have changed the topic of conversation, but the wind altered its direction again, blowing the snow directly into the windshield. My attention concentrated instead on searching for the roadway and navigating it.

After that, we traveled in silence. Well, not quite silence, because the blizzard howled and attacked the car as if it were attempting to get inside and swallow us in its icy maw. It began to seem as if this usually short trip between Riverton and Shoshoni might go on forever, but finally I saw, barely, the curve leading into the little town.

The lights of the Desert Inn Motel glimmered weakly on the left, and I carefully steered toward them. When I arrived at what I thought was a curb, I tentatively braked and slid into cement with a bump.

"We're here," I said, and Ernie said, "Yeah."

I shut off the motor and I said, "I hope they have a room," and Ernie said, "Yeah."

He continued, "I didn't get my things out of my car," and I said, "That's all right. I'm sure that I have whatever you need."

Out of the corner of my eye, I checked to see what was his reaction to that bit of dialog, which I regretted the moment the words left my mouth. But I didn't detect a response, probably a good thing. I got my suitcase from the backseat. I locked the car. I thought that was no doubt redundant; who was going to trek outside in these conditions to rob me? But the action was second nature.

Ernie and I struggled through snowdrifts into the motel lobby. No one was at the front desk.

"Anybody here?" I called.

After a moment, a man came out of the office and said in an accusatory tone, "Well, I certainly didn't expect anyone today."

"We didn't expect to be here either," I responded. The man and I stared at each other, until at last I said, "So, can we register?"

"Yeah," he said, unenthusiastically. "My housekeepers didn't come in today, and I cleaned only one room myself, so that's all I have available."

He paused, as if he hoped that statement would discourage us from staying and send us back out into the blizzard, but I said, "That's fine."

"Okay," he said, doubtfully. "Sign in. Please."

I wrote my name in the ledger, and I asked Ernie what his last name was.

"Jones," he told me.

I wrote that in the book.

"Credit card," said the clerk, in a tone that indicated he could have been less interested only if he were dead. He regarded the card suspiciously, then told us, "The terminal's not working," and laboriously wrote down my information. He gave me a key and said, "The room's on the first floor, right down the hallway."

I thanked him, and Ernie and I headed toward our night's accommodations.

The room was a typical motel room. I was glad to see that there were two beds.

I put my suitcase on the stand and asked Ernie, "Do you want to shower?" It seemed that whatever I said might have a double meaning.

"You go first," Ernie replied.

The hot water felt good streaming down on me. The heater in my car was an efficient one, but the cold had crept in through every opening in the vehicle, and just the short trudge to the front door of the motel had erased every bit of warmth in my body.

After I was done with the shower, I shaved. I wasn't sure why. I'd taken a robe into the bathroom, and I put it on and went into the main room. Ernie was on one of the beds watching TV.

"Your turn," I said, and he got up. When he went into the bathroom, he didn't close the door completely.

I lay down on the second bed and looked at the talk show on the TV and listened to the shower.

When it stopped, Ernie swung the bathroom door most of the way open, to let out the steam, I supposed. From where I was lying, I could see into the bathroom, and I watched Ernie, naked, go to the mirror.

"Mind if I use your razor and shaving cream?" he asked.

"No, go right ahead."

He lathered his face and began to shave.

From the side, he appeared in shape, not excessively toned but with the look of a man who took care of himself. His arms were muscular and sculpted, and his legs were bowling pins. The peninsula of his cock stretched out from the continent of his body. His balls were like two plums in a sack.

He lifted his jaw and ran the razor down his neck.

"Do you like what you see?" he asked, not looking at me, still regarding himself in the mirror as he rasped the razor on his skin.

I contemplated his question. What would be the wise answer? Was it advisable to speak the truth? What if I said yes and he objected? Was he going to wreak some sort of havoc on me? Yeah, maybe. On the other hand—

The other hand won.

"Yes," I said.

He rinsed the razor and laid it on the sink. With a hand towel, he wiped the foam from his face. Did this mean that I hadn't angered him? Perhaps. But it could mean that he was thinking about how to punish me for letting my desire rule my reason.

He turned from the mirror and walked out of the bathroom toward me.

From the front, his cock was even wider than it had appeared to be from the side, and it was more than substantial.

He stopped at the bed. He laughed and said, "You obviously like what you see," and took hold of my prick. I hadn't noticed that it was poking up through the front of my robe, which it was, and it was definitely, approvingly stiff.

He climbed onto the bed and straddled me so that his crotch was mere inches from my face. "Show me how much you like it."

I lifted his cock. It was warm and hefty, so I hefted it, and I slid as much of it as possible between my lips. It tasted of soap and water and something that I couldn't put my finger on, but could and did put my tongue on, and I tantalized it, and it stiffened. Then it was a promontory jutting out from his flinty flesh, and I encircled it with my fingers as a sort of boundary because I couldn't take all of it in. He grabbed my hand and put it on the pillow beside my head and held it, and he did the same to my other hand, and he drove into my mouth more and more of his lengthening, thickening prick.

I wanted to tell him to slow down, to relent, but I was so full of him that I could barely breathe, let alone say anything, and he struck again and again, until it began to feel as if somehow he had enlarged my throat and I was increasingly able to ingest him. More and more I could savor the flavor of him, the soap and the water and his fire and the singular taste that I couldn't identify but that was somehow brisk and bracing and that impelled me to seek further his tartness and his tang. I tried to make as much contact with his still-enlarging cock as possible, but was thwarted by his size and length and vigor.

Were my intermittent tongue touches to his dick giving him pleasure? Was he stimulated by my lips pressed tightly around his cock? Or was any satisfaction he experienced because of the fact that he had complete dominance over me?

I was getting a certain fulfillment from running a sort of oral race with him, as his cock went one direction and my tongue went another. I decidedly wasn't in control of the situation, but that lack of control was unexpectedly exciting, the feeling that nothing I might do could really affect his actions, or that I might as well not try resistance, that all I could do was accept his insistence and persistence.

My own cock was responding impetuously to the situation, whatever the situation was, and I wasn't the least sure what the situation was. I felt an ache in my groin, and I knew that an elemental part of me had responded and risen.

His eyes flickered as he pressed down harder on my hands against the mattress.

Suddenly, his cock wasn't in my mouth, and he seemed to flow off my chest to stand at the side of the bed.

"Get up," he said.

I got up.

"Take off your robe."

I took off my robe.

"Turn around."

I did.

I felt rather than saw him move from his side of the bed to mine. He pressed against my back, bending me over.

"Wear protection, please," I said.

"What?"

"Wear protection," I repeated. "I have condoms."

After a pause, there was an amused exhalation, and he said, "Man, you and your boyfriend must really trust each other."

"We do. But it's an open relationship. I mean, he lives in Casper and I live in Riverton, so . . . "

What else should I tell Ernie, and why had I told him this much?

"So . . . " I repeated.

"So," he echoed, his tone mocking, or so I thought. "See? I'm using protection."

I watched him tear open a package and slip the sheath onto his imposingly rigid dick, and I thought that it was fortunate that I had brought more than one size, including large.

"Now," he said, and he made a peremptory gesture that told me to bend over again, and I did. I waited. It was almost a surprise when his hands settled on my hips, and it was a shock when without preparation or preamble he propelled his dick into me. I gasped, and he said, "*Shh.*"

The suddenness of his attack and the mass of his entire cock abruptly inside me seemed for a moment to be all that existed, my throbbing asshole and his hard burning dick. He became all of my awareness and experience, the agitation that was a hurt and an ignition, and he had thrust into and out of me two, three, four times before everything resolved itself into a pattern as he fucked me.

It was an odd fuck.

It wasn't a bad fuck, just an odd fuck.

He hit the right places at the right angle with the right pressure and in the right tempo, but he was strangely rhythmic as he assailed me. Men who have fucked me before varied their speed, their twists and turns, their delivery. But Ernie was deliberate, purposeful. Yes, every fuck has a purpose, for both the giver and the receiver, and even if I wasn't sure what satisfaction Ernie was getting, I certainly knew what effect he was having on me.

I groaned.

"*Shh,*" he hissed again, and with no modification in rhythm or angle or pace, he continued to fuck me.

No matter how singular was his method of fucking, it was also efficient, as evidenced by the rousing effect he was having on my crotch, and I closed my eyes in pleasure. When I opened them again, I was looking at a cowboy riding a horse. Then I realized that I wasn't really looking at a cowboy riding a horse, but was instead gazing at a belt buckle, attached to a belt, attached to a pair of jeans, attached to a man who stood in the doorway.

"Well," said the man, regarding my upturned face, "you seem to have made friends quickly."

"He who hesitates," said Ernie, hesitating not one stroke in his screwing.

The other man laughed. He was shorter than Ernie and chunkier and not, in my slanted viewpoint, as appealing as Ernie.

"Can I get in on the action?" the man asked.

"Sure . . . Bert," responded Ernie. "I have a feeling that Hal won't object."

I was momentarily annoyed that Ernie had invited Bert into our action without consulting me, but not after Bert shrugged off his coat and unzipped his jeans and produced a prick that was already firm and stuck it into the mouth that remained open from my initial surprise at seeing him in front of me.

His cock did not taste of soap and water as Ernie's did; it tasted of perspiration and musk. But it was goodly sized, and, I confess, in my sexual enthusiasm, I was quite pleased to accept its insertion.

And so I was fucked at both ends with mute, brute force and in a coordinated cadence of cock, and I felt like an accordion squashed from two sides, their cocks squeezing me simultaneously, or a set of drums being pounded in a percussive duet, and all of this sexual symphony in silence.

Abruptly, there was a pause. Ernie's cock remained in place, at rest, and Bert withdrew his prick.

"Protection, Bert," Ernie said mockingly, and after a brief intermission I heard Bert open and put on a condom. Ernie's cock was pulled out and Bert's ramrod was shoved into my ass as he began his rhythmic battering.

Ernie lay on one of the beds and watched us, stroking his dick. His eyes and his smile were enigmatic. He was enjoying seeing his friend fuck me and seeing me fucked by his friend. And was there something else in his expression? It seemed that both men were still within me, banging together, impelling my own cock to an almost painful expansion.

Ernie closed his eyes and his body arched and his cock spurted like the wind and snow outside, onto himself, and shooting up onto his chest and arms and into his bush and over his balls.

Bert drove into me with a final blast and his fingers gripped my hips so strongly that I thought he must surely be leaving permanent indentations. His body bent over me so that he was almost lying on my back, and he came inside me, and his breath was hot on my skin, and even though I knew that he was expelling himself into a condom, his explosion seemed to scorch my asshole with its fire.

I jerked and shuddered and shook in the climax that streamed down onto the rug and lasted forever and was too short, and I also was noiseless even though a shout was building inside of me. We were all silent in our spasms.

Exhausted by the fervor that had racked me, I fell asleep.

When I awoke, the other two men were whispering together.

"Boy, that was some piece of ass," said Bert. "I want more."

"We've got to go," responded Ernie. "When the sun rises and if the storm is over and if the streets are passable, we've got to go. Are you parked in front of the motel?"

"Yeah, I found a car where some idiot from the farm

had put his keys under the mat. Boy, will he be surprised tomorrow to find that it's gone. I can just see him running around looking under every snowdrift. It was a bitch getting here."

"It's a good thing Hal happened by when he did. I thought I was going to freeze out there."

"And see how warm it got in here," Bert said and laughed.

"I was nervous waiting for you," Ernie said. "There were a couple of times when I thought you weren't going to make it."

"There were a couple of times when *I* thought I wasn't going to make it. I followed the directions you phoned me on your cell to this motel."

"We'll take your car in the morning," Ernie said. "The other car, the one I stole and that broke down, can stay out there in the middle of the highway. Hal can drive his car to Casper or wherever he's going. I mean, I don't want him to get totally screwed. It's going to take a while for the authorities to get their shit together, and by that time, we'll be gone."

I understood then what I should have at least presumed before. Bert's words "the farm" were the trigger. Bert meant "the Farm." "The Farm" was the Honor Farm, frequently referred to by its neighbors as the Prison Farm. It was a medium-security detention center located about a mile north of Riverton. The inmates, generally incarcerated for fairly minor crimes, worked in several outdoor jobs, including farming and training wild horses. The facility's recidivism was low, and so was the escape rate. Bert and Ernie were obviously exceptions.

Bert and Ernie—shouldn't their names have alerted

me that all was not well? But by the time Bert made his entrance onto the scene and into me, I was so enveloped in a sexual fog that I couldn't see the lighthouse of reality that was directly in front of me, and I continued on my way toward the collision with the facts that I'd willingly, willfully ignored.

Perhaps the fact that they had been prisoners explained their singular method of fucking. By necessity, they would have grabbed sexual pleasures when they found them, and their fusions had to be as quick and as noiseless as possible so that satisfaction was achieved before other prisoners or the guards reached the clandestine couplers. A moan issued at just the wrong moment might give away illicit activity. Silence was not only golden, it was a necessity.

And did their confinement, I wondered, cause the strange flavor of Ernie's cock? No, that was too fanciful a thought. Wasn't it?

"I want to fuck him again," said Bert.

They were sitting at a table, nude, and their cocks surged down between their legs and my own cock issued its response before I did or said anything.

I was lying on the sticky rug, and I stood up, and my dick stood up.

"I guess that means he's willing," said Bert and laughed.

The three of us moved into position.

"Don't forget the protection," Ernie said with a grin, and Bert nodded somewhat exaggeratedly and slipped a condom over his broad dick.

Bert was behind, and Ernie was in front. In wordless coordination, they entered me.

I was still smarting from their last assault, and so their

cocks felt bigger and longer and stronger in this new intrusion. After the beginning discomfort, I welcomed all of the hardness, the speed, the strength, the vehemence, even the strangely rhythmic fucking.

Ernie's cock was expansive in size and taste, and Bert's cock was remorseless in its bombardment of my stinging, hospitable hole. My own dick felt as rough and tough as a brick, and the juices boiled in my stomach as the two men struck me over and over, silently, deeply, powerfully.

Then Ernie, with just the slightest moan, exploded into me. His come was copious and tangy as I had expected, and I wanted to hold it in my mouth and relish its taste, but there was so much that I had to swallow, and the surfeit overflowed my mouth and ran down my chin.

And Bert, with just the slightest moan, heaved into me with a final lacerating thrust and gripped my hips with his hands and burst inside of me, and even through the condom the waterfall of his fluids seemed to flow into me.

And I, with just the slightest moan, because that was all I could achieve with Ernie's dick still in my mouth, had a climax that earned that name, an explosion that shook me and poured out onto the rug in a violent venting that seemed to endure in a forever that all too abruptly ended.

Then we three, with just the slightest moans, toppled onto the floor.

And I, again, fell asleep.

When I awoke, there was no one with me.

I was naked, sticky, and alone.

The air was heavy with the redolence of spent sperm and faded passion.

I stood and went to the window that looked out onto the parking lot. Only my car was there. A snowplow was slicing through the heavy mounds of white. Bert and Ernie were gone. There were two roads at the other end of Shoshoni. Maybe Bert and Ernie had taken the one to Casper and from there down I-25 to Denver. Perhaps they were on the road to Thermopolis, or they might have taken one of the cutoffs that led to another of Wyoming's myriad of small towns.

Maybe, perhaps—whatever, the guys were gone.

And I was sorry that they were.

I would shower and dress and drive to Casper and visit my boyfriend, Jared. At one time, I had loved Jared, but my affair with him had turned predictable and boring, and periodic visits to him had become more of a duty than a real pleasure. Jared never visited me. I seldom made contact with gay men in Riverton. It was very obvious that Jared made contact with other gay men in Casper. Our association was hardly satisfactory. But I didn't want to scissor it. I needed someone, and Jared was someone.

I wished that Bert and Ernie, or whatever their names were, had taken me with them. I was a law-abiding citizen, and I didn't know what the men had done to get them in prison and what other crimes they might have committed and what they might have required me to do if I were with them. I was an accountant in Riverton, but the figures of that existence didn't add up. Conformity and respectability seemed, at that moment, just dreary conventions.

The connection with Bert and Ernie had been nothing more than physical, and it was one in which they had demanded and I had acceded, albeit getting some satisfaction in the process.

My jaw was sore, and my ass ached, and my spirit was as depleted as my sexual fluids.

I didn't want to think about what the three of us had done together, and I didn't want to forget, and I knew that sooner or later our screwing would turn into daydreams for my jerking off, although it wouldn't ever be only that.

It was time to leave sucking and fucking and the flash and fury, and I walked out the door to my car and prepared as well as I could for the shadows of reality.

Author's note: Wyoming is a real state, and there are in it such towns as those in this story. And in Shoshoni, there is a motel called the Desert Inn. All of these locations have been used, as may be quite evident, fictionally, and no resemblance to the truth should be inferred.

his face with experience lines. The blue uniform showed off a muscular frame, kept lithe and strong, no doubt, through strict diet and strenuous exercise. He was delicious, for a human. "You are aware that your people, your government, has given us full control of you?" he said.

"I am of peace and love. I submit completely."

"This is a delicate procedure." The general continued, shaking his head. "I must ask you to play spy as well as emissary."

I cocked my head, trying to read him. "What do you need?"

General Watson leaned slightly over his desk, trying to hold me with his blue ice gaze. *So open to me*, I thought. I released a few pheromones, sighing inward as his nostrils flared and his pupils widened into darkness. Dazed, he stumbled. "We need any information concerning the Trahaiten and Kisha Borders, the conflicts on Rosa Two and Three, the planet Aslyian."

With a shrug, I slipped my robe off. Naked, I stood before him, breathing deeply. His eyes would read me as a human male, perhaps in his late twenties or early thirties. I shifted slightly, reading him better now that he was responding to my scent, to my probes. My skin and hair darkened to chestnut brown as my eyes widened and became blue. I grew taller, my muscles filling out my frame. I became the vision of a memory that once brought him to orgasm and shame. His hands fumbled at the crotch of his suit. His penis strained the cloth. He fidgeted as hunger roared within me.

I knelt down before him, gently taking his trembling hands into mine.

"I will spy for you," I said. "What else do you need?"

"I need to fuck your mouth," he blurted out.

I smiled, bowing my head. I tore his suit open with my teeth. I took his hard cock into my mouth and I sucked him, deeply, until he trembled. I took his seed, draining him fully. I left him calm and centered. I left him no longer ashamed of a memory.

In my head swirled the complete tactical designs of the human race in their war against the Blayling. It was very valuable information to possess. So much at stake in war, after all.

In the small carrier, the humans anxiously stirred. It was a long drift to the Blayling ship. Space is eternal. I find that both terrifying and soothing. I touched the window glass, covering up the stars. It is a fact that by the time we see their lights, those stars are dead. The twinkling lights we see are the stars' death cries.

"I don't get it, Lieutenant," one of the men said. "Is he gonna fuck all the Blayling?"

Soldiers snickered. I pressed my face up against the cold glass. It is said that all of us contain the same genetic material as stars. Up close, space smells like metal and ice. I looked at my hands: in human form, hands are star shaped. I smiled at the irony. Humans also taste of salt and musk. I hummed, thinking of General Watson.

"That's enough," Lieutenant Agroyerra growled. "Stapleton. You have a problem, you deal with it after mission completion. Until then, we're locked and loaded, correct?"

Another soldier took the bait. "Some mission this is. We're babysitting while Omega gets to play rescue."

No, Omega would not be playing when it came to

facing the Blayling during Colonel Jessing's rescue. Omega Unit would be running, praying, and dying.

"I am . . . " I said to none of them in particular. They waited for me to say more. I took my time, spinning around to face them, the smell of space and stars clouding my thoughts, lulling me into a dreamy state not unlike what I render unto my lovers. "I am most willing to fuck all that I must to complete this mission."

Silence reigned for the rest of the long ride.

The Blaylings are a tall, heavy, long-limbed race. Humans use the word *troll* to describe them. I don't know what that word means, but the image that comes up in the human mind does resemble the Blayling race. As heavy and cumbersome as they appear, Blaylings move with an unexpected speed and grace. Indeed, they move constantly. They do not tire easily and they fight to the very end. As an enemy, they are formidable. The safest way to kill them is to wait until they are finally eating or fucking. At least then, they are long enough in the same spot.

I suspect that the only reason humans and Blaylings are at war is because they both want to control the universe. Otherwise, they'd probably get along, and then the rest of us would be in trouble. In other words, it's a good thing they are both such stupid races.

"Christ, it smells," one of the troop said as we followed the Blayling greeter to the assembly chamber.

"That is because Blayling saliva has toxic properties," I said, gesturing at the walls of the warship. "Blayling clean with their tongues. The acidic residue protects ship-metal, but leaves behind a residual poison." I turned to smile at my human soldiers. "Blayling saliva can melt human skin, tissue, and, in large quantities, human bone. Perhaps you shouldn't touch the walls or floor?"

"Perhaps we won't," Lieutenant Agroyerra returned darkly. "It doesn't affect you, though, does it?"

I shrugged in human manner. "I submit willingly."

The assembly doors opened before us, displaying the waiting Blayling captain, officers, and crew. To human eyes, they would appear clumsy, stupid in their expression. But I read them true: I see the strength in their arms, the dark, bloody life experience in their eyes, the cunning intelligence they hide, and the harsh brutality that they barely keep in check. Blaylings fuck slowly, deep, and hard. It is a well-earned joy to be fucked by them.

I read something else in the easy swaying stance of the Blaylings: a tense air of anticipation and hidden knowledge.

Somehow, the Blaylings knew that the humans were trying to rescue Colonel Jessing. This was a trap. Omega Unit must be dead. How human to underestimate the enemy. For the Blaylings, this was going to be an amusing slaughter.

I spun around to warn my group when the Blaylings opened fire from the ambushing flank behind both the human soldiers and the Blayling assembly. Some of the humans slid into secure positions to cover both sides of the attack. The core center pulled together, surrounding me until they could get me out of harm's way. It saddened me to realize that these humans were willing to sacrifice their lives to keep me covered and safe.

Lieutenant Agroyerra leaped forward to shield me, her laser firing carefully over my head and shoulders. I dropped to the floor, unwilling to endanger her further. A shot rang her shoulder from behind and she twisted, calmly returning fire. Another shot sliced into the side of her neck. Slowly, she reached up to stop the blood flow. Her dark eyes met mine and I reached out to stroke her face. It was a small gesture, for death was coming for her. Another shot opened her chest, followed quickly by two or three that found her belly. Her hands held her wounds as she slid farther into my lap, nearly a child now in her dying.

A man to my left hissed in pain before his body exploded under a rain of fire. His blood splattered me, and for the first time in my life as Emissary, I wanted to scream, to cry out. Behind me, a soldier lost the top of his head, and I did finally scream, my star-like hands covering my ears. Lasers took them, then, my human soldiers, blue fire dancing along their bodies until at last only I sat there alone, unharmed, in the middle of the dead. I cried out when the Blayling came for me, my training undone in the face of horror and war. One of the Blayling stood over me, grinning, baring rows of rotting teeth. He backhanded me with his hot laser just before darkness took me.

I came awake to violent shaking. He repeated the question that took me several moments to translate. Human speech, a stranger. He was asking me if I was a spy.

Yes, of course. I am Emissary. We serve the greater good even when it destroys others.

I nodded once in human manner as I tried to sit up. Thundering blackness hit my eyes, and I fought an urge to vomit. I shook my head to clear it. After a moment's hesitation, the human helped me by leaning my back against the wall. When the world stopped spinning, I opened my eyes.

I could only assume that this was Colonel Jessing, the

man the humans had been seeking. I stared in wonderment. He was dressed, if just barely. I was naked.

Imprisonment often thinned, broke, damaged, and mutilated a being. Colonel Jessing had not only held on during his capture, but seemed stronger for it. Beautiful as he was for a human, an inner light seemed to radiate from within him. I reached out to touch his face and he let me, although confusion ran in his green eyes as his full-lipped mouth anxiously twitched. Tiny blond hairs on his cheek and chin bristled under my hand. I ached suddenly to taste him, to run my tongue over those bristles, suck at his chin, and then kiss his full mouth. I ached suddenly to wrap my legs around him as he fucked my ass, his tongue deep in my mouth, dreaming of his cock.

"You're not human," he said.

I croaked out, "No, I am Gevarian." I took a breath to center myself. "Your people petitioned for an Emissary to distract the Blayling while they tried to rescue you. I am Emissary."

"My, my," Colonel Jessing said. "Great job then, Emissary." At my confused look, he added, "I guess you got everyone killed?" I opened my mouth to protest and he snarled at me. "Save it."

He then retreated far away from me.

They came for him next, leaving behind food and water for me. I ate quickly, shoving the pasty cold slop into my mouth, nearly drowning myself with the pitcher of water. Then I heard him screaming. I vomited up everything. When they brought him back, he growled when I came near him.

It took me hours to convince him to drink water. He

drank sparingly, his head against my chest, his trembling chin cradled in my palm, his curving torso in my lap. It would be nothing to kiss him, to lick the water drops from his mouth. I would have a moment's feast from it and he'd gain a second of relief from me, but I resisted. And then, when I would have given in, he rolled away from my lap and lay down next to me. He was wiser than I. I stretched out next to him and stroked his back until he fell into a troubled sleep.

It was several days before they brought us any more food or water. Not that I needed it, but Jessing suffered greatly. I knew his mouth was dry from his endless coughing. I listened to his stomach rumble like music. And so, when he finally passed out and was too far gone to fight me, I came to him and kissed him: long, hard, and wetly, so very wetly. Jessing drank what I gave him and was satisfied, finally falling into restful slumber.

I should have sucked his cock. The mere thought of it filled me with desire. Said cock answered while he dreamed and snored. That is what I really needed, what I really wanted. Watching his sleeping face, I slid my hand in to feel his hot flesh. I stroked as his cock stiffened further, rising, thickening. Hunger threatened to overtake me. I leaned my head forward to drink more of him, just as he murmured, "Ian?"

I stopped. *Ian.* I slowly removed my hand. What was I doing? I'd been thinking of my own needs, my own hunger. But to do it while he slept, when I had no idea if he was welcome to my intentions? It spoke of a darker Emissary urge. We try to control that part of us, the taking part. Usually, we are successful. Everyone wants to fuck, right? Or be fucked. I couldn't, however, feed from a sleeping man. It was dark and unspeakable. I'd starve first.

But there was this Ian. Darkness sang in my head. Wouldn't Jessing love a visit from his old friend? I could be Ian. Another kiss would secure the image for me. Then, as Ian, I could fuck the man until I was full and fat. I snarled at Jessing as he lay there sleeping, completely unaware of my turmoil. I moved to the other end of the cell and sat there, angry and frustrated.

It was a relief when they came for me.

I shed my robe in the cell and followed my guards down the hall. They brought me to a room containing three other Blayling, including the captain. I spread myself across the table for fucking. They quickly filled my ass and mouth with Blayling juice. Satiated, I rolled over on my stomach, while a Blayling underling sucked come from my ass. At last I was happy. Hunger pains were no more.

The Blayling captain smiled down on me. "I have gift for Emissary."

I smiled, my eyes closed. "More of your cock?"

The underling nibbled one asscheek and then got back to licking my rosebud clean. I moaned under his intentions. I hoped that we were nowhere near done yet. I shoved my ass into his face as he tongued my hole.

"You must finish," the captain said. "The Gevarian Council wishes attendance."

I pried opened my eyes and found myself addressing a High Lord. I sat up quickly and in utter surprise as I dislodged the underling. I knew of this Lord. He was the Gevarian known as Athelen. I was either in serious trouble or in serious service. I bowed my head and waited.

"Emissary," Athelen purred. "I see our gifts are not wasted on you. Fair greeting."

I murmured back, "Fair Greeting, Lord."

"We have a mission, a need for one of your talents, Emissary."

I merely nodded.

"If you will, Good Emissary," he continued, "we only want you to ask questions and listen to this man the humans are seeking. Ask the human about his mission, about the human goals in this part of space. Ask and listen. Be accommodating as only Emissaries can be. Be pleasing. Gain the human's trust and feed on him freely. Tell us everything you discover."

I peered at the High Lord. He smiled, waiting for an answer. Again, I nodded.

Of course I would do as he commanded. It was a mission for a finger, a favor not asked but expected, commanded for the good of community. Our entire culture is based on this. We are unity and harmony. This also meant that I was not the only Gevarian Emissary with access to a human. If I was a finger, then there were others out there, too, working for the whole.

Naturally, I would spy for my people. Obviously, based on my Lord's request, they'd chosen a side. This was a concept so foreign, though, that I wasn't really sure I could be thinking it. Probably, I was wrong. Gevarians never choose a side when they can play all sides against each other. This then was bigger than I could envision, but I was simply a finger. Does the finger tell the hand to make a fist or to be still?

I blinked up. The Lord seemed to still be waiting on something from me.

I said, looking intently into his black eyes, "I will ask and listen, and then tell you everything."

In the spare light they'd left us, Colonel Jessing said, "They don't torture you."

I answered, "They do not."

Silence reigned then for a long time as he chewed on this. I waited him out. "Why are you spared?"

"I am Emissary. Torture is useless. I willingly submit. Rape cannot be used against me. I am always more than willing to do as instructed. Pleasure is my currency. Pain is merely a sensation. Same coin. I serve the greater good, always. I am of peace and love."

I stopped then because Jessing started laughing at me. "What is that exactly?" he choked out. "What kind of animal are you?"

And in that moment, that animal he mentioned stirred in anger. It was good that the light was sparse, for my teeth clenched as my inner harmony drifted toward chaos and my breathing fell off center.

"I am an animal who survives. I am an animal that will still exist long after you and the Blayling have destroyed one another. I am Gevarian. I blink my eyes and you have already died. You are history to us. We were here when the first star gave birth. We were already gods when your people crawled out of the swamps and onto land."

Jessing stopped laughing. He was listening to me, and yet, despite my training, my anger was controlling me. I blamed my hunger for him. I blamed my lack of experience as a high-level Emissary. I blamed my need for physical contact. If I were to truly survive, I was going to have to fuck him soon. I had to have him inside me. And I needed to be inside of him, too. I wanted to tear him apart from the inside out. I wanted to rip the human from the animal and let chaos reign. Despite the amount of sex I'd had with the Blaylings, I wanted the starving human so bad that it hurt.

The colonel again started to chuckle as he pointed around. "And just look at how far you've come."

The door opened then. They'd come for Jessing.

He was gone for a long while. It's hard to tell time in semidarkness, so I counted to occupy my mind. Then I thought of Jessing's soft blond hair, of my hands gripping his hair while I fucked his mouth, of my hands tangled in his hair while he took my ass and I screamed. These images helped pass the time.

When they were done with him, they threw him back to me. I crawled over, touching him gently. I pulled him up into me and held him. He cried long into his sleep. I stroked his head and hummed old songs as if he were a child. While he slept, I set my mind to healing some of his injuries. I couldn't fix him completely, but I did what I could. Human biology can be so difficult and stubborn. Resistant. Just like humans.

I thought of planting seeds in his mind: images of me, copies of the ones I'd used to keep me company in his absence, but I resisted. Mostly. I did whisper a few into his mind. If he'd not already been thinking of me in this way, it wouldn't hurt for him to do so now. It might even take some of the sting out of the Blayling inquisition.

I was taken to the captain's quarters. Blaylings never act alone. They are pack animals, with severe rank discipline. The Blayling guards opened the door to the officer's quarters, and I was met with four Blayling high officers and their captain.

Once the door closed, I shrugged off my robe and stood before them naked. To Blayling eyes, I am long-limbed and strongly built, my rows of teeth clean and sharp, my eyes dark, hair long and black and enticingly tangled. An officer licked his lips, and I knew that my appearance pleased. I spread my legs, swinging my hips and crotch forward. Another officer fidgeted. I smiled, awaiting their pleasure.

"Emissary," the captain grunted, nodding his head in greeting.

I nodded back and started stroking my cock, coyly tugging on my balls, my voice a low-pitched rumble. "What's your pleasure?"

One of the officers dropped his pants, openly stroking his own cock. Two others started undressing, their eyes on me and my rising prick. I pulled at one of my nipples. The captain gestured for me to come to him. I came, and within inches of him, I sprayed him with pheromones. His dark eyes widened, nostrils flaring. He grabbed my upper arm to guide me. I leaned over his desk. He reached for the jar of lubrication and started slapping it thickly on his massive, hard cock. Rough sticky fingers probed my ass, widening the crack. I pushed against these digits, grunting, riding his hand, a moan building in my chest.

In my ear, he barked, "Where are the human ships? What has the human told you?"

I closed my eyes. I saw clearly the tactical reports from Colonel Jessing's mind. I saw both man and machine placement. I saw action plans and movement. I opened my mouth to speak, but it was then that I saw humans dying to protect me, humans giving up their short meaningless lives to save my own meaningless one. I thought then of my longing for the handsome colonel, tortured in darkness, laughing to keep his hopes up. I closed my mouth, biting down on my bottom lip.

The captain thrust his cock into my ass so hard that I slammed into the desk. He started fucking me then, long and slow, steadily building up desire. His thick fingers pulled on my nipples, one moment a caress, the next a painful pinch. I thrust back to take him in fully, my own cock painful and straining. I gave in to the pleasure of it. I was so fucking tight and he felt so damned good inside me.

The captain bit my shoulder. "Emissary?"

"I don't know yet," I lied and nearly choked. We don't lie, after all; we don't need to. An officer crawled between our legs to suck at my cock. I moaned, my prick down his capable throat while the captain thrust himself into my ass. The officer sucked my balls, then came back to my cock, his tongue rolling over the fat head. The captain threw himself into his work, nearly lifting me up with each plunge. My hips rode wildly, giving my ass fully to the captain's hot cock, giving my own prick to the officer's suckling mouth. I moaned, enjoying the sound of slick flesh pounding rhythmically and the wetter sound of saliva, sweat, and lubrication.

I thought of the human war plans. I lied some more, the words strained as juice and sweat dripped down from my ass. Another officer licked at my legs and slick ass and the captain's swinging balls. "You're going to win this war, Captain," I panted. "Another Blayling victory."

The captain shouted as he came, his hips a fierce dance that left me dizzy and dazed. He pulled out slowly, and I instantly missed his glorious cock. I whirled around, sucking at his mouth and long tongue with desperation. His rank breath filled me, and I inhaled it willingly. Blaylings taste of honey and sweet rot.

I read him then. He was pleased with the news, vanity winning out. He wanted to fuck me more, but alone, long after the officers were done. I nodded at him, agreeing with those plans. His cock was full and long, and he could fuck like a strong machine. Yes, I wanted him, too. In my ass, in my mouth.

Alone, without his pack of officers to censor him, I was sure I would find the captain a most willing and talkative playmate. It is always wise to know how all the players in a game think. The Blayling officers came to me as the captain stepped aside to wait his turn, and then we all came and came again.

Satiated, my mouth tangy with come, my ass and cock sore and happy with use, they gently put me back in the cell with Colonel Jessing. By Emissary standards, it was a good day's work. I had enough Blayling in me to keep me fat and happy for at least a week.

War plans mixed in my mind with Blayling desire and countless positions. The one I played over and over in my mind was the delicious one where I rode the captain's cock backward as he sat in his big chair. His large hands nearly tore my nipples off while his teeth chewed on my neck and shoulders. The Blaylings had spies in the human assemblies on Rosa Three and within the Kisha Border. They had smart bombs pointed at Charion Moon and Rosa Two. The Trahaiten Border was unprotected on the Blayling side, but intel confided the rumors of civil unrest on the Aslyian Planet.

Colonel Jessing came over to me the minute the door closed, human concern washing over his beautiful face. I reached up dazed, stroking his cheek, my fingers slipping for a second into his full mouth. I then sucked my fingers, tasting him. I tasted bitterness with an underlying sweetness, all with that wonderful human musk.

Worn out as I was, I could feel my hungry cock stirring. My hand under my robe, in the cover of the poor light, I cradled my cock, lightly pulling on it. Bruised as it was, it started giving in to hunger. I rose up on my elbow as the colonel leaned over me. I wanted to kiss him. I wanted to pull him down on top of me and put his cock inside me.

"Are you okay?" he asked. "Did they hurt you?"

"I didn't tell them anything," I whispered.

The colonel paused, confused. He didn't know that I had a lot to tell to both sides.

"I know how the humans can win this war," I whispered, just before I kissed him. At first he froze, then he responded, his tongue wrapping around my own, lips grinding. When he finally pushed me away, I realized that I hadn't even thought to use the pheromones. That was more shocking to me than the rejection. I hadn't thought to seduce him. I'd wanted him to respond to me because he wanted to, not because he had to.

Colonel Jessing moved to the other side of the cell. In the dark, his husky voice cracked. "Why are you screwing with my head?"

"I'm not."

"Then why did you do that?"

"I . . . I don't understand."

"They sent someone like you in here to break me," the

colonel said softly. "How did they know exactly what I like?"

Days passed, maybe a week or two. Time is hard to tell when one is imprisoned. We sat in complete darkness once the light went out. Sometimes the colonel would forget to hate me, to mistrust me, and we'd have a conversation. He started to understand my humor. I could make him laugh, until he remembered I was the enemy. Talking to him was simply putting off the inevitable. It was facade. It's hard to leave training behind. In the end, we all fall back on what we know.

We are, after all, what we are.

In the blackness, noises echoed and exaggerated. It sounded like the Blaylings were either having parties or making war. It was hard to tell which. But after an eternity of that, hunger drove me. I was starving now, the Blayling lust having worn off. Memory of the colonel's kiss sharpened the blade on my hunger, making me feel edgy and temperamental. Now when the colonel goaded me with his nasty quips, I growled in response. Eventually, I stopped responding altogether.

I'd not used my pheromones. I'd wanted a natural response to my lovemaking. He'd rejected me, pushed me away. No one rejects an Emissary. We are of love, always. It's impossible, unbelievable, to consider such a rejection, and for him to do that meant, well, I wasn't sure what it meant but it couldn't be good. And now I was going to die of hunger. I wasn't going to reach out to him again. Colonel Jessing was going to kill me, after all.

It's true, Emissaries die. Stars burn out and fade. Emissaries die without love.

We really are sexual parasites. Our food is desire, come, longing.

The colonel crawled closer to me. He whispered, "What is going on with you?"

I ignored him. He reached out to touch me, and I cried out, the feeling of his hand on me overwhelming, the desire to live, to love, nearly overcoming my fierce proud urge to die, leaving him and me unsatisfied. I shook under his hand. He rolled me over to face him. I was blind in the darkness, but I could feel his breath on my face. I longed for him.

"I'm dying," I said, plainly. "Now, go away."

Colonel Jessing chuckled dryly and I cried out. I was going to miss that, his double-edged laughter, his strange human hope for something better, his bitter doubt that he deserved it. He asked me, softly, his hand on my chest, "What do you need? What can I do for you?"

"I told you," I said with a pause, making him wait for it, wanting him to hurt for it. I tried to shove his hand off me, but instead I clung to it. "I told you to go away."

Colonel Jessing lowered his mouth to mine until we were only a hair's breadth away. "What if I told you I was also dying? The Blayling have forgotten all about us and now we're going to die together."

"I'm dying first," I insisted, waiting one beat before adding, "and it's your fault."

"Blame God, blame warmongering planets, blame greedy industrialists and savage aliens," Colonel Jessing said with a sigh, "but how is it my fault?"

"I can't live without love," I replied. "But you can."

Silence then.

Finally, Colonel Jessing said, "Is that the truth?"

I turned my head away, closing my eyes. Softly, I said, "Nothing is the truth."

The colonel reached for me in the darkness, his hands gently finding my face. His mouth was hesitant on mine at first, a sweet kiss, a testing kiss, and then, as I responded, that kiss deepened. I moaned into it.

There were images in his mind of his first tender kiss as a teenager. It was a kiss shared with his best friend, Justin, under a bridge one rainy afternoon. Then there were the kisses in college: drunk, wild kisses in public places with a steady line of boyfriends. And then the most tender, secretive kiss of all: the one he shared with another officer just before boarding a war cruiser.

Colonel Jessing found my stiffening cock. My back arched as he stroked it possessively. I pulled my robe up so that he could handle me completely, touch my bare flesh. I groaned when his warm mouth folded around my prick, his tongue lapping gently at the underside of the mushroom head. He took my cock fully into his mouth and throat, his plump lips gently brushing my aching balls as he sucked and swallowed. My hips jerked under his control, feeding his hungry mouth with my cock.

The colonel pulled away for a moment, adjusting himself. I whimpered in the sudden chill, my cock pulsing without the warmth of his mouth. It was then that my hands found the colonel's own cock, rising in his tattered military uniform. Together we released it from his pants before his mouth was on my cock and mine on his.

I sucked his thick tool, breathing in his musk, his warm balls slapping my chin. Our hips danced in unison: slow, circular waves, then quick pulsating beats. When at last we came, it was so close to being at the same time that it was hard to tell who did it first. I just know that I licked the colonel clean from the tip of his juicy prick to his warm balls.

We lay in darkness then, resting. When the colonel had enough energy to laugh at a private thought, I knew it was time. After all, he'd kept me starving for him long enough.

I pulled him up to a sitting position. I sucked his fingers until they were wet enough, and then I guided his hands to my ass. I rocked on my knees as he fingered my tight chute, loosening me up for a good, hot fuck. I took in as many of his digits as I could, riding his hand, nearly buckling under the pleasure of it. He spit down into my asshole, adding saliva to his fingers.

When he was hard again, the colonel got on his knees and slid his cock into my waiting ass. He fucked me hard, his balls slapping into me from behind, his hand pulling tightly on my cock, jerking me. I strained against him, willing my ass to take him completely. I rolled my butt into his hips, giving it up to his thick prick. This time I came first, splattering his hand with warm, gooey spunk. Moments later, he came inside me, his body writhing behind, his come hot inside before trailing down my cheeks and legs. The colonel tried to pull out, but I reached behind me, holding on to his asscheeks, letting his cock jerk inside me. I was reluctant to lose even this much of him.

"God," Colonel Jessing panted, pulling free at last, his cock soft and happy. "That was a good fuck." Idly, he stroked my cheek with his knuckles. "I needed that, needed you."

I smiled, playfully sucking on his fingers. Then, in the calm silence of the dark, distant shots rang out. Shouts followed before the sound of metal crashing, more gunfire, screams that were distinctly both human and Blayling.

"Look," Colonel Jessing said, "here comes the cavalry."

Temptation rose inside me. I wondered if we had enough time before they arrived, before I would have to Emissary again someplace else, to control the outcome of total and complete war. We are not supposed to take sides. As Emissary, we are entitled to sex in exchange for partial and sometimes misleading bits of intel. Long after other civilizations fall, Gevarians live on. We will still be here when the final star dies, and then, loveless, we will finally fade away as well.

But I really couldn't help it, and so I gave in to temptation one last time with him. I rather liked humans, after all. They did surprisingly senseless things just to do them. It was stupidly sweet. Perhaps I even owed them one. I mean, humans had saved my life twice now.

And so I rolled on top of Colonel Jessing. Even in the darkness, I could feel him smiling. He gasped when I took his soft cock into my mouth, but he quickly responded when I started doing things he'd only dreamed of before. In other words, sometimes being an alien man-whore, mind-reading parasite is its own reward.

THE GAG GIFT

Lee Minxton

"Well, boys, looks like another Welcome Back Party has gone off without a hitch." Brad chuckled as he surveyed the scene around him. The faint of heart would shudder at the potato chip crumbs crushed into the sofas and the scent of stale beer, but he knew that his fraternity brothers wouldn't have it any other way. "And this year's gift exchange was downright impressive, wouldn't you say?"

Every party needs a gimmick, and the Sigma Chi Welcome Back Party gift exchange was the most beloved and feared one on Fraternity Row. The guys would draw names out of a hat, then find gag gifts for their chosen recipients. The gift ceremony, the traditional climax of the party, always resembled Secret Santa, but on crack. Presents were chosen with an eye toward irony or complete tastelessness, preferably both.

Dylan, the frat's resident wine connoisseur, held up his bottle of Ripple bedecked with a shiny red bow. "Impressive? Absolutely. But hey, how come Kyle beat the rap?"

"He didn't. I'm about to take care of him personally."
The glint in Brad's eyes was positively evil. "Come on up,
roomie."

Kyle made his way through the throng of fraternity
boys, taking the gift as he sat in the overstuffed armchair.
While the guys tapped out a fake drumroll, he tore off the
paper. "Oh . . . my." He turned over the box in his hands.
Below the garish pink lettering that read PLEASEMASTER
5000, a scantily clad woman gazed up at him.

"Why, what is that, Kyle? Hold it up." Brad barely
suppressed his giggles.

Kyle did as he was told, turning red as he heard the
exaggerated gasps.

Never ones to let an embarrassing situation get resolved
quickly, the good brothers of Sigma Chi began to chant,
"Read the box! Read the box!"

Kyle mumbled in resignation, eager to end the travesty.
*"The PleaseMaster 5000 combines space-age technology
with quality Swedish design."*

"Speak up!" Brad crowed. "What kind of communica-
tions major are you?"

Kyle raised his voice. *"Waterproof for the utmost
versatility, this device's awesome power requires just two
triple-A batteries."* He shot Brad a glare.

Brad put on an angelic face, making a *Who, me?*
gesture. "Please, continue."

Kyle spoke haltingly. *"With three speeds and five pulsa-
tion patterns, the whisper-quiet PleaseMaster 5000"*—he
sighed—*"will send you into orbit."*

The room exploded into laughter, but Brad remained
stone-faced. "You're forgetting something, Kyle."

"For novelty use only," the hapless junior dutifully

intoned. "Consult a doctor before using on unexplained calf pain." He narrowed his eyes at Brad. "This isn't over," he then mouthed.

Brad grinned, unaware of what he'd just set in motion.

Brad had to give Kyle credit. He had handled the whole gag gift incident with much more grace than he himself would have, given the circumstances. Understandably, Brad's bed had gotten short-sheeted the following night. Of course, Kyle had swiped the chocolate-chip cookies in the latest care package from Brad's mom, leaving only the bone-dry oat bars. Still, by the end of the week, Kyle was all sunshiny Midwestern goodwill, just like before. Everything was back to normal.

Yet, Brad couldn't shake the strange visions that had been haunting him since the party. He'd see his roommate napping, and be confronted with a fleeting mental image of Kyle on his back, shaggy blond strands fanning over his pillow as he teased the PleaseMaster 5000 down his body. As he sat in the stands at Kyle's water polo matches, he became inexplicably fascinated by the droplets shimmering along his roommate's broad shoulders. When Kyle raised his head and arched his back to launch the ball, it was too easy for Brad to confuse exertion with ecstasy.

To make matters worse, life in the frat house wasn't helping. From the pickup games of touch football to the toga parties, every bonding activity was like the setup for a gay porn movie. Kyle was always at the center of it all, laughing and sweaty as he emerged victorious in shirts versus skins, gripping the cue so assertively as he won another round of pool, etc. At least, Brad thought ruefully, they hadn't had the budget to put in a hot tub.

That's right, wasn't that vibrator waterproof? Brad pondered this as he watched Kyle stalk through the bedroom in a skimpy towel before closing the bathroom door. He nearly had a coronary as he heard a loud buzzing, followed by Kyle's yelp.

Kyle poked his head through the door. "This is the worst electric razor ever," he muttered. "Are you all right, man? You seem short of breath."

Brad nodded weakly, praying for winter break to come early.

A glimmer of hope shone through a few days later. Obviously, Brad realized, this wasn't really about Kyle at all; the vibrator was to blame for the whole thing. Who wouldn't be curious about something called the Please-Master 5000? Being the raging heterosexual that he was, Brad was drawn in by the large-breasted woman on the box, and then intrigued by all the hype in the product description. Kyle only figured into the scenarios because Brad had given him the toy.

Brad had slept through most of Psychology 101, but this explanation would have to do.

Relief washed over him as he devised his plan. He'd pick a day when Kyle was at water polo practice, and then he'd find out for himself. Brad wouldn't try it, of course; he was way above that sort of thing. He'd simply take the toy out of the box and see how unimpressive it really was. He smiled, ignoring the flutter in his stomach. This was one letdown that he really looked forward to.

When Kyle left for practice that Thursday afternoon, Brad rushed to Kyle's closet like a shot and gingerly opened the door. Adrenaline made his hands shake as he pulled out the blindingly purple box, but he managed to remove it without dislodging the rest of Kyle's gear. He then sat on the edge of his bed and went to work with his pilfered prize.

Brad hadn't considered the toy's actual attributes when he bought it. He basically chose the most indiscreet package in the store. And so he now hefted the PleaseMaster 5000 in his hands, not knowing what to expect. The blue, plastic oval fit squarely in his palm, with three small buttons on top. Thankful for the toy's non-phallic shape, Brad started to relax. *Why, Mr. Innocent probably hasn't taken the thing out of the box yet*, he told himself as he randomly pressed buttons. *He certainly wouldn't put in the batteries . . .*

At that moment, a loud buzz startled Brad, and the ticklish sensation made him drop the toy. When he picked it up, he noticed that the bottom was coated with some sort of softer material—silicone, the box said—which dragged a little when he rubbed it along his wrist. The clingy sensation was not unpleasant, Brad had to admit. He continued to run it up the inside of his arm. He couldn't really tell much from that, he decided. Brad's shoulders were tense lately from all this Kyle business, so he'd see if it really worked as a massager.

A few pushes of the middle button changed the tempo to a deep thudding pulse, which felt pretty good on Brad's neck. His sweatshirt's material muffled the sensations on his shoulders, though. Better to take it off, he realized. He tossed the shirt across the room, rubbing the vibrator along his collarbone as he did so. His pulse started to quicken. Apparently, he was more uptight than he'd thought. He needed to lie down. He stretched out on his bed and started to rub the PleaseMaster 5000 over his chest, closing his eyes as he circled it around his nipple.

The toy's hum was strangely soothing, except for that weird clicking noise in the background . . .

"Whoa, dude."

Brad bolted upright to find Kyle intently staring at him. "What the hell are you doing here?"

"I live here." There was a strangely hoarse tone to Kyle's voice. "Practice got canceled. The question is—"

Brad hadn't heard a word, so intent was he on shutting the damned thing off. Failing miserably, he threw the PleaseMaster 5000 on the bed in desperation. The toy continued to shake, as if it were laughing at him. He saw that Kyle, on the other hand, wasn't laughing at all. "Swear to God, Kyle . . . " Brad looked up into the blue eyes that continued to fixate on him. He gulped. "I swear, I never tried it before."

"Obviously." Kyle shrugged. "Everyone knows it's much better when you're totally naked."

All the blood in Brad's body rushed away from his brain. That had to be the reason why one nod from Kyle had him scrambling for his zipper. It was the justification for Brad's jeans and briefs hitting the floor in record time, for Brad's willingness to hand the dangerous weapon over to his roommate without a second thought.

"I like the low speed here." Kyle touched the tip of the toy to the peak of Brad's nipple, smiling mischievously as he watched it blush and harden. He pressed another button as he teased down Brad's ribs. "A little faster here." Brad shuddered, but opened his legs slightly in spite of himself. "And there?" Brad gasped as Kyle made circles over his inner thigh. "The escalation pulse is very nice."

For more than a year, Brad and Kyle had been inhibited around each other in the way only college roommates can be. Brad's head spun as he thought of all the effort he'd spent hiding morning erections or pretending he didn't need to jack off. Now, he was more aroused than he'd ever been, and this same roommate was not only a witness, but the cause of it. Kyle explored Brad's body with abandon, pressing the toy against his balls before stroking it over his perineum. Yet, Kyle wasn't touching Brad's cock at all. Even in his lusty haze, Brad knew this had to be an oversight. Brad's hand drifted downward, but Kyle blocked it quickly.

"No, Brad. You're not supposed to touch your room-mate's things." Kyle's voice hitched as he moved Brad's hand away. "And right now, this thing belongs to me." Kyle looked him in the eye as he closed his hand around Brad's cock, moving upward with a light but deliberate stroke.

The playful contact contrasted tantalizingly with Kyle's forceful tone, and Brad wondered what else lay beneath his roommate's rapidly crumbling gee-whiz facade. While Ridgeston University had outlawed hazing a few years earlier, a large paddle, emblazoned with the Sigma Chi letters, was still displayed in the frat's basement. Brad wondered if it ever came out for special occasions. As he writhed under the competing sensations of silicone and skin, Brad pictured himself bent over the basement sofa, bracing himself for a blow. Kyle would loom naked above him, the muscles in his arm clenching as he whacked the paddle against Brad's flesh. Heat rushed through Brad at the fleeting fantasy, and his hips bucked to meet the imaginary smack. "Please . . . "

Kyle placed the toy squarely on the root of Brad's shaft, teasing it along the length. He bit his lip as he felt Brad tensing beneath him. "Come for me, Bradley."

Brad didn't know if it was the wicked vibration hitting

his glans that did it or the feel of Kyle's breath in his ear. All he could do was moan as his spunk flew in graceful arcs, hitting his neck and chest. Kyle's free hand moved along Brad's thighs and belly, working the last remnants of sensation free.

It took a long time for the both of them to catch their breath. Kyle gazed in wonder before leaning into his shell-shocked roommate. "You okay?"

Okay was not an adequate description, but since Brad was having trouble forming complete thoughts, it would have to suffice. "Yeah." He noticed something as Kyle brushed against him. "You're . . . hard."

"Hottest thing I've ever seen." Kyle's voice was low. "Why wouldn't I be?"

"I don't know." Brad smiled in amazement, just beginning to comprehend the whole situation. "But you're really hard." He couldn't resist grinding his bare hip against Kyle's denim-clad crotch, and he chuckled as his roommate groaned.

"You'll see." Kyle grinned wickedly at Brad. "I'm going to be very satisfied before we're through. And so will you." He raised an eyebrow. "First, we need to clean you up. You could use a good, long rinse." He caressed Brad's sticky chest with real affection.

Brad's head lolled as Kyle moved his hand lower to enclose him. "And a safeword," he panted.

Kyle stole a quick but ardent kiss that left Brad breathless. "That, too," he whispered into Brad's mouth. His eyes sparkling, Kyle took Brad's hand and led him toward the shower.

GHOSTLY AFFAIR

Karl Taggart

Jason Stark, the stage actor, had been keeping me for about a year when he announced we were moving. "Pasadena," he said, drawing out the word as if he were playing to a full house. We'd been living in a Hollywood Hills rental. I was happy there. Pasadena conjured up images of the Rose Parade, little old ladies, restraint.

"Don't frown," Jason scolded. "It doesn't become you, and besides, the new place is twice as big. You'll love it once we're there. It was left to me by an uncle, and I'm ready for a change, a bit of character, some old-world charm."

Jason was as close to old-world as I wanted to get, but no amount of pouting could sway him, and so we moved into what I initially called—under my breath, of course—"the home." Since I'd come to depend on the relationship, it was worth my while to see things Jason's way.

The house had been built in 1914. It was a mansion, stately and dark, with five bedrooms, four baths, a grand salon, a library, a den—well, the list went on and on.

Jason was energized by the change, as if the older house made him feel younger. He fucked me in every room and outdoors as well—in the gazebo in broad daylight, on the lawn under the cover of darkness—and while I loved this revitalization of our physical relationship, I always had the feeling we were being watched. There was nothing visible, no objects moving or doors opening without explanation, just a presence. Often, when Jason had me on my back, pumping his cock into me, I'd look over his shoulder to see if someone was there.

And then one day someone was.

The funny part is, when I finally saw the ghost, I didn't even flinch. I was so accustomed to sensing the presence when Jason and I had sex that the embodiment merely served as confirmation rather than surprise. Jason's dick had been buried in my ass at the time and I was working my own prong when the most gorgeous man suddenly appeared beside the bed. He was blond, naked, slightly translucent, and possessed a big, dangling cock that he gripped with his left hand.

He watched us go at it, working himself all the while, and when I came, he fixed on the sight, tongue hanging out as if he longed for a taste. Jason, meanwhile, was nearly there, grunting and pounding away, out of breath, as usual. The ghost had a good vantage point, and let his gaze slide down to focus on the action: Jason's prick going in and out of my well-lubed hole.

It was when Jason finally came that I noticed the ghost's dick was soft, which made me wonder whether erections might be something tied to material life. *Poor ghost*, I thought. As Jason spent himself, then quieted, the ghost let go of his cock, backed away, and disappeared.

Jason collapsed onto me, pulled out, and rolled over. Breathing heavily, he instantly fell asleep. I hit the bathroom to wash up, then returned to the bedroom to stand at the foot of the bed in the hope that the spirit might return. Sadly, he didn't.

I never mentioned anything to Jason about the intruder. When it became apparent that he hadn't seen the ghost, I figured the visitor meant to connect with me alone. I decided to find out who he was and what he wanted.

Jason was appearing in a play downtown and spent much of his time rehearsing at the theater. Left on my own, I decided to entice the ghost into making an appearance. So, one afternoon I undressed, picked out a few choice pieces from our dildo collection, set out lube and a towel, then climbed onto the bed for a good solo session.

I was greasing a big pink ten-incher when I felt the presence. Without reacting, I lay back, raised my legs, and started working the rubber cock into my hole. My dick was already hard from just the idea of what I was about to do. I began to fuck myself while jerking my cock, and this—as I had hoped it might—brought the ghost to me.

He stood off to one side, a beautiful specimen, maybe thirty, with curly golden hair and piercing blue eyes. His skin was pale, of course, but not so much so as to turn me off. He had a substantial build as well: broad shoulders, smooth, thick chest, narrow waist, strong thighs, and that big cock, which was still soft even though he had it in hand.

I steadily worked the dildo, making a show of popping it out and then pushing it back in, groaning as if some hot guy was attached to it. The ghost moved closer, watching me intently, so I pulled the dildo out and worked my muscle instead. When he fixed his stare on my pulsing sphincter, I ran my finger over the rim, then went in. With this, my dick started throbbing, and I would have come had I not backed off. I wanted to get this guy involved, sensing he wanted something only a mortal could provide.

I thought of asking him to join me, but before I could say anything to that effect, he sat down on the edge of the bed. His look was calm, with no hint of urgency, and it made me wonder if people could fuck in the next world; if spirits invisible to us were going at it in our midst. The ghost smiled, and I realized he could read my thoughts. Then, slowly, as if it might frighten me away, he reached a hand toward my ass. I withdrew my finger but kept squeezing my prick. He then slowly moved a single finger to my hole. Eager to get him into me, I spread my legs and pulled my buttcheeks wide. As invitations go, I couldn't get more blatant.

When he stuck his finger in my ass it was like an icy rod going in. I flinched. He pulled out, and we shared an awkward moment before I offered him another welcoming thought. Then he stuck in two fingers. I smiled, despite the frigid cold.

He was tentative, which was fine because I was acclimating to the chill, wondering what his dick would feel like, forgetting, until he took hold of the member in question, that he could read my every thought. I quickly recovered and thought of sucking him off. He stopped working my hole; I think he was surprised by the offer. I hesitated for a moment, and then put my legs down and crawled across the bed to him.

"Who are you?" I asked.

"Graham Ellis."

"Why are you here?"

"It's my house."

"Are you related to Jason's uncle?"

"It's my house," he repeated.

"Okay, I'm not going to quibble, but you have to know that I've never met a ghost before. That's what you are, right? A ghost?"

When he didn't respond, I went on. "Right. Well, that's what I think you are, only I've never heard of naked ghosts sticking their fingers up asses."

He looked down at my stiff cock, then back up to my face. "Will you do it?" he asked.

"Suck your dick? My pleasure. Why don't you get comfortable?"

I had him lie back, head on the pillow as I positioned myself between his legs so I could see his face. He was cold, so goddamned cold. Everything—balls, cock—but I did it. It was like giving a Popsicle a blow job. The best part was that the big dick finally got hard. As it began to stiffen in my mouth, I realized that was why he'd made himself known to me: you can't arouse yourself in the hereafter. If he was putting in an appearance with me, maybe he wasn't quite resigned to his fate.

I couldn't get all of him into my mouth, but I gave it the old college try, deep-throating his frosty pole until my tonsils were numb, licking and sucking until he finally became animated. He began to gently thrust, so I worked his balls as I sucked him toward his long-awaited climax. As he bucked up into me, releasing his icy load, I wondered how long it had been.

The come made my mouth ache, but I took it all, knowing that of all the dicks I'd sucked, his was the cleanest. He let out a long moan as he emptied, with-drawing only when he began to soften.

"Quite a payoff," I remarked. "Been a while?"

He uttered a dismissive laugh and slowly stood. I thought he might disappear again, so I said, "You want some more?" I began to stroke my dick, then eased back and raised my legs. "Do you want to fuck me? I could sure use it."

He started working himself again, and I saw the longing in his eyes. His cock remained soft. "Come here," I said. "Let me help you with that."

He slid down next to me, and I began to pull his big sausage. It came to life in my hand. Seconds later, I had him thrusting into my palm. "How about it?" I said.

He nodded and crawled between my legs, pushing them up as he stared at his target. I pulled my cheeks apart.

"Go ahead, stick it in. You might want to grease it up a bit first." I pointed to the lube, which he picked up and squeezed. "Great stuff," I said. He smeared his shaft and then guided it to my waiting hole. "Do it, man," I coaxed when he hesitated. "Isn't this what you came back for?"

He nodded, then rammed that iceberg into me, which made me cry out from both its temperature and size. He didn't wait for me to acclimate to either; he began a full-out ride, pounding my ass while his mouth opened to a silent cry. I heard our flesh slapping, and had to remind myself this wasn't real, that he'd materialized from the next world, and yet the sound was a totally human squishy fuck-slap. He got the bed creaking as his cold dick seared my chute.

When he let go his load, it felt as if a garden hose was turned on inside me. Cold come flushed deep into my bowels. That got me to pump my own dick, balls churning out another load. My hot cream, his cold one—what a pair.

"Don't leave," I told him when we'd finished and he started to get up. "Not yet," I added. He hesitated, then sat beside me and let me run my hands over him for a few moments before finally saying, "I shouldn't be here."

"Why? Are there rules? No cavorting with the living?"

"Something like that. Only . . . "

"What?"

"You're in my house. It's been quiet for so long, and suddenly all this . . . this . . . "

"Fucking?"

"Yes. It's just so difficult."

"To watch?"

"To only watch."

"Why me and not Jason?" I asked.

"I don't find him attractive."

I took hold of Graham's dick, which immediately began to harden. He drew a long breath and started to thrust.

"You're really more my type," I said as he fucked my palm. "We can make this a regular thing if you want. Jason's gone a lot, rehearsals and all. He's an actor."

He shook his head, even as he unleashed another come. I worked him until his chest had jizz all up it. It was while I was caressing his body that he dissolved, come and all. I lay immobilized for a few seconds, thinking he might reappear, feeling more alone than ever when he didn't.

The house suddenly seemed cavernous. Cold and lonely. I got up, put on some sweats, and built a fire. When Jason arrived hours later, I made martinis and embarked on a serious effort to get drunk.

"What is it?" Jason asked, but I told him nothing of

my day, insisting instead that I was simply pining for him and that he should fuck me on the living room floor. As he complied, I waited for the being-watched feeling, but it didn't arrive. Jason, tired from his day, took forever to come and, as he pumped and pumped, I wondered if Graham Ellis had, now that he'd gotten what he wanted, moved on to his final reward.

Loneliness crept over me the next few days. I clung to Jason. He kept asking what was wrong, and I kept assuring him everything was fine, although I knew it wasn't. I wanted Graham to return. I was pining after the hereafter.

Oddly, it was during an outburst that he reappeared. A rehearsal had gone poorly. I was consoling Jason, but when I suggested sex, he got miffed, and things went downhill from there.

"It's not always about sex," he shouted. "If I could solve my problems with my dick, don't you think I would?"

Wounded, I went silent. That's when I felt the presence. Looking past Jason, I saw Graham standing to one side. He was naked and pulling on his cock.

"Fine," I told Jason. "I'm sorry. I won't bother you further."

"I'll be in the study," he said, leaving me alone—or so he thought. Graham approached. I knelt and took his soft cock into my mouth.

After that, our encounters became a way of life, though maybe that's the wrong expression. Graham, however, became more real to me than anyone else, even Jason, and I found myself longing for him, lost in thoughts of his touch even as I sat across from Jason at dinner. Months passed, and then time—as it invariably does—got me to thinking about what was next. Life with Jason had a finite quality. What, then, did I have with Graham?

He didn't retreat now after sex, and I knew he'd fallen in love with me, as I had with him. "We must be breaking all kinds of rules," I said one day as we lay in bed after a rousing round of sex. He was stroking my dick and issued a soft chuckle. "You know, I've fallen in love with you," I added. He sucked in a long breath—so human—and closed his eyes. "So, what now?" I asked.

When he finally opened his eyes they were moist. I had my answer. "We keep on keeping on, don't we?" I asked. He nodded. And then I thought of that movie from the forties, *The Ghost and Mrs. Muir*, where the woman spent years waiting to die so she could join the ghost she loved. Graham knew what I was thinking and said, "We're not a film."

"What are we then?"

"An affair," he said, luxuriating in the sound. "A beautiful affair that need never end."

He kissed me then, with the cold lips I'd grown to savor. I thought of how Jason, being so much older, would die before me, and that when he did I wouldn't be alone; Graham would be there. And when my time came, it wouldn't be such a bad thing. "So we've got, like, eternity?" I asked.

"Yes," he said. He then rolled me over and pressed himself against me, his dick awakening in my crack.

"What's the other side like?" I asked.

He shrugged. "Pasadena," he said, his lips cold on my neck.

THE BALLAD OF
COWBOY SPRINGS

Louis Flint Ceci

It was time to go. Donny had already left, taking his mandolin and coffee grinder with him, and leaving two months of unpaid phone bills and his share of the lease behind. I had stupidly put the phone in my name, so I was on the hook for that, but the three months left on the lease wouldn't be a problem; the way rents were going up in the Outer Mission, my landlord would have our place rented before I was down the steps with the last box of books.

San Francisco was getting too expensive for a writer/ performer of satiric folk songs—especially one who hadn't written anything new in half a year. You'd think this city would be an endless fount of subjects for satire, with its colliding populations of preening politicians, inflamed activists, and gaggles of cash-rich conscience-poor techies teetering on top of an understory of the homeless and undocumented. It was a real layer-cake of irony, but I just wasn't feeling the love. So I chucked or gave away maybe two-thirds of my stuff (including some of Donny's, but he wasn't coming back for it, was he?) and put the rest of it in my sister's basement in Oakland. I threw my camping gear into the back of my 2003 Toyota 4Runner and got the hell out of Dodge.

But where to now? Well, when you're about as far west as the West Coast gets, and you can't seem to find the gumption to run your four-wheeler off the cliff at Fort Funston (putting the "fun" back into Funston), your only choice is east. It was June. The Central Valley would already be hellish, but the Sierras beckoned. Maybe the thinner air up there would clear my head, allow me to write. And so I headed for Yosemite.

It rained. In June. In California. If a fully decorated Christmas tree had sprung overnight from my fore-head I couldn't have been more surprised. Or disap-pointed. (I don't particularly like Christmas trees.) The Tuolumne was flooded, so the campgrounds were closed. I turned around at the entrance, but still felt the urge to keep going. I headed for the Tioga Pass that would take me over the Sierras and down into Mono Lake and the high desert. It felt like the right thing to do. I'd been deserted by my boyfriend and my muse, so why not go all the way?

I camped that night at Big Bend above Lee Vining. The campground was oddly empty. It was too dark to pitch the tent, so I just rolled out my sleeping bag in the back of the Toyota and burrowed into it.

The sound of the door opening barely woke me. In fact, I felt it was important to keep my eyes shut, even if I was awake.

The warm length of a naked leg slid down my thigh

as he slipped into the sleeping bag with me. "*Shh*," he said, though I had said nothing. Then his stomach pressed against mine. I could feel his abdomen inflate and contract as he breathed. He slung his hips forward and pressed a remarkably hard cock against mine as he wrapped his arms around me, pinning my arms to my side. I knew that cock. Knew its size and shape and throbbing pulse. "Donny?" I whispered.

"Aw, now you've ruined it."

My eyes flew open. I saw nothing but the pitch-black interior of the car. There was, of course, no one in the sleeping bag with me. How could there be? When Donny and I went camping, we zipped our bags together and did our best to zip our bodies together, too. But there was only one sleeping bag in the back of this car. There wasn't room for two. I looked down at my cock. It still believed we had company, but I shook my head. "Sorry, fella; it's just you and me."

It bobbed at me, refusing to give up, but when I tried to give it what it wanted, it refused. It would spark a little from the friction, but then the heat would dissipate into the mountain air. I lay back with my eyes open, staring at the inside of the car. I should have pitched the damned tent. Then at least I'd be looking up at stars.

The next day was better. I drove up north on US Highway 395 along the east side of the Sierras, getting lost looking for a hot spring that I'd read about in *Hidden Treasures of the Eastern Sierras*. It was too well hidden, apparently, because I didn't find it, but as I came around the corner of a twisting mountain road, I suddenly faced an expanse of wildflowers. They were Clarkias in full bloom, spreading up the rocky slope in a carpet of pink dotted with maroon. My eyes lit up as a wide grin spread across my face. There was a tickling in my brain as words and the sketch of a tune trickled into place. What was this weird sensation? Joy? Or simply altitude sickness?

The words and music bounced around inside my head as I drove to my next stop, a primitive campsite above Mammoth Lakes. I thought the internal chatter might keep me awake long into the night, as it often did back when I wrote tunes for a living. But I fell asleep almost as soon as the sun disappeared behind the peaks.

The next morning, I drove back down into the valley and headed south on US 395. The landscape of the eastern Sierras continued to pull me in two directions: up to the peaks and out into the desert. I took many side trips, finally stopping late in the afternoon at a private campground. I drove in looking for the pay station or the campground "host," but didn't see either. Signs along the way promised NATURAL HEALTHFUL HOT SPRINGS! in the CLEAR, RESTORING WATERS OF A MOUNTAIN STREAM! guaranteed to be NATURE'S OWN CURE FOR WHAT AILS YOU! But the rains had swollen the stream to a river, and the hot springs were now a good twenty yards from the bank. Any attempt to wade out to them would have swept you away and cured what ails you for good.

I was not the only one disappointed by this turn of events. Several disgruntled campers lingered around the soggy semicircle of logs that constituted the NATURAL AMPHITHEATRE! A family of five bickered at one end; I sat at the other with a middle-aged man in a red-and-black flannel shirt and jeans whose contours made me wonder if perhaps he might be good for what ails me. His dark mustache showed streaks of gray, which were echoed at his temples. There was a tuft of black hair waving at me from the open collar of his shirt, so I struck up a conversation.

"Too bad about the hot springs," I ventured.

"Is that what brings you here?" He smiled at me, a big, open smile with eyes that looked straight into mine, eyes I didn't want to let go of.

"I've been driving around, looking for inspiration," I said. *You might be it*, I added to myself.

"I do that, too. Have you found any?"

I could mention the spark in his eyes, the bulge of his crotch (were those 501s?), the promise of firm turf beneath that flannel shirt. Instead, I said, "I saw something yesterday, a field of wildflowers. It made me want to sing."

He laughed and looked up. The sky was beginning to pearl over into evening. "Oh, yeah, I get that, too. So, did you?"

"*Hmm?*" I'd been distracted by the music of his laugh.

"Sing. Did you sing?"

I thought a moment. "I haven't written anything in months, but yeah, something did come to me. Well, the start of something, anyway."

He leaned back, holding himself up by his outspread arms and letting his knees fall open. "Care to share?"

I had to close my eyes to clear my head, but once he was hidden from sight, the words and melody came back readily enough:

Be simple in your sorrow,
Care less about your fate,

For if you need tomorrow
To be happy, you're too late.

I opened my eyes hopefully. He was looking down, a small smile on his face. But he said nothing. "It's just a start," I apologized.

"So, we should be like wildflowers?"

I smiled. *This guy gets me*, I thought. "Kinda."

"But that isn't true, is it?"

Or not. "What?"

"Those wildflowers will be gone in a day or two. Withered. Dead."

"Well . . . "

"You have to think about tomorrow. You have to make decisions today, or your tomorrow is in the hand of other powers."

"Of course, you—"

"Every day, every moment, you have to decide to live in Christ or outside Him."

And that was that. *Well*, I thought as I drove out of the campground, *at least I haven't paid a camping fee.*

I made camp in the dark and ate an MRE whose flavor and consistency left no impression. As I looked up at the stars through the netting of my tent, the words started dancing again. I let them. If I were still the singing satirist of San Francisco, I would have flicked on the camp light and written them down. Instead, I just let them caper in the dark of the mountainside:

"The flowers wither, the grasses curl!"
So said Saint Peter to Saint Paul.

Come, my love, let's give it a whirl.
Who cares if summer leads to fall?
For summer ever leads us all.

Not great, but as the border between thought and dream dissolved, I had the feeling that whatever had been blocking me was being carried away down the river of stars.

Morning was sharp and clear. "Right, then," I announced to the manzanitas. "Enough mountains; into the desert."

The *Hidden Treasures* guide told me I was in Long Valley, the caldera of an ancient lava plume that had moved east ages ago and was now parked under Yellowstone National Park. It had left plenty of heat behind, though, and the desert floor was dotted with small, locally maintained pools and springs (called "tubs"), and even a river so hot it could boil a dog alive (and apparently had, or else why bother mentioning it?). It gave directions to several less lethal spots, all of them off an intricate web of unpaved roads that seemed to follow no particular pattern in their layout or direction.

GPS was useless out here. After an hour and a half of dusty futility trying to find one of the local "tubs," I gave up and simply drove through the desert. I didn't tear up the roads; I just meandered wherever my 4Runner felt like running. I couldn't get lost. The Sierras, still shining with the remnants of the snow dropped by the storm three days ago, clearly marked which way to go if I wanted to get back to the 395 and civilization. Finally, feeling pleasantly loose and relaxed, I stopped the car and got out.

The rain had done its magic here, too. The desert plants bloomed in yellows, reds, and colors I would have thought possible only in neon signs. I took a deep breath. The morning air was still cool but warming up. It carried the creosote smell of coyote bush and sage with a hint of . . . wait, was that *sulphur*?

I looked around. About fifty yards away was an outcropping of dark rocks, a few of them a little taller than a man, the whole group no larger than a school bus. From behind them, a thin plume of vapor trailed into the morning sky.

Well, I'll be damned, I thought. *I've found one.*

There was no one else around and no cars visible up or down the road I'd been wandering, but I locked the Toyota anyway and headed for the rocks. Looking down, I could see there was a faint trail in the desert crust leading around to one side. Could this be one of the local hot springs I'd read about? And was it one suitable for human soaking, or was it a real dog boiler?

Feeling like an intrepid prospector and grinning from ear to ear, I rounded the corner and pulled up short.

There was a naked man sitting on a ledge of rock above a pool of steaming water. The pool was about the size of two large oblong bathtubs side by side. The man's legs dangled over the edge and disappeared into the hot mist. His clothes lay neatly folded beside him, topped by a cream-colored Stetson. My sudden appearance caused him to start and look up.

"Sorry," I stammered. I looked away quickly, but not before my eyes had registered significant details: blue eyes, straw-colored hair, small mustache of a slightly darker color, lightly muscled chest and abdomen, smooth, and a crotch sporting even darker hair. By glancing away, I caught sight of a horse tethered to a sagebrush. It regarded me with calm indifference, which was more than I would be able to muster if I looked back at this golden cowboy.

"No problem," he said evenly. "Didn't hear you, is all."

If I continued to look away, it would be obvious that I was trying not to be obvious, so I turned around. He was looking at me with a bit more curiosity than the horse. I told myself to relax. "I parked a ways away and walked in." My brain emptied. I looked at the water his legs disappeared into. "Is it hot?"

"Hot enough," he said, without the slightest trace of mockery.

Feeling I couldn't look or sound any more idiotic (where were all those words that had danced in the starlight?), I asked, "Do you mind if I join you?"

"Make yourself at home," he said, a small smile on his face.

I turned away as I stripped, piling my clothes on the desert floor in a neat imitation of his.

"You'll want to put those up here," he said, patting the rock ledge he sat on. "Bugs."

I nodded my thanks and set my bundle next to his, then stepped into the "tub."

This was indeed one of the locally maintained hot springs. The bottom was rough concrete, and I soon made out the PVC pipe that brought the water from the actual spring about twenty yards away to this rocky shelter. The water near the pipe was scalding, but it dissipated through the pool; close to the rocks it was tolerable, but just. The tub wasn't deep. I was completely immersed only if I sat on my butt and leaned back on my elbows. If I knelt, the water only came up to my navel.

After a few minutes of full immersion, I began to feel

dizzy. "Whew!" I said, sitting up. My heart was pounding.

"It does it to you, doesn't it?" my cowboy companion said.

"Yeah." I felt a little out of breath. The water was cooler near the rocks, but still hot. There wasn't much room on the ledge for two. How would he take it if I sat next to him? Would he feel I was coming on to him? There was no one around for miles. If he panicked and got tough, there would be no one to stop him or come to my aid.

Screw it. I was boiling in there. And so I hauled myself out of the pool and sat on the ledge. There was just enough room for the two of us and our two piles of clothes. Our legs dangled in the water. Our knees touched.

Steam curled up from my skin and a light breeze tugged the wisps away. As my brain simmered down from a boil, I took a glance at the man next to me. He must have cooled down already. His skin, smooth and tanned, glistened in the sun, but did not steam. He was looking down at his crotch. I looked down, too. His cock was sticking straight out between his beautiful thighs, hard as the rock we perched on. He didn't look at me.

I gazed out over the desert. My heart rate was picking up again, but it wasn't from the heat. I knew if I got back in the pool and faced him, there was a good chance I'd pass out before I could find out if his semaphore was meant for me or just a kind of morning salute.

I took several slow breaths and got my heart back under control, then took another look. Yup. It was still up. I reached into the water and pulled up a handful and ladled it slowly on the golden thigh next to me.

He exhaled audibly, his shoulders simultaneously

relaxing and expanding as he leaned back and closed his eyes.

I scooped up another handful of water and poured it over the same thigh. He breathed deeply. Another scoop, this time poured on the other thigh, passing over his cock, which bobbed up and brushed my hand as it passed. A bead of precome stuck to my wrist.

"*Mmm*, that feels good," he said, eyes still closed, face completely relaxed.

I stood in the water and faced him. Leaning down, I took a handful of steaming water in each hand. But I didn't pour the water on his thighs this time; instead, I dribbled it on his shoulders. Then I placed my heated hands on his cool shoulders and slowly ran them down his chest. There was a sharp intake of breath as I passed over his nipples. When I reached the top of his thighs, his legs spread and I knelt down, my knees resting on the rough concrete bottom of the pond. I was no longer worried about the heat.

I ran the length of my forearms slowly up and down his thighs, then I reached my hands around his hips. His legs rose behind me and rested on my back. I leaned forward and took his cock in my mouth.

His precome was salty and sweet. For a moment, I just held the head of his cock in my mouth, savoring the flavor and running the broad flat of my tongue around the ridge of his meat, teasing the slit with my tip.

His breathing had become audible. Looking up, I could see his chest expand with each inhale. His harms were hanging loose at his sides.

I slid my mouth down the length of his shaft. It thickened in the middle, then narrowed at the root. As my lips reached the bottom and my nose buried itself in the reddish hair sprouting there, I felt the head of his cock slip into the back of my throat. I heard him moan. The sound rumbled through his torso and turned me on something fierce. Despite the heat soaking in from the waist down, I knew my own cock was hard as the magma bed beneath us. I deep-throated him again and again. Looking up, I saw his muscles contract from his rib cage to below his navel.

Oh no you don't, I thought. *Not yet.*

I pulled back. My man was panting, his eyes open, imploring me with blue intensity. I blew on his cock as he took several deep breaths.

I moved my arms under his legs and lifted them slightly. His balls now hung down between his legs and hovered above his ass. I leaned in again and took one of the nuts in my mouth, rolling it around from cheek to cheek. His breathing started coming short again. I got the second nut in my mouth and pulled back slightly, stretching his scrotum.

He grunted and put both hands on my head, pressing down slightly.

I knew what he wanted. I released his balls and let my tongue slide down his taint to his asshole. The second my tongue touched the rim, he let out a whimper. I flicked my tongue in and out of his hole, which opened and contracted around it in waves. I flattened my tongue and ran it over his puckered hole, then up to his balls and back again.

He was now moaning with each breath. He reached down and grabbed his cock. I knew there was no stopping him, and so I focused on getting him his release. I took both balls in my mouth while I inserted a spit-slicked finger up his ass. I slid it in and out in time to the strokes on his cock.

The base of his shaft seemed to grow thicker and harder. His thighs tensed and clamped my face to his crotch.

When he came, he convulsed so hard I thought we'd both pop off the ledge and into the water. His abdomen contracted and he doubled over, bellowing one continuous animal sound as he came. I could feel his urethra pulse beneath my tongue as spurt after spurt ripped out of his cock and spattered over my face and hair. It seemed to go on forever.

His bellowing soon faded to silence. His cock still throbbed and shudders shook his frame. He was panting, exhausted. I started easing my finger out of his ass. A final shudder as one last pulse of come pushed its way up his cock and squeezed my finger from his hole.

And suddenly I was very, very hot.

I gently let his balls roll out of my mouth and, with my strength quickly fading, pulled myself out of the hot springs and onto the rock ledge beside him. He collapsed sideways into me, and I nearly collapsed myself. Mercifully, the breeze picked up again, and in a few minutes I realized I was not going to pass out.

I looked down at my cowboy. His head lolled against my shoulder and his chest rose and fell regularly. His cock was slowly deflating between those two powerful thighs, dangling a thread of semen that trailed to the hot springs at our feet. I looked down at my own legs. Two bright red disks marked the point where my knees had met the bottom of the pool.

"Wow," my man said.

"Wow," I agreed.

I didn't want to ruin this by saying anything more. There was a time for words and a time for the desert silence.

Sometime later, we did say a few words more, but they were mostly the ordinary things strangers say when they pass each other on the trail. We dressed. He mounted his horse and rode off to the north, where he worked at a kind of adventure ranch for rich kids. I stayed behind, sitting on the rocks beside the pool. Soon, an SUV pulled up with its radio thumping, and some local kids got out. It was time to go.

I returned to San Francisco, that ironic city, but I brought two things with me from my time away: the first faded away after only a week—the second-degree burns on my knees; the second, however, lasted long enough for me to find my voice again.

The Ballad of Cowboy Springs

'Twas in the perfect desert air
Beneath the rising desert sun
I found a cowboy stripped down bare
Beside a hot springs, all alone.

"Oh pardon me if I intrude,"
I said as I approached the spot.
"I'd like to join you in the nude
And soak there if the water's hot."

"Oh yes," he said and grinned, "it's hot,"
And by his look said something more.
I wondered if, as like as not,
There might be something else in store.

The breeze that teased our skin was cool.
The desert blossomed all around.
I blew him there beside the pool
His sighs and moans the only sound.

The desert air is clear and sweet
And sweet the desert solitude,
The perfect place for men to meet
And come upon each other, nude.

COMING HOME

Andra Dill

The text alert ping saved the fool from being throttled. Tomas leaned forward, his wide hands on the desk, glaring at his two subordinates, neither meeting his eyes. Just under six feet, he had an intimidating build: short, thick neck that flowed into broad shoulders and chest, thickly muscled arms and thighs. Dark brown eyes glanced down at the phone. *Carter* shone on the screen. Clenching his teeth to grit back the tongue-lashing he wanted to deliver, he picked up the phone.

He read the text: *Need to talk. Wake me nmwt. POD people.* And just like that, the red haze of fury died. How did Carter do that? Tomas believed his husband was psychic. He had the uncanny knack of reining in the tempest that was Tomas's emotions with a word, a look, a touch, and, in this case, a text.

He smirked at the message. *Nmwt* was Carter's shorthand for "no matter what time," but what was *POD people*? Payable on death, print on demand, passed out drunk? What the hell?

He rubbed a hand over his long-past-five-o'clock stubbled jaw.

"Paul, can you take over the Barron negotiations?"

The young fool opened his mouth to protest. Tomas lifted a hand, silencing him.

"Yes, I'll get my team up to speed this weekend." Paul fidgeted with his cuffs, looking at a spot just over Tomas's shoulder.

"Good, let's hope that we can salvage this." Another ping; he glanced down at the new message, this one from his daughter. "Gentlemen, I haven't been home in four days. Fix this. We'll talk on Monday."

The built-up tension from the meeting in Portland, the mess he had found when he returned to the office, and the too-long commute home dissipated as he walked through the front door. Coming home was a gift. Twenty-one years. They had built this home, this life together. The entry hosted a soul-soothing display. His hand came up of its own volition to touch their wedding photo. His fingers stroked over Carter's image, looking dashing in his tuxedo, the two of them grinning like fools. His fingers glided down to tap the photo directly below of the four of them taken this summer as they hiked through Yosemite.

Inhaling deeply, familiar aromas greeted him: the signature scent of orange from products the cleaning lady used twice a week; from the kitchen, the lingering aroma of bacon and tomato sauce. He flinched, looked down at the partially unzipped duffel bag on the steps, the pungent smell of a teenage boy's gym clothes. Zipping up the bag, he went upstairs.

It was peacefully quiet; unusual that one or both kids weren't still up. He dropped the offensive duffel into

Brandon's room, then peeked into his daughter's room before making a beeline to Carter.

Tomas threw his jacket over the ancient chair, one of their first purchases together. The television volume was on low, its flickering light the only illumination in the bedroom. His attention was riveted on Carter, on his long, lean body propped up by a mountain of pillows in the center of their king-size bed, mouth open, softly snoring. Tomas removed his tie while watching his husband's sleeping form: golden skinned, bare chest rising and falling rhythmically; head resting on one arm, his brown hair just starting to gray and in need of a trim, the other arm resting on his thigh. Tomas smiled at the garish red-and-orange plaid sleeping pajamas, a Christmas gift from the kids. They were seriously ugly, but still Carter's favorite pair.

He clicked off the television, the countdown in his head ticking off the seconds, knowing what Carter would say. He wasn't disappointed.

"Hey, I was watching that," Carter grumbled three seconds after it shut off. He rubbed his eyes, blinked a few times before squinting at Tomas's shape.

"Sure you were." Carter usually fell asleep to the drone of the television. Tomas couldn't stand the noise. The first year living together, it had been one of their most persistent fights. Funny how it was a little joke between them now. Tomas leaned down and kissed Carter, pressing him firmly into the mass of pillows. He breathed in his scent, vetiver and pepper, before breaking the kiss.

"Hi." Carter's fingers twined into Tomas's sable brown hair, now edged at the temples with white, messing up the meticulously combed strands. Carter's hands drifted down to embrace Tomas's nut-brown face, thumbs brushing over cheekbones. He pulled him in for another kiss, deeper this time, slower, more demanding.

When they parted, Carter asked, "What time is it?" He twisted toward the nightstand, turning the lamp on.

"Just after midnight." Tomas walked into the bathroom, fingers combing his tousled locks, and flicked on the light. "POD people?"

"You remember that movie? You know, pod people." He looked expectantly at Tomas. Getting no response, he huffed, "*Invasion of the Body Snatchers.*"

"Okay," Tomas said neutrally. Picking up his toothbrush, he applied a thin line of toothpaste.

"Aliens replace normal, rational people with pods that have aliens who look like the sane person, but they're really aliens who want to take over the world. Or something like that."

Tomas stuck his head back into the bedroom. "Who have the aliens, uh, podded?"

"*Your* daughter—"

"Ah, that good, huh?" He couldn't wait to hear what their twelve-year-old demon/angel child had done. The Longfellow poem about "the little girl who had a little curl" flashed through his mind. When she was "really bad," she was *his* daughter.

"*Your* daughter had a meltdown about dance lessons. Let's see, in addition to ballet and pre-pointe, she wants to add lyrical. Of course, lyrical is only taught on the same night as karate, and she is willing to forego that class to fulfill her dreams."

"What the hell is lyrical?" Popping the toothbrush into his mouth, he started brushing.

"A class that Petra, Ellie, and Mia are taking, according

to Brandon. He got smacked for that answer, by the way. Anyway, Zoe is willing to drop karate and volleyball so that she can take this extra dance class."

Speaking with a mouth full of paste, Tomas interrupted. "Volleyball is over."

Carter nodded. "Uh-huh. The teacher is brilliant." That last word was accompanied by air quotes. "Personally asked Zoe to join the class. I could go on, but I'm too tired. She was so worked up that she carried on the argument-slash-conversation for ten minutes before she realized I wasn't answering her. Zoe screamed, actually screamed, at me that we would be 'ruining her dreams' if she couldn't take lyrical. She stormed out, slamming her door for good measure. I didn't see her for the rest of the night." He added, sotto voce, "Thank god."

Tomas rinsed his mouth. "You'll love this." Striding across the room, he dug out his phone and handed it to Carter.

Carter read aloud, "*Daddy, we need to talk. Wake me nmwt.*" He smiled and returned the phone. "Daddy, huh? When was the last time she called you that?"

"When she was nine?" He shrugged out of his shirt, watching Carter watch him, that intense hazel-eyed perusal igniting a familiar need within him. Tomas's fingers twitched, wanting to touch that golden skin.

Carter flopped back on the pillows, sighing heavily. "I talked to my mom. She says this is normal. The next few years we'll get to see an escalation in dramatic outbursts and far fewer glimpses of our beloved daughter until the summer before she goes to college, at which time she will be, more or less, back to normal."

"Your mom is such a smartass." He sat down on the

bed picking up Carter's bare foot and began massaging. "Anything going on with Brandon?"

He worked his fingers between each of his partner's slender toes, rocking them gently. Pressing his thumbs into the arch, he received a satisfied moan in response.

"No, we need to go grocery shopping again. He's inhaling food at an alarming rate." Carter's other foot restlessly rubbed up and down Tomas's thigh. "I don't care if she takes the class. I don't even care if she stops the karate lessons."

He waved off Tomas before he could protest. "No, seriously, she's been doing it for five years. This past year she's been whining more and more. She can break boards. She kicks every boy's ass in the class. I know you want her to continue, but I think it's time to let her leave. She may go back to it later. She may not. But she is going to start hating it soon if we make her stay. You know I'm right." Carter let out a contented sigh. "I love your hands."

Tomas smiled, tweaking Carter's big toe. "I miss the days when we were concerned about Zoe's unhealthy obsession with all things *American Girl*."

"Me too." There was a pause. "You need to talk to her. She—you need to talk to her."

"I will."

"So, how was the meeting? Did Horton sign the contract?"

"Yeah, they did. I'll have to go back out to Oakland in a few weeks, but it will all be wrapped up soon." He didn't want to talk about the fiasco with Barron right now.

He kneaded the ropy muscles of Carter's calf, enjoying the sensation of coarse hair under his palms.

"Take these off." He tugged at the flannel sleeping pants.

Carter lifted his hips. Tomas helped him slide the plaid pants down, cock springing free. *Happy to see you, too,* Tomas thought as he tossed the ugly pants onto the floor. Bending Carter's knee a little, he kissed his inner thigh.

Carter sighed again. "I missed you."

Dark brown hands glided up Carter's hamstrings and back down. Little nips and kisses sprinkled along the taut inner thigh. Tomas gripped Carter's cock and stroked. There was a protesting moan when he let go so that he could lean over to pull out the top drawer, to pluck out a bottle of oil.

He rearranged Carter's legs to settle between them. He kissed across a hip, down to the pubic bone, licking and sucking at spots he had learned over the years that drove Carter crazy.

Carter tugged on his dark locks. "Tomas," he pleaded.

Smiling, but not stopping his exploration, he made his way across the other hip. He would not be rushed. Fingers slick with oil, he stroked the sensitive tissue around Carter's hole, working in one finger, then two. A groan of pleasure, Carter's hips lifted, trying to get those diabolical fingers to push in deeper. He got a smack for his impatience.

Tomas massaged the rim, slipping his fingers in and out of the rosette. He focused on Carter, listening as his breathing changed, watching his face contort.

Tomas licked the cock bobbing in front of him, his mouth lightly sucking the head, lips sliding down the velvety shaft. He alternated between playful licks and intense sucking, knowing what his lover liked best. Carter's hips rocked restlessly, both hands now tangled tightly in Tomas's hair.

Tomas's tongue kneaded the thick vein under the plum-colored cock. Fingers stroked and massaged in rhythm with his tongue strokes, making Carter moan even louder. God, he loved that sound. He dragged his fingers back slowly, only to thrust them in again, Carter's hips pumping in earnest. Curving his fingers up, he pressed into that knot of flesh that made Carter's spine arch violently. Tomas increased the pressure of tongue and suction of his mouth. With his other hand, he cupped the scrotum, playing with his husband's heavy balls. He could feel the tightening leg muscles, Carter's breath coming out in gasps and pants now.

"Tomas, ah god." A faint sheen of sweat had broken across Carter's golden skin.

Tomas abruptly stopped sucking, letting the cock slide from his lips.

"Oh god, don't stop, please, Tomas."

Tomas looked up at the bowed body of his mate. He loved to hear Carter beg. Smiling, he resumed treating the throbbing cock like a candy treat, Carter's pleading groans music to his ears. Allowing his jaw and throat to relax, he suckled more deeply, taking Carter in to the root, enjoying the taste of him, the weight of Carter's cock in his mouth. Tomas pinched tender flesh, kneading the ball sac. He could feel the large muscles of Carter's thighs contract even more, his hips moving spasmodically now.

"Ah god." Carter came in a torrent, Tomas swallowing all of it, not losing a single salty drop. He suckled as the flesh softened.

Carter's body was lax now. Sounds of breathing, harsh and uneven, tried to draw in more air. Tomas's lips feathered over Carter's, the kiss lazily changing as tongues and teeth became involved. "I love you," Tomas whispered against Carter's temple.

"Love you, too." He nipped Tomas's lower lip, scraping his short nails over a darkened nipple. Tomas sucked in a sharp breath.

"Roll over," Tomas said.

"I can't. My brain has shut down and my muscles won't work. Wait a minute for my body to reboot." Carter's husky laugh rumbled out as calloused fingers continued to torment the puckered nipple.

Tomas captured both wrists and trapped them high over Carter's head. "Behave," he snarled.

With a gentle push, Tomas stood, removing his pants, his cock taut against his stomach. Picking up the oil again, he flicked the cap.

Carter lifted his hand, reaching for the bottle. "Let me."

Slowly, Carter sat up, stroking Tomas's prick, slicking the oil up and down, twisting and teasing. His hazel-eyed gaze locked with his lover's coffee-brown eyes.

Breathing roughly, Tomas repeated, "Roll over."

Carter bestowed a rough, demanding kiss before complying.

Tomas planted kisses along the spine, lapping at the sweat there. Lightly biting Carter's right cheek, his hands kneaded the muscles, spreading flesh. He placed the tip of his cock against the rim and slowly pushed in as Carter pressed back. They both groaned. Tomas held still, enjoying the sensations, the tight grip of muscles.

"Move, old man," Carter growled.

There was a smack of palm against ass. "You're so impatient. And I'm not old."

A rough laugh came from Carter. "Move, now."

Tomas obeyed, albeit slowly, enjoying the leisurely movements of their bodies. No rush, just absorbing the feel of them together, the air painted with sighs, moans, entreaties. Tomas leaned over Carter's back, caressing his flank, the flex of muscle playing against his palm.

Carter wiggled under him, rocking back and forth to urge Tomas along. "Faster. Fuck me faster, Tomas." His voice strained.

Tomas lifted off Carter's back, digging his fingers into his mate's hips, his mind shutting out everything but this right now. Awareness honed on movement, sound, emotion, sensation. Carter moved in opposition to him, his tempo crescendoing, the sounds of flesh smacking together. Heat and desire built. Breath sawed in and out of lungs. Tomas's heart galloped against his ribs as he thrust harder. "So good." There was nothing but the two of them.

"Faster," Carter urged.

When his verbal demand was ignored, Carter set to clenching and relaxing his muscles, spurring Tomas on. Teeth gritting, Tomas tightened his hold and expeditiously complied. His torso was covered in a thin gleam of sweat, their bodies gliding, pulsing, flying together.

The runaway train that was his orgasm ripped through him. Spasming, nerves zinging, he laughed. Tomas felt his muscles contract violently, then melt. His chest crashed onto Carter's back. Sweat-slicked skin pressed to sweat-slicked skin, Tomas waiting for his body to come back online. His breathing synced with his lover's. When he could, he eased back, rolling to his side. Carter flopped across him. The weight felt wonderful, comforting. He stroked Carter's back.

"So," Tomas said, a moment later, after he cleared his throat, "no more karate, huh?"

"No, if we force her to continue, it won't be pretty." Carter petted him, fingertips skimming over his chest, playing with his collarbone.

"I'll talk to her," he promised. "Grocery shopping tomorrow?"

"Yeah, boys are so much easier."

Laughing, Tomas shifted, pulling Carter onto him more. "Think your folks would take the kids so you can go with me on the next trip to Oakland?"

"In a flash."

"Good, I missed you." He pressed a kiss against Carter's brow.

"Welcome home, Tomas."

UGLY-SEXY

Gregory L. Norris

Did you hear the one about the two married dudes who were fucking in a leather sling, and how the sling broke, spilling their asses all over the basement floor? No?

Well, it went something like this:

Let's begin with our cast of characters. There's Flynn. Flynn's the hero of our story. Flynn's a construction worker—a man of tools who can sometimes be a tool. Dude swings a mean hammer. He built the house where the above-referenced disaster occurred. Flynn constructed the sling, too. At last report, the house was still standing.

Flynn. Your typical former jock. Still plays sports at forty, but comes home creaking to that house with the former sex sling in its basement. He ices up now more than when we first crossed paths, back when I was in my early twenties and he'd just hit the big three-zero. Flynn plays first base on a summer weekend hardball league that's made up of other wannabe jocks that never got their big breaks. Fucker stands at six-two, doesn't have an ounce of fat on his lean, ropy mass of muscles, drinks beer, scratches and grunts. He's a modern caveman. A penis with feet—size-thirteen boats, by the way.

I'm Flynn's costar in this mad piece of performance art known as our life. You can call me Charlie. That's sort of Flynn's pet nickname for me. Okay, under full disclosure, it's what he calls my asshole, which he first fell in love with at a rest stop men's head just after the witching hour on a humid Sunday night a decade ago. We don't have your typical meet-cute story—it doesn't get trotted out at parties or shared with relatives, most of which still refer to us as "roommates."

It's sort of an ugly story. Sexy, too, because something miraculous happened when Flynn was buried balls deep in me in that stinky men's stall. It was the best sex of my young life. Turned out, it was also the best of Flynn's, pre and post-divorce. We exchanged phone numbers after flushing that second cock-sock full of his juice down the drain, then started to walk away from each other, but wound up watching the sunrise together at that house he was building.

We've been together ever since.

Relationships can get ugly. The ones with legs, with staying power, go through a predictable evolution. First up is the nonstop fucking or honeymoon stage, where you can't keep your hands off each other and you're doing it everywhere, at all hours: in the shower; in the mudroom the moment he swaggers home from work and kicks off his gigantic steel-toed boots; in the car after you make a run to the grocery store for ice cream, and you not only get caught by the driver of the minivan you're parked next to while humming up and down on his dick but also the fucking ice cream melts.

Then you arrive at a kind of Limbo—land of lost souls, according to the ancient Greeks, who, as goes the legend, understood the joy of that wondrous honeymoon stage, and also the dangers of getting stuck in a place between living and death. In modern speak, Limbo is when he's sprawled across the sofa in the basement's man cave, his giant feet kicked up on the coffee table, and one big toe poking through a hole in his white crew sock. He's wearing old shorts and a T-shirt that's overdue in the wash, hasn't shaved for two days, and his face is almost as hairy as his legs. You go down there to ask him what he wants for dinner, listing the options. He grunts, his eyes no longer seeing you, just the ball game playing on the flat screen.

There's something galling about being overlooked for baseball, football, pucks, hoops—whatever sport is playing in high-def. Heck, it could be fucking bowling that owns his attention. But also, there's still that image of cuteness as he flexes his toes, scratches his chin, thinks a man's most basic thoughts. Yeah, sexy.

Changing tactics, your eyes wander over those athlete's legs, that one big toe sticking out of his sock triggering breathlessness. You drink in his manly scent, piney and potent, lean down and kiss his furry cheek. Your mouth lingers, moves up to his ear, licks. He shrinks, pushing away from you.

"Quit it," he grumbles.

You don't, and then cup his cheek, drawing his mouth to yours.

"Charlie, the game!" he complains.

The only game involving a bat and balls you care

about waits between his legs. You kiss him, your free hand walking down, lower and lower. By the time you reach his furry belly button, visible through the gap between T-shirt and the top of his shorts, he's getting into it, kissing back. You find his dick hard, his piss-slit damp with a drop of his juice when you pull his shorts aside, and those big, meaty balls that won over your heart spill out. He works one of his gargantuan mitts through your hair, urging you to suck his cock. Which you do—after attending to those low-swinging nuts, funky with his sweat. You even take a few licks at his asshole, which he permits. In the honeymoon stage, when he was mostly straight and fresh out of a miserable marriage, you had to warm him up to the idea. But once you did, there were times that you ate that fur-ringed knot between his sports-toughened ass muscles for what felt like hours, made him bust more than a few loads merely from licking him where no one else ever had.

Flynn flips you onto your stomach and returns the favor, his tongue wet, warm, hungry. He lines up that fat head of his dick with your knot, and pushes into you, his cock at long last scratching the itch that's now always there. He grinds on top of you, fucking in and out, his shorts hanging off one of his ankles. He moans warm breaths into your ear, presses his cheek against yours, humps, and sweats. You take care of your own dick, jacking off in concert to Flynn's fuck-thrusts, a trend now that you're in Limbo.

"I love you, Charlie," he pledges, his fat balls gonging against you with every inward charge.

You believe him, and you love him, too. But at some point, you notice his eyes are back on the television. He's a man only half there.

Yeah, that's Limbo for you.

But then there's the End. That's the place where a week passes between fresh lays. Fucking becomes part of a schedule, penciled in like an appointment to see the dentist or your mechanic. Sometimes, you reschedule it for another time, or you skip it altogether. He's down in his man cave jerking off between innings or at halftime to stay sane, and you're upstairs doing the same thing to the latest sausage-fest of bachelors on your favorite bad reality TV show.

Where do you think Flynn and I were, leading up to my ill-fated swing in the fuck-sling? You get one guess.

Yup, it was the End.

He forgot his wallet. So, aggravated, I hopped into my car and drove downtown, where Flynn's construction company was renovating an old brick mill building into luxury loft apartments. It was seasonally muggy out, and when he strutted up to my window, hardhat on his head, the musky smell of his sweat riding up my nostrils, I wasn't turned on.

"Here," I snapped, and handed Flynn his wallet.

Flynn narrowed his blue eyes. I hated the look of his nose and the threads of silver visible above both ears. "Is there a problem, Charlie?"

"Clearly," I lobbed back. "I've got things to do today, and you keep piling more on my shoulders."

"I'm sorry," he said, though by his tone I could tell he really wasn't. "Jesus, I'm sorry I forgot to take my wallet with me."

"You forget to lock the front door, you forget to empty your pockets before you toss your pants in the laundry, and you'd probably forget your head if Doctor Franken-stein hadn't sewed it onto your shoulders."

A bead of perspiration slipped out of Flynn's hairline and dripped down the side of his face, telegraphing that his temperature was rising, and that my husband of a decade was growing angrier.

"Charlie," he growled through clenched teeth.

"Try a little harder; that's all I'm saying."

"Fuck," he sighed. Straightening, Flynn pocketed his wallet.

At that moment, it was easy to forget that we cared for each other, that we *loved* each other, even if we'd fallen out of love through the natural progression that links two horny males together and potentially drives them in search of other partners for excitement.

That potential living wedge moseyed over from the direction of the construction waste dumpsters in the form of a tall, lean tomcat dressed in old blue jeans, a navy T-shirt, dirty work gloves, and dirtier shit-kickers. Flynn's face hardened, but he didn't say anything as the young man leaned down, all smiles.

"This the main squeeze, boss?" the tomcat asked, his voice a youthful but manly baritone.

In the next second or so, I drank in his magnificence: clean white teeth showing from a gesture more wolf's snarl than actual smile, a prickle of five o'clock scruff at just after nine in the morning, bright blue eyes, some ink protruding from the cuff of one sleeve, hair in a classic athlete's cut, a total jock's body. He was, dare I say, a younger version of Flynn.

Still hacked off and avoiding direct eye contact, Flynn said, "Cory, this is Charlie. Charlie, this is the new dude, Cory."

My annoyance evaporated, a shiver teasing the fine

hairs at the nape of my neck. I wanted to believe that the handsome, younger version of Flynn was experiencing a sliver of the same attraction that held me in its grip. His scent, pretty much the same as my husband's, made my insides ignite. I extended my hand, intending to shake, but Cory took it and kissed the back, like a handsome prince from a fairy tale.

"Enchanted," he said.

I resisted the urge to smile, but failed. "What a gentleman."

"Hey, Big Flynn here's a lucky dude, I hear. I should get so lucky to have a Charlie waiting for me at the end of every long, miserable shift."

Our eyes connected, and I fell madly in lust with the handsome young stranger: the Before to Flynn's After.

"Okay, that's enough," After said. "Get back to work. Charlie, we'll continue this later at home."

No, we wouldn't, I figured. I'd be in my room, exhausted after jerking off nonstop to thoughts about Cory, who winked at me on his way back into the building. Flynn would pop open a beer, turn on his flat screen in the basement, scratch his nuts, and throw a bone as a result. The words, unspoken, would get lodged in our throats until the next shouting match sent them flying.

Ugly stuff, yeah.

"All right, Charlie, out with it."

Flynn shuffled into the room, hands tucked in his pockets. While waiting for me to respond, he rocked on his heels. I saw that he'd at least remembered to lose his work boots in the mudroom, though not the sweaty white socks. Even so, I cut him a break.

"Go on," I said.

A smile attempted to form on Flynn's tense lips. The best he managed was a smirk. "You're pissed at me? I'm pissed at you."

I faced him, my arms folded. "Oh really?"

"Yeah. What was with the doe eyes at the job site? Did you expect to offer it up for Cory right there on the spot?"

"No, the porta-toilet—I'm a rest stop fucker, remember?"

Flynn's smirk sagged. "Charlie, that dude's a dog. He can't keep it in his pants—chicks as well as other dudes. He's a one-man army of dick. If that's what you really want, well, you should be aware that it won't require too much effort. To Cory, you're just another notch on his belt."

"I didn't know you cared," I said.

I started past him. Flynn caught me and drew me back by my wrist. "Charlie," he sighed in that grating tone that had grown more fatherly in recent years than that of a husband.

"Maybe what we need to fix this broken thing of ours with is a good old-fashioned threesome," I answered. "Dust off the cobwebs, shake up the status quo. Something other than bachelors on TV and summer baseball games."

It happened a few days later. Two handsome, strapping studs pulled into the driveway, Cory in his big, new truck, all shine and torque, Flynn in his older model, which showed a few dings and paint scrapes: the Before parked beside the After.

I gazed out the window, struggling for breath. After their Saturday afternoon baseball game, Flynn had agreed—or at least conceded to—my request that a three-way with Cory was exactly what our relationship needed. For three hours and nine innings, I paced our house, resisting the urge to jerk my erect dick and fearing that, with my luck, their weekly game at the ballpark would go into extra innings. It didn't. Flynn had texted, *on our way*, and my hands were shaking so badly that it took me three tries to reply, *OK*.

Flynn stepped out of his truck, clad in his dirty home-white baseball uniform, expensive shades over his eyes, a fresh grass stain across one knee. He carried his smelly old cleats by their shoe-tongues, and had changed into an old pair of sneakers that reminded me of how sexy I'd always found his feet, how often in that honeymoon stage I'd sucked his toes, something he'd found odd but had tolerated.

Before followed After into the mudroom. My heart attempted to throw itself into my throat. Cory's uniform fit his body even tighter, better than Flynn's, as though it loved him. A pang of guilt worked its way through my nerves and arousal, because at that moment, I wanted this shiny new toy with his handsome, scruffster's face and obvious bulge from his jockstrap more than my husband of ten years.

I wanted Cory more than any man in the history of Planet Earth. That's what happens when you reach the End—you start to fantasize about random strangers, men you see on TV, the dude who delivers your mail.

I pulled two longnecks out of the fridge and greeted the men at the mudroom door with beer.

"Hey," I said, and flashed what I hoped was my cutest grin.

Flynn avoided eye contact and gave me that tip of his

chin that men of his design use when addressing others, a primitive gesture left over from the cave.

"*Charlie*," Cory exclaimed, and grabbed hold of me for a theatrical spin.

I laughed, going along for the ride.

"Okay, none of that shit," Flynn groused.

Cory smacked a kiss on my cheek. I drank in his incredible smell: sweat and sunlight, the dregs of whatever deodorant he'd slapped on before the game, the minty scent of his breath, likely owing to gum chewed in haste between dugout and destination.

"Hey," Flynn barked. "I mean it. None of that romantic stuff, even in joking. That's Rule Number One."

"Yessir," Cory said, and saluted. I wanted to blow him right then and there.

"The rest of the rules are, in order—"

And here they were: no kissing; Cory was instructed to wear a condom if things went that far; and this was only a one-time deal, no repeat performances allowed.

"And just to be clear, this is all for Charlie," Flynn said. "I'm doing this for him."

Cory groped my ass. "Anything else, boss?"

Flynn shrugged. Our glances crossed paths as I handed him his beer. I could see he was nervous, not exactly into it. Doing this for me? I'd assumed when he agreed that this was for *us*.

I faced After, my husband, and the heaviness on his brow, the scent his masculine body exuded—clean sweat with a hint of ocean or summer rain, testosterone working up through his epidermis—again made Flynn the handsomest man on the planet, and the only man I ever really wanted.

"Flynn?" I asked.

He unscrewed the bottle cap with his big hand and pitched it at the sink, his aim perfect.

"If you'd been able to do that out there on the field, dude, we'd have won today's game," Cory chuckled.

Suddenly, I resented Before. I despised myself even more for letting one of my secret fantasies escape the bedroom, turning it loose onto the world. I started to toss a wet blanket over the whole threesome idea when Flynn's handsome mug broke with the fakest smile I'd ever seen on his face.

"Okay, let's do this."

It was sex, only sex, I told myself as we tromped down to Flynn's man cave for the sweaty synthesis that followed. My husband had granted me one of those ultimate fantasies: a threesome with two men, *real* men. Men of a quality that pushed all of my triggers, dressed in dirty baseball uniforms, their sanitary sweat socks on huge feet, said socks not so white nor sanitary following the game.

"He loves feet," Flynn said, as though reading my thoughts. After so many years together, perhaps he could.

"Feet?" Cory chuckled. "Go for it, dude."

He pressed the damp toes of his right foot to my face, while I deeply breathed in his funk. In my imagination, this moment had been so much sexier. It always was with Flynn, sexier I mean, when I'd found myself in a similar position, between my husband's hairy legs, worshipping his gigantic feet. I should have loved this. Cory certainly was, pawing at his meat through his baseball uniform pants. But . . .

"Feels weird but good," he said after I liberated him of his socks and stirrups, and was licking the buttery stink from between his toes.

A porn flick played on the flat screen, something directly from Flynn's extensive DVD collection. His attention, I noticed, was more on the action taking place between your typical, rugged stunt cock and two hot blondes than what was happening in the room directly beside him. He and Cory, sitting bare buttcheek to bare buttcheek, sipping beer, the air infused with their manly jock scent, might as well have been light-years apart.

"Keep going," Cory said. "*Dude . . .* "

Ten minutes earlier, I'd have sold a kidney, maybe my soul, to be where I was, high on Cory's smell. Now, I wanted to get up, walk out, run away, and not look back.

"You got a hot tongue," Cory said.

I drew back, feeling colder on that hot July afternoon than in the middle of a January snowstorm.

In any case, we went through with it. I licked Cory from his hairy ankles up to his hairier balls. Flynn took me in that place of mine he loved more than any other while I sucked his friend, his coworker, and his teammate's cock, and did a fairly great job—after all, early on in the honeymoon stage of our romance, I'd gotten plenty of practice on Flynn's bone. I ate his asshole, which Cory loved, and when he nutted, he played the role of the man, the stud, the victor.

"You ought to turn this place into a sex dungeon," he said on his way out the door.

He and Flynn punched knuckles. Cory slapped my ass, said he was looking forward to the next time, despite Flynn's list of rules, and winked at me.

As his truck pulled out of the driveway, I hurried upstairs and brushed my teeth. After showering, I scrubbed my mouth out twice more, unable to get Cory's taste off my tongue.

I pulled into a fetal curl on the bed. The scuffle of footsteps from big, bare feet drew my haunted eyes to the bedroom door. Flynn leaned against the frame, clad only in boxer-briefs and T-shirt, arms crossed, his face difficult to read.

"I thought you wanted this."

"I thought I did, too," I said.

Flynn shrugged. My eyes wandered over his body. So handsome, my tall and rugged After, proof of a long and mostly happy life lived together. "Okay, so we gave it a shot."

"Yeah. Maybe you should try being with a woman again."

Flynn scowled. "What makes you think I want anyone other than you?"

I uncurled my body, eased up to my elbows, and saw Flynn, my Flynn, through what felt like new eyes. "Really?"

"After all this time, do you still have doubts?"

I struggled to answer. Flynn uncrossed his arms and strutted over. My heart galloped. He leaned down, crushed our mouths together, and hugged me with a gentleness I'd forgotten him capable of expressing.

"I love you, Charlie," he said.

And then, over the course of the next few days, he proved it in actions as well as words.

So here's the part where the fucking sling comes in.

Flynn and I had pretty much arrived at some conclusions following our tryst with Cory. First, no more threesomes, because what looks good on paper doesn't always translate into the real world. And last, we had reached that part of a relationship that follows the End: the Afterlife, a state in which we both needed to work harder at keeping the passion between us fed. Also, that parting shot from Cory offered Flynn the opportunity to put his carpentry skills to use.

He bought fine leather, grommeted it, fixed it to chains, and secured the chains to eyehooks drilled up into the basement ceiling. During this time, while he screwed and hammered, I was forbidden from entering Flynn's man cave.

"It's a surprise," was all he said.

Days after he started, Flynn shepherded me down the stairs blindfolded and walked me into place. He removed the blindfold, and there it was before me: a leather sling, suspended from the ceiling, in clear view of the flat screen for those fucking occasions when a ball game happened to be on.

"What do you think?" asked Flynn.

I could tell by his excited tone and the look on his face how proud he was of his creation. I reached for Flynn's gorgeous mug and drew him down to me. "I think it's amazing—just like you."

Our mouths crushed together as clothes came off through a series of rough fumbles and rips. I stood naked before Flynn, who was now clad only in blue jeans. I hadn't forgotten how magnificent his torso looked, with all that coarse chest hair and the treasure trail cutting him down the middle to the top of his underwear's elastic band, though the pleasant reminder stole my breath. I dropped to my knees and gawked at his big, bare feet— heavenly distraction! I unzipped, fumbled down his jeans and boxer-briefs, and then licked his balls until I was stoned on their musky scent.

"Oh, yeah, Charlie . . . just like that!"

I sucked the helmet of Flynn's cock between my lips and again grew intimate with his thickness, opening wider until his thatch of pubic hair tickled my nose. I toyed with his nuts, caressed his athlete's legs, tasted the first salty-sour tang of skeet from his balls.

Flynn scooped me up and set me in the sling. Clearly, he'd put plenty of thought into the deal. My ass was now at the perfect height for him to access—first with his tongue. After feasting upon me, he straightened, held his cock by the base of its shaft, and entered. My entire body came alive, as it had in days long passed.

He pushed in, all the way to his balls, drew back so that only the head of his dick was still lodged inside my asshole, and slammed back, again and again. Sweat flowed, along with a whole stream of obscenity-laced endearments. "*Fuck*, I love you, Flynn," I moaned.

And then the sling broke, spilling us both down to the floor in a tangle of limbs, torn leather, and busted chains.

"What the fuck?" Flynn roared.

His cock was still inside me, beyond hard. Our wide, unblinking eyes locked together. I began to laugh as the silliness of our situation worked past my shock. Then Flynn joined in, and we were howling, bawling, unable to catch our breaths. And I remembered one of the biggest reasons I fell in love with him way back when: his wonderful and sexy sense of humor.

Oh, and a nice set of feet sure doesn't hurt.

So here's what happens in the Afterlife of any relationship lucky enough to prevail, as Flynn's and mine had. If you remember that you love that handsome, strapping man's man as much as I love Flynn, and you understand how easy it is to get lazy, then together you'll make a conscious effort at keeping things fresh. Flynn had, and I found myself happier and hornier than ever before.

THE INSTRUMENT

Dale Chase

Beethoven was my passion. Richard favored Mozart, but I loved him anyway. When his mother died and left him a Russian Hill apartment and season tickets to the San Francisco Symphony, we settled comfortably into our Victorian digs and fall concerts. We liked to think our passion for music had been there all along, reminding ourselves we'd amassed a good-sized musical library, but in truth our concertgoing had been sporadic. We soon found that regular attendance took music appreciation to an entirely new level.

Even though Richard considered Beethoven too dramatic, he nevertheless paid homage, his hand discreetly traveling to my thigh during a performance, promising that he would do as well by me as did the maestro. I would make similar gestures when Mozart played, even though I considered the music highly predictable. For Bach, we usually held hands.

Symphony nights were events: dinner beforehand at a

fancy restaurant, drinks afterward, then the ride home, already hot for each other, both of us hard. We'd scarcely be inside the door before we'd be pulling at each other. I'd then mount him on the floor, evening clothes scattered, Oriental rug beneath us.

Richard was a glorious specimen, ten years my junior. I'd picked him up in a bar years before and kept him, his lithe body nurturing my own, staving off the inevitable. He'd proven to be spirited yet pliant, readily admitting to needing direction. Over the years, he'd gone to such great lengths to distance himself from a stifling upbringing that he'd lost his way in, and so I helped him find it again, choosing his career, his look, returning him to the culture he'd abandoned, all the while fucking him. I found him receptive to everything, and if I plied him with liquor, receptive beyond that. I'd had my prick in that delicious ass of his in every corner of the apartment and repeatedly on the terrace, which was, in fact, his favorite playground. In our twelve years together, we seemed to have done it all, or at least all we wanted. We had, I suppose, slipped into habit, and so, when Bach appeared on the symphony schedule, I anticipated nothing new.

"It's that young British violinist," Richard said one Saturday morning. "Trevor Conley."

"What will he be doing?"

"The *Sonatas* and *Partitas*, *Two* and *Three*."

I put down my *Chronicle*. "Really?"

Richard nodded. "Have we seen anyone do them?"

"The number three prelude once as an encore."

"Well, he's doing it all."

Richard knew these pieces ranked high with me, especially the Chaconne from *Partita No. 2*. That final fifteen-minute movement took me beyond words. "You'll go then?" he asked.

"Don't act so surprised; of course I'll go."

"I usually have to break your arm to get you to a weekday performance."

"It's not usually the Bach sonatas," I replied.

The violin had, over time, proved to be my musical undoing. Richard had learned to appreciate its erotic effect, trusting a good performance by the soloist would result in a good performance by me. During the same period, Richard gradually became enamored of the piano, and while he loved to suck me off to the strain of Mozart, he did allow that Beethoven's *Emperor Concerto* was a piano masterwork and became embarrassingly erect during those wonderful opening chords.

In my honor, he tried to assimilate my passion for the violin, but his cock would sag as he labored through a sonata, and I was left on my own, so to speak, fucking him to the haunting Chaconne that often made me weep and come simultaneously. As time went by, Richard decided the violin itself had become an erotic tool. "You'd fuck one if you could," he once said.

"Fuck a violin?" had been my response.

He'd pulled away from me, limp cock in retreat. "You'd find a way," he'd said, disappearing into the bathroom.

"Richard," I called after him that day, but he didn't respond. "Oh, Richard."

It was then that I noticed that the Sunday paper had a piece about young Trevor Conley, a relative unknown to us. As Russian, Israeli, and Japanese violinists prolifer-ated, the British remained a bit obscure. We'd seen the charismatic Nigel Kennedy in his prime, ever the adorable and talented punk, and he'd even done the Beethoven *Violin Concerto*—I liked to think for me—but Kennedy was aging now, while Conley was a mere twenty-two. How vain of me to look to youth. Richard, himself now forty, noted this as I looked at Conley's picture.

"He's straight, you know."

I sipped my latte. "You have it first hand?" He went quiet. "Richard, love, it's a concert, a hall full of people adoring the boy."

He turned to me with that smile I loved. He knew me too well. "As if that matters," he said with a mock pout. "He'll be alone onstage, just him and his instrument."

"Which means?"

"You'll be doing me in the men's room at intermission."

"You flatter me."

Unlike Kennedy, Conley appeared to conform. He wore white tie and tails in the photo and his expression seemed quite agreeable. For a moment, I thought I saw that same willingness I saw in Richard.

"Turn the page," Richard said.

"I beg your pardon?"

"You're staring. Turn the fucking page."

As if to fortify me, or perhaps himself, Richard refused to dress on the night of the concert, idling up beside me, naked and fondling himself. I was at the dresser, buttoning my shirt. "Richard," I said, trying for some measure of discipline.

He began to work himself with languid strokes that I watched in the mirror. His body had not changed in our time together, still smooth, lightly muscled, a silky blond bush caressing his long narrow prick. "I want to go to the concert with my ass absolutely tingling," he said, reaching for my crotch. I didn't stop him.

"I don't want to get sweaty, " I objected.

He began to unbutton my shirt. I looked at the night-stand clock. "We can have supper after the concert instead of before," he said. "Late night at a greasy spoon."

"You're certainly in a mood."

He pulled open my pants and freed my cock. I had no intention of succumbing to him, and yet I did.

Phillippe was going to be in a tiff about the dinner reservation, I thought as I stripped and joined Richard on the bed. I'd be scolded next time I booked. Considering this as I lubed Richard's butthole, I fingered him a bit too long.

"You're wandering," he said. "Put it in."

I looked at him, cock high, legs higher. He loved fucking face-to-face, while I preferred the rear mount, but, as this was his show, I acquiesced, running a hand down his chest, stomach, prick, taking his feet in my hands as I eased into him.

He always responded as if I hadn't been in there before, vocal to the point of parody, contracting his sphincter to retain the illusion of a road less traveled. I could have done without these efforts—I loved him, loved his ass without reservation—and yet I appreciated what it meant and fucked him with abandon, unleashing a good-sized load that would surely leave his ass as tingly as he desired. That he orchestrated his own climax to coincide with mine was further testament of his devotion, and as I rode him I thrilled to the sight of great dollops of cream spurting from that knob I had so often sucked.

There was, I had to admit, a certain decadence in

entering Davies Hall knowing I'd just had Richard. He stayed close, brushing my arm as we moved through the crowd. We stood at the bar for a drink, and while I read program notes on Bach and Conley, Richard whispered to me that his sphincter was quivering. "It's getting me hard," he said. He pulled my hand from the program to his crotch. As I groped beneath the bar, I was amazed, as ever, how much we managed in public. Richard was a true master.

Once seated, he had a way of placing his program over his crossed legs that allowed one hand free rein. He would then lean my way if he was so engaged, knowing it amused and interested me. To his left were a couple so elderly I doubted they could hear the performance, much less pick up on Richard's doings, and so when he took my hand under the program, I was ready for a bulge, but not a fully exposed prick. How he had managed this without the old couple's notice was one thing; without my noticing, quite another.

The stage was seldom empty at Davies Hall. At the very least there were usually violinists and an accompanying piano. Solo pieces were few, Bach the most stellar example. From our fourteenth row center seats, everything looked vast and hollow. That is, until Trevor Conley strode in.

Even in white tie and tails he looked the handsome schoolboy: shock of dark hair above pale skin and pink cheeks, slightly hesitant in his movements. He started to smile at the applause, then stopped, and I feared him lost until he put the violin to his chin and began to play.

Richard's under-program erection had gone soft. I could feel him staring at me. I pulled my hand from his

lap and heard him draw a long breath. Ordinarily, I would
have offered some sort of reassurance—a look or touch—
but I was away just now, watching the boy and his violin,
listening intently.

The *No. 3 Sonata* was first, which meant the *No. 3
Partita* next, and that meant a similar order for the *2's*. I
felt smugly complicit with Conley in saving the *Partita No.
2* and its haunting Chaconne for last. As I watched him
bring Bach to life, I felt a heaviness in my chest, a longing
for the music, and for the boy. This bittersweet ache spread
throughout my body, and I soon found my cock hard and
my recently emptied balls swelling with desire.

Richard shifted in his seat, pointedly removing the
program to show me he'd zipped up. I gave him no more
than a glance. I couldn't offer more. Everything in me was
directed toward Trevor Conley.

The first sonata concluded with a rousing Allegro Assai
that sounded like two violins instead of one and sent the
crowd into cheers and applause. Conley acknowledged
these with a single bow, then began the *Partita*. Its prelude
was equally exuberant, and I found myself riveted.

My erection, which had never waned, began to
ooze. Richard, of course, knew what was happening,
and I silently pleaded that he not put a hand under my
program because I would come at the slightest touch, so
primed was I. I then watched Conley's long fingers glide
up and down the instrument's neck, stroking powerfully
yet with a sensuality that took my breath away. Indeed,
I found myself not breathing, discovering it only when a
gasp escaped me, which, of course, set Richard fidgeting.

When Conley had completed all seven of the piece's
movements, he took his bows with less hesitance than

before. His cheeks were flushed, and though I knew the lights obscured most of the audience from his vision, I still had the feeling he looked directly at me. He paused, noticeably, as our eyes locked, and at that moment I fell absolutely and totally in his thrall. I watched him leave the stage, catching Richard looking at me. "I could use a drink," he said, and I nodded and followed him out.

Wine in hand, I could say nothing. I didn't want Richard at that moment, didn't want anyone but the boy. I sipped repeatedly and looked about, hating the entire assemblage, Richard included. Everything and everyone was an intrusion.

"So . . . " Richard said. "Not bad, is he?"

"Quite good."

"He looks like an absolute child."

"Yes, doesn't he."

"Plays incredibly well."

"Yes." I felt myself nodding.

Richard let me alone then, allowing me my thoughts, however much he might object. When it was time to go back inside, however, he tugged my arm. "He's straight."

No, he's not, I wanted to say, but didn't.

Richard took my hand as Conley began the *Sonata No. 2*. I maintained our connection throughout the piece, but when Conley began the *Partita*, Richard let go. I appreciated the concession and let myself submerge into the music. I found, as the Chaconne approached, that I wanted more than anything to free my cock and pump it to eruption. When I moved my program to my crotch, I knew Richard took note, but I didn't care. While I didn't go so far as he had, didn't set my throbbing dick free, I did allow the pressure of my hand against the swelling.

Halfway through the Chaconne, as Conley gave it to me like no one ever had, I came prodigiously.

When the performance ended, I was out of breath and apparently weeping. Richard brushed tears from my eyes as I watched Conley leave the stage, my heart pounding as he returned for another bow. When he settled us with an encore, I didn't think I could stand it, yet I dissolved in gratitude as he offered a snip of Mozart. I forgave him the digression. Anything to keep him before me.

"You're awfully quiet," Richard said as he drove us home. He waited patiently as I worked up a reply.

"I think maybe our little preconcert tryst was too much. You don't mind skipping supper, do you?"

"No."

Once in bed, I took Richard into my arms, kissed him, then turned over and closed my eyes. Trevor Conley was still playing for me, and the ache I felt, and the erection I bore, were for him alone.

When I saw in Thursday's *Chronicle* that Conley would play at a free noontime outdoor concert at Justin Herman Plaza on Friday, I said nothing to Richard, hoping he wouldn't notice the item. I worked so hard at being nice to him—attending him, fucking him—I was certain he had no idea of my intentions.

I left work at eleven on Friday and said I wouldn't return, then strolled the few blocks to the plaza. The crowd was sizeable, and I noted a piano had been brought out. Other performers had been added to the program. Just as well. I liked the idea of Conley not being the main focus. It made him seem all the more accessible to me.

When I saw him approach, my breath caught, everything in me pausing in sublime anticipation. He had on faded jeans and a royal blue silk shirt open at the neck. I pushed through the crowd to intercept him, jostling strangers for the desperately needed eye contact. As he passed, he glanced my way and hesitated ever so slightly, then moved on. The crowd surged in around him as I withdrew. I had what I wanted.

He played Beethoven's *Kreutzer Sonata*, accompanied by a young female pianist from a local conservatory, and encored with Bach's *Allegro Assai*. I stood some distance away, confident now, and when the performance was over, he hung back, fussing with his violin, chatting until the crowd thinned and people went back to work. He closed his violin case as I approached.

"Magnificent," I said.

He looked up at me. "Thank you."

"I heard you Wednesday night as well," I said. "Also magnificent."

"Thank you again."

His accent was delectable. I'd always had a thing for the British and could be coaxed quite far with the simplest conversation. "If you haven't other plans, I'd like to buy you a drink," I said.

He didn't look old enough to be in a bar, would certainly be carded, and yet I saw knowledge in his eyes. "There's a bar at my hotel," he said.

"Oh, where are you staying?"

"The St. Francis."

"Fine, shall we walk or get a cab?"

"Walk."

We said nothing en route, both understanding the situation. I enjoyed having him beside me, enjoyed glances from passersby, which I chose to interpret as acknowledgment of the suitability of our pairing.

At the hotel, Conley passed the bar without a glance, heading directly to the elevator. He had a small room, and once inside set his violin case on a table and, much to my surprise, opened it and removed the instrument. I stood just inside the door as he played the few notes every violinist does at the start of a concert. Tuning up.

For the first time in my life I had no idea what to do. I watched him, dumbstruck, my erection sagging. And then I saw him drop his bow hand, and I let out some sort of half exhale, half cry, which caused him to smile as he turned and presented me with an open fly and a long prick not quite erect. He then began to play the *Partita* I so favored. I found myself stunned into near paralysis.

When I didn't approach him, he came toward me, playing all the while, as if it was the most natural thing in the world for him, like breathing for the rest of us. I kneeled as he reached me and put a hand to him, caressing his stiffening cock and tracing the knob, which was already wet. I glanced up at him and the violin, then closed my mouth around his cock, savoring his feel, his taste, before I began to pull, to lick and suck his delicate meat, my hand running through the silky black hair that engulfed it.

He continued playing above me, moving from the first to second movements, and I pulled back, undid his jeans, lowered them. He never missed a note as I stripped his lower body, as I lifted each leg, pulled off his shoes. And when I had him naked from the waist down, he took a wider stance. I reached up to cup his sac, squeeze his balls, going in to suck them as my hand kept his cock working. When I took him back into my mouth, he lasted until the third movement before he withdrew and erupted, shooting great spurts of come onto my face. I turned from side to side, taking it all, and when he went soft, I settled into a gentle licking. He didn't stop playing until he'd completed the entire movement.

I sat back and only then did I realize I hadn't even taken off my jacket. He grinned as if he'd just noted the same thing, and I rose and removed it. "What about the rest?" he asked. He put the violin aside and took off his shirt. I laughed too sharply—I seemed the schoolboy now—and undid my tie.

As I disrobed, he opened a bottle of water and casually paraded about the room. He glanced at me periodically— I'm certain to see what kind of body he'd landed—and I was glad I'd kept myself trim. Richard had helped inspire me. You don't, after all, hang on to a younger partner without looking good.

When I stood naked, Conley offered me his bottle and I finished it, only then realizing how dry I'd gone. All my fluids had gathered inside my balls. My cock stood stiff above them, waiting.

"There's protection and lube in the nightstand," Conley said, and I took a moment to savor the idea of my finger up his butt, my prick up his butt, before retrieving things and setting them beside the bed. He then said, "Not there," and I picked them up again. He motioned me over, and then he took up his violin.

When I stood, momentarily lost, he sighed and offered an all too brief explanation. "It's the ultimate," he said, putting the instrument to his chin.

"You mean while you're playing?"

He didn't answer. He started into the fourth move-ment—the energetic Gige that precedes the Chaconne— turned his back to me, and spread his legs. Apparently, I was to take him standing; apparently, it was up to me to find a suitable angle; apparently, he had done this before and knew it was feasible.

I'd taken Richard standing many times, but always there had been that adjustment from him, that bend that encouraged both penetration and ride. Now I simply stared at this gorgeous specimen while he flexed his butt as if to hurry me along.

The Gige is just under four minutes, and I wanted to be inside him for the Chaccone, so I slipped on a condom, took a fingerful of lube, and thrust it into his hole. His muscle responded, closing around my digit, and I prodded him briefly while he played brilliantly above. I was so occupied when the Gige ended that Conley allowed a brief respite between movements, as if to say *now, do it now,* and so I slathered my prick, planted my feet firmly between his, pulled him open, and shoved in.

He was shorter than me and had bent slightly forward to receive my cock. He stayed that way briefly, allowing me a few glorious strokes before he righted himself to begin the Chaccone. I had to adjust my position to accommodate him and felt my age as leg muscles complained at the posture. Yet I did not waver, so elated was I at fucking the boy, the violinist.

In seconds, my body acclimated to the angle. I began to ride him with full abandon, shoving my cock up his chute with energy newly born. I pumped him in accompaniment to the Chaconne, savoring his tight hole and the fact that the movement was fifteen minutes long. It was like some exquisite timer set in motion. I found myself thrusting with the music, easing to a slow sensual rhythm where it did, then picking up speed as the music began to build, plowing to my root in an orgiastic frenzy that set my entire body reeling. I kept on reaming Conley's ass in this great musical fuck until time finally ran out and my swollen cock began to throb, juice rising, pulsing, begging. I tried to hold back but couldn't. I experienced that ultimate sweet agony as I came, while the boy began Bach's final minor key passage.

When I was spent, I slid out and tossed the amply filled rubber, then rested my chin on Conley's shoulder in time to watch him come unaided, cream shooting from his stiff prick onto the carpet in a great arcing show. He played all the while, never missing a note, spending himself in this most dramatic manner as the Chaconne's final notes died away.

His chest was heaving, body wet with sweat; his eyes were closed and I knew to remain silent. I slid my arms around his chest as he lowered the violin. He took his time now, as if return was difficult, as if he'd been somewhere the rest of us aren't allowed. When he finally turned, he gently pulled away. Tears were all down his face.

"What is it?" I asked, instantly aware the question was an intrusion. "I'm sorry," I added. "It's just that it was such a . . . so incredible, the music . . . "

"And the fuck," he said quite bluntly. "My two passions."

"And you like to combine them."

"Every time I play, I want to come."

"Do you?"

"No, I just want to."

"But have you ever? I mean, in concert?"

He looked at me with suspicion now.

"I only ask," I explained, "because it happened to me

Wednesday night when I heard you play. I came right there in my seat."

He remained guarded, as if only the music was trustworthy, and I saw then how he'd trapped himself, how his music and his sexuality had become one. My reaction, unfortunately, leaned toward rescue. "How long are you in town?" I asked.

"I leave in the morning."

"I have the entire afternoon free," I said. I thought of Richard and our Friday nights out. "Longer if I make a call."

He held the violin parallel to his flaccid prick. I took in the image, knowing at day's end it would be all I had left, the instrument and that beautiful cock.

"I don't think so," he said, offering nothing more, trusting me, in my maturity, to understand.

"Of course," I replied, grabbing my clothes. "Yes, I understand. Certainly." I left my cuffs unbuttoned, shoes untied, and shoved my tie into my coat pocket. At the door I hesitated, something inside me breaking apart. I turned just as he lifted the violin and began the Chaconne, but I didn't linger to watch it make him hard.

BLACKOUT

T. Hitman

A restless autumn wind scattered sheets of rain and shook the trees around Hampshire House. Most of the dorm's residents were gone for the night, partying or fucking or home for the long weekend. I felt alone on the second floor, though I wasn't the only soul left in the place. Jim was working out in the weight room when the lights went dark. I knew he was down there, sweating and pumping and half-mad with nicotine withdrawal, due to the fact that he'd recently quit smoking. I'd seen him an hour earlier on my way up to my room, but now I could *sense* him under the floorboards, dripping with sweat, a force of nature, just like the storm itself.

My bed sat directly above the weight room, and when the lights cut out, blown dark by the storm, I heard him huff, "What the fuck?" as I dropped the paperback I'd been reading in bed, too tired to jerk off for what would've been the third time that night.

Jim was a year younger than me, twenty, a tall jock

with a killer body who got hooked on cancer sticks young and was waging a private war to banish their power over him. Hampshire House was a Greek Revival–style manor that had become home to a mix of college athletes floating through on sports scholarships, as well as liberal arts students. He was one of the former; I hailed from the latter.

James Bowden—his official name—lived in the dorm room two doors down from me. I met him for the first time at the end of August while he and a pair of his buddies from the football team were talking loudly, their butts planted on a mattress destined to be soaked in buckets of come, judging by Jim's amazing good looks. He pushed six-two in height, sported an athlete's cut of dark brown hair, eyes that of the same color, and, on that day, he was clean shaven. He wore a T-shirt, a ball cap with a frayed bill, white socks, a pair of old sneakers on big feet, and black workout shorts that showed off decent leg muscles and lots of hair.

"Welcome to Hampshire House," I'd said.

We shook hands. I was instantly smitten.

Just over a month later, about an hour before the lights went out, I saw Jim pacing around his dorm room on my way to mine, the dude clearly unable to sit for any length of time. The school had kept the original hardwood floors during Hampshire House's renovation after the building was donated for student housing by a generous bene-factor. Those floors groaned and squeaked constantly, loudly. I swore Jim had to have been sliding across them in his giant, socked feet. Or fucking cheerleaders by the twos and threes, though I never saw a single one hanging out there with him, just his jock buddies. When I couldn't stand the racket a moment longer, I got up and wandered out of my room.

Jim paced the floor.

"You okay?" I asked.

He told me he had quit cold turkey and offered up a smile that looked half-crazy.

"Better for your health, dude," I said. "You don't want to stroke out in the middle of a game-winning touch-down."

Jim again flashed that grin, showing a length of white teeth, the gesture more snarl than actual smile. I told him that if he needed anything, he knew where I was. He grumbled something about working out in the downstairs gym. I returned to my room and jerked off to thoughts of licking the sweat off his hairy nuts and gulping down a load of his skeet, one of my favorite new hobbies when not studying or trying to figure out what the hell I wanted to do with my education.

Then the lights went out, and out they stayed.

Hampshire House's downstairs was divided between a main gathering spot with couches and a long study table, the boiler room, and an oblong area that got converted into a residents' gym with weights, step machines, a pair of mismatched exercise bikes, and mats over the ancient hardwood floor.

Jim went down there a lot. If he wasn't pacing back and forth, the cadence of his nervous footsteps audible on the squeaky floors, even two stories up, if he wasn't jamming to music on his earbuds or banging away at a video game when he should've been cramming, he was in the weight room. At ten o'clock that Friday night, with

Jim in the desperate throes of craving a cancer stick and probably willing to sell his soul for one, fate played the ultimate fuck-you and knocked out the power, plunging half the town in darkness.

Dressed in boxer-briefs and a tatty old T-shirt, with the scum of two loads dried or drying on the hairs of the happy trail that dissected my stomach, I bolted upright in my dorm room as the whole world was plunged into shadows. The world shifted from light and the white noise of the desktop computer in the background to pitch-black darkness that was just as extreme and immediate. After it happened, the only sounds were the throb of the windblown rain against the windows and then the angry, exasperated groan of Jim's voice from beneath the floorboards.

Jim and I weren't friends, not in the real sense. We weren't guys who confided about our problems or high-fived over exaggerated tales of a hot weekend fuck; we were guys who greeted each other in the hallway, or if I passed through the downstairs on my way to take out the trash and happened to catch sight of him lifting weights, the hair on his legs damp with sweat. Which was often enough, because the guy had great ones and was determined to keep in top physical shape. I'm a leg guy, so Jim probably thought I had the cleanest room in all of Hampshire House, considering how many times I hit the dumpster by way of the basement door.

Anyway, though not really friends, I did however feel protective enough of my dorm brother to ensure he wouldn't break his neck stumbling around down there in the dark. And so I fumbled my cell phone off the nightstand and headed out of my room dressed in my undershorts.

The hallway was cloaked in total darkness, broken only by the battery-powered exit signs. Heart in my throat, I trudged toward the staircase, then down the twenty or so steps to the weight room. I aimed the phone's screen toward the mats and exercise equipment. Just as the piney, masculine stink of fresh perspiration ignited in my nostrils, the beam touched upon glistening leg muscles. Jim was stretched out on his spine atop one of the weight benches, an arm thrown over his eyes. For a second or two, my gaze lingered on his crotch, long enough for me to see that he wasn't wearing underwear. One sweat-soaked, hairy nut hung loosely out of his workout shorts.

I forced my gaze up to his face. "Yo, dude," I said.

He startled out of the thoughts he'd fallen victim to and bolted upright. "Hey, man," he said. "What the fuck's up with the lights?"

"They're out, numb-nuts."

He huffed an exasperated sigh and absently scratched at his crotch. "I was waiting to see if they'd come back on, but that don't look like it's gonna happen any time soon."

"The way this storm's blowing through, they could be off all night," I said. "Anyway, I heard you down here and wanted to make sure you didn't kill yourself going up the stairs."

"Thanks," he said. "What else you up to?"

"Nothing. I was reading a book, about to crash early, so it's no big loss to me."

Jim shook his head. "I won't be able to sleep. Can't."

I blame what I said to him next on the crisis atmosphere. "Jerk off, then. It works for me."

He snorted, stood, stretched. His T-shirt rode up his stomach, revealing a decent pattern of fur just above the top of his shorts. "If I abuse my dick anymore, it'll fall off."

I unintentionally shot a look at the meaty fullness of Jim's crotch. "Whatever works, dude. You want to borrow this? I have a few games on it." I extended the phone in his direction. Jim smiled, then shook his head. Since quitting the smokes, he'd sprouted a mustache and goatee on his handsome mug, and at that moment I realized how much I longed to kiss him. "You sure?" I yammered, my mouth suddenly bone dry.

"Yup," he said.

"Well, if you need anything, just knock."

He promised he would and I started back up the stairs. My room welcomed me into its throbbing stillness. I briefly considered reading my paperback by phonelight and beating off again, which I'd done less than an hour earlier. I settled instead for passing out. Sleep, however, eluded me.

After a while, I heard the cadence of pacing footsteps on the other side of my door. They began, stopped, started up again. Jim, I assumed, was in the grip of a merciless nicotine fit. Back and forth he went. Eventually, I heard a furtive rapping of knuckles. I peeled myself off the bed, grabbed my phone, and padded barefoot to the door.

For reasons I couldn't identify at first, my heart began to pound. A step short of the threshold, I realized it was thumping around in my chest so hard because I knew it would be Jim waiting on the other side, because it was a crazy, stormy night, a night when anything could happen.

Jim's handsome face glowed at the open door in the light cast by the phone screen. "Hey," he said.

I flashed a sleepy smile. "S'up?"

"You mind some company?"

I didn't, especially not his. "Come on in," I said, extending a hand. Jim strutted in wearing white socks, no sneakers, and the same clothes he'd worked out in. The piney smell of his sweat trailed him into the room.

I closed the door and plunked my ass on the edge of the bed. Jim remained standing with his arms folded, and fidgeted in place, rocking from foot to foot. Had he not been so damn handsome, just looking at him would have worn me out.

"This fuckin sucks," he growled. "Can't watch the tube, play videos, listen to tunes, and my laptop can't hold battery power worth a shit."

"Relax, man," I soothed. "Pretend you're sitting around a campfire."

"Yeah, like that would ever happen."

"Have a seat," I said forcefully. I rose from the bed and reached into the fridge. I pulled two sweaty bottles of beer from the darkness inside and handed one to Jim. He twisted off the cap and knocked back a swig. The suds, still cold, seemed to calm us both.

"So, what are you up to?" he asked.

"Nothing. Sleep."

Jim let loose with a goofy chuckle. "Yeah, right. You were probably beating your meat, dude, just like you said."

The comment momentarily caught me off guard. When I could think clearly again, I said, "So what if I was?"

A flush of embarrassment rippled over his face, the redness visible in the phone's glow. Large beads of sweat appeared across his forehead. "I sort'a wish you would," he said. "Anything to distract me from how bad I need a smoke." His eyes briefly met mine before darting away.

My heartbeat hammered in my cars, sounding twice as loud thanks to the imposed silence surrounding us. It grew steadily harder to breathe, to rationalize. Before I could stop myself, I said, "If that's what you need, I'll whip it out if you do."

In the broken light, I saw Jim's hairy throat knot under the influence of a heavy swallow. "Okay," he grunted in a broken voice. He was serious. Just how serious didn't sink in until he spread his legs and went fishing. I watched, mesmerized, as he hauled out his fat tool, already half-stiff, a good thick seven or eight inches of cut meat with a head shaped like a fleshy arrow. His sac spilled out with it, loose and furry, heavy with his as yet un-spilled seed. Jim yanked on his balls and moaned. "Your turn."

My dick had toughened, too, I discovered, and had quietly put a tent in my boxer-briefs. I kicked off my under-wear and saw the moist tip glistening in the phone screen's wan glow. Mine wasn't as thick or as long as Jim's, but it was enough of a handful for me and anyone else to enjoy. "Sorry, since there's no power, we can't watch a DVD or video. We'll have to use our imaginations instead."

"That's okay," he grunted while stroking on his impressive tool.

"Besides, all I have are gay movies, guy-on-guy," I confessed. Nothing like a little power outage to make you forget the usual rules of hospitality. "And I'm sure you wouldn't be interested in seeing any of that."

"Maybe I would," Jim said. "At this point, anything."

And then he leaned closer. Without warning, his hand was on my knee. I flinched, gasping in surprise. In the murk of the shadows, it still hadn't fully sunk in how blurry the boundaries had gotten in the darkness. His hand inched closer to my straining cock. The back of it brushed my shaft's sensitive underside. He fondled my nuts. I about came from the rough fumble of his shaking fingers.

"What are you telling me, dude? That you're into it?"

"Tonight, I'd do just about anything to get a blow job. Even give one," Jim growled. "Help me out, man, and I'll take care of you."

I looked into his eyes and found myself captivated by their intensity. It was true. The guy I'd whacked off thinking about for a month now held my dick in a choke hold. Seconds later, my head was between Jim's hairy spread legs.

I lapped at his ripe-smelling balls, tasting the funk of the night's long workout. Breathing in that acrid musk, I gave each giant nut a gentle sucking before opening wide to accept as much as I could take of his dick. I gobbled; Jim moaned.

Jim voiced his approval of the job I was doing through a string of breathless groans and half-muttered expletives. Not long after I started blowing him, he pulled me off his knob, and saying nothing, made good on his promise. I honestly didn't think he would. Part of my racing consciousness even wondered, jokingly, if his oral fixation for cigarettes was what made him suck my dick. You know how quitters chew on pencils, suck on lollipops, or in Jim's case, another dude's erect dick. But he went down, and I didn't protest. The helmet of my tool and about four inches of shaft vanished into his goatee.

I'd given my share of head since landing at Hampshire House, but I'd also gotten enough to know mine wasn't the first cock Jim had ever hummed on. I briefly remembered his teammates who visited his room, and now had new thoughts as to what they were doing in there.

Next, he slapped his tongue over my balls. The sensation sent shudders through me, from my nipples on down to my toes. It was too good to waste on a quick orgasm; I wanted this to last.

"Come up," I gasped, and at first he misunderstood the meaning of my words for something else. Spitting out my dick, Jim raised his wet mouth to mine. I kissed him, tasting cold beer and hot precome on his lips.

Jim shucked his T-shirt, his shorts, then finally, one at a time, his socks. This left him completely commando. I sat on the edge of the bed and studied his magnificent physique in the dying phone light for a few moments before again sucking his dick into my mouth.

"Aw, fuck," Jim groaned. He wrapped one of his big mitts around the back of my skull and proceeded to ride my face. Standing up left his nuts to dangle heavily under the root of his cock. I toyed with his low-hangers until he tackled me onto the bed and pinned me beneath his frame in an awesome sixty-nine.

Jim's tool flopped back into my waiting mouth. Being on my back also put me in the perfect position for a taste of his asshole. I stared up at the hard muscles of his butt, the twin hemispheres of a lightly forested globe, with a thin line of dark hair cutting it down the center. I massaged his cheeks, pried them open. Leaning up, I drilled my tongue into his hot pucker.

He seized in place. "Yeah, dude, eat my hole!"

Tugging on his cock, I drilled deeper, licking and lapping and probing until, at last, Jim started to squirt.

His spunk sprayed my face and dribbled down my neck. I licked the tip of his over-stimulated dickhead and tasted salt and sourness as my entire body shuddered. My own orgasm shot partly in Jim's mouth. The rest splattered off his goatee to land on my nut sac and drip down my inner thigh.

Jim pulled off me and spun around, putting us face-to-face. Then he kissed me and we tasted ourselves. Our spent cocks ground together. Fresh sweat mingled with the staleness of his earlier workout. Jim collapsed on top of me and nibbled on my neck.

I wrapped my arms around him. That's pretty much where we were when the lights came back on in a thunderous surge of power, and life returned to normal in Hampshire House—whatever normal really is.

THE LAST TIME
I SAW HIM

Jonathan Asche

I was with Jason when the old man first appeared.

We were in an abandoned house, the one I passed by walking to and from school. Cruising grounds. That's what it was. The house was dark, but enough of the hazy afternoon sunlight peeked through boarded-up windows to highlight his blond curls. He was leaning against a crumbling wall, thumbs hooked in the front pockets of his jeans, feet crossed, his package bulging enticingly. He took one hand out of a pocket and slid it down the front of his pants.

"So . . . " He finished the line by squeezing his crotch.

That's all it took to seduce me. "I thought you were straight," I said, putting my hands on Jason's waist.

His laugh was almost ethereal. "Yeah, I thought so, too."

Still, he was hesitant when we kissed, though he warmed quickly to my lips. Warm turned to hot as he urged me lower down—and I was eager to go. I slowly unbuttoned his blue jeans, his underwear bulging forward as his fly parted. I grabbed the waistband of his briefs, looking up at him for assurance, to make sure this wasn't about to be revealed as some cruel practical joke. In four years of high school, this guy never noticed me, but now that we'd graduated, he suddenly wanted me to suck his cock? It was too good to be true.

Still, Jason nodded, a slight smile on his lips. "Go on," he whispered. "Take it out."

I slowly pulled down his underwear, letting out an impressed gasp upon freeing his cock, which was as long and fat as I had always imagined it would be. The shaft was hot and throbbing in my grip. When I guided his dick into my mouth, Jason let out a moan that sounded as if it was out of relief as much as pleasure.

His cock filled my mouth until it was hitting the back of my throat, and still I wanted more of him. Gripping his waist, I pulled him forward, encouraging him to bury the full length of his prick in my gullet. He groaned too loudly for my comfort. *What if he's heard from the street?* I thought to myself. I'd endured cruel taunts and threats of violence throughout most of junior high and high school because of classmates' suspicions that I was, in their words, a *fag*; I didn't want to find out what would happen if their suspicions were proved true.

Jason thrust his cock deeper into my mouth, groaning louder than before. If he wasn't concerned about discovery, why should I be? For a few moments more I continued sucking, worried about nothing more than the possibility that he might come before I could fully experience all the pleasures his beautiful body had to offer.

Fear punched me hard in the gut as a cracking sound

reverberated through the empty house, followed by the sharp, piercing whine of rusty nails being pried from wood. Though I didn't hear footsteps, I knew someone was entering the house to try and pull me away. Maybe Jason could stuff his hard-on back inside his pants in time before the intruder (or intruders) found us. Maybe we'd just be suspected of smoking dope.

But Jason's hands came down on top of my head, holding me in place. "Don't stop," he sighed. "Don't stop."

I didn't, yet I couldn't escape the fear that we were about to be discovered at any second. I worked on his cock at a furious pace, now hoping he'd come quickly and we'd be over and done with, our secret safe. Then Jason cried out, practically shouting: "I'm going to shoot! I'm gonna shoot!"

Panicky as I was, I wanted to see his face when he came, and I looked up at him. And that's when I saw the old man, looking down at me, grinning as I sucked his cock.

I leaped back, scuttling away in a backward crabwalk, screaming as if he were coming after me with a chainsaw. I shouted—

"What?"

My body shuddered and I opened my eyes.

"You say somethin'?" a male voice asked sleepily.

As my eyes adjusted to the light, so did my mind adjust to my reality. I was in bed—a futon, actually, the only new piece of furniture in the room. Everything else was second- or third-hand. On one wall, Steve Reeves's muscles bulged as he raised his sword against unseen attackers in *The Slave*; on another wall, Bette Midler's bosom loomed large in a poster-sized blowup of the photo that graced the back of her *The Divine Miss M* album cover. I squinted to make out the time on the clock on the dresser, determining that it was around two. There were voices outside, probably from people walking home from the bars off the square, just a couple blocks from the tiny apartment.

"Russ?"

"You expecting someone else?" he chuckled.

I rolled over to face him. "I was dreaming. I was going down on this guy I had a crush on in high school. Should've known it was a dream. Don't think he said two words to me the whole time we were in school, until . . . Anyway, last I heard, he got sent over to 'Nam. It just seemed so real, though. It *felt* real."

That detail elicited one of Russ's goofy-adorable grins. "Did it? Let me check." One of his hands traveled beneath the sheets to my crotch. He groped my hard-on through my briefs. "Yeah, *that* feels pretty real. Why'd you wake up?"

"It got . . . weird."

Russ's fingers slipped under the waistband of my underwear. "How weird?" he asked, while fondling my weeping cock.

"Ah . . . it doesn't matter," I said, pushing my boner against his roving hand. "We're awake now."

Russ snickered softly, leaning in for a kiss. I gave him a quick peck on the lips, and he asked what the hell was that. "Morning mouth," I reminded him.

"I'll just kiss something else, then," he said, licking the side of my neck. His left hand slid over my chest, stopping to tweak a distended nipple.

His mouth followed his hand, kissing one nipple, then the other, before taking the stiff brown nub between his teeth and biting, just hard enough to make me gasp. I looked down to see Russ's head disappear under the sheet as he continued kissing and licking his way down my torso. The uncomfortable tickling sensation of his tongue dipping into my belly button sent a shiver through me. I shivered again when he reached my crotch, but for entirely different reasons. Russ mouthed my hard-on through my briefs, my cock pulsing as his hot breath soaked through the thin cotton. I clenched my fists and closed my eyes, bracing myself for the moment he peeled off my underwear and took my dick down his throat.

Russ's mouth went to my right thigh instead. The stubble on his chin scratching against my skin was oddly pleasurable, though not nearly as pleasurable as his mouth on my cock would've been. In the two semesters we'd been seeing each other—me, an undergrad, he on the cusp of getting his masters in English Lit—I'd grown accustomed to such teasing misdirects, though I didn't always find them endearing. Now was one of those times. I was about to smack him on the back, tell him to stop wasting time, when I felt his breath against my taint. His nose pushed against my balls as he bit at my drawers.

"That's more like it," I sighed, raising my ass off the mattress so that he could pull off my underwear with his teeth.

Russ flung off the top sheet, rising up on his knees with my briefs hanging from his mouth, looking like an excited puppy with a toy. The puppy comparison went to his face as well. Russ had a round, friendly face with big brown eyes and an upturned nose. He was more cute than handsome. His body, though, brought to mind less good-natured beasts, bulls and stallions, specifically. His physique was on the stocky side, his torso closer to a rectangular shape than Steve Reeves's inverted triangle, though it was, to be fair, all muscle.

He also had a great ass and a pretty penis, both of which were finally revealed after he tossed away my underwear and removed his own. My eyes were immediately riveted to his hard-on, artfully lit from a shaft of light cutting through a gap in the curtains.

"If you're not going to suck my dick, then I'm going to suck yours," I said, getting a thrill out of saying words I'd have been embarrassed to think just a year earlier.

Russ didn't accept my offer. He didn't suck my cock, either. He did dive between my legs, though, taking my thighs in his hands and lifting them until my ass was pointing toward his face. His fingers caressed my splayed cheeks, tickling the hairs lining my crack and making my butthole twitch in anticipation. The tip of his index finger pushed against my contracting sphincter, as if testing its resistance. I closed my eyes, bracing myself for the invasion of that single digit, even though it would be nothing like the invasion to come. Then my eyes popped open and I let out a cry that was half moan, half chortle, overtaken by the pleasurable shock of Russ's mouth on my hole.

I rested my legs on his shoulders, bearing my weight down on them to simultaneously push Russ down and lift myself up, ensuring his face was locked into position. His tongue poked and prodded, working its way past the tight ring of muscle and into my chute. I moaned softly and reached down to stroke the top of his head, running my hands through his straight brown hair. A year ago, a man licking my ass would've been out of the question, I mused, rim jobs being outside the realm of my sexual imagination. In any case, Russ wasn't the first guy I'd had sex with, but he was the most experienced, the first one to show me that gay sex was more than hasty blow jobs and quick fucks to be approached like a robbery: get in, get off, and get away. He'd eat my ass until I was quivering on the brink of orgasm and begging him to fuck me, then tease me with the promise of his cock, either batting it against my lips or nudging it against my asshole, then resume tonguing my hole until *he* could stand it no longer.

This early morning butt-munching session promised to be as excruciatingly glorious as all the times before it. Already my cock drooled so profusely that my belly was slick with precome. If he stopped boring his tongue into my chute and started wrapping it around my dick, I'd be shooting a thick load down his throat in less than a minute. As much as that idea excited me, I held off suggesting it, not wanting things to end too soon. I thought of another diversion instead.

"Hey, babe," I said, my voice hoarse with lust, "how 'bout letting me take a turn eating *your* ass."

Russ slowly raised his head from between my thighs. Except it wasn't Russ. The old man looked at me, dead eyed, yet still managing the suggestion of a smile through his white beard.

I kicked him away, pulling my body up into a ball as I cowered against the wall. "No, no, no!" I shouted, my eyes shut tight in denial. "This isn't happening!"

Only the intrusion of distant laughter convinced me it was safe to again open my eyes. The old man had disappeared. And so had Russ.

I heard the laughter again, and then the door to the

master bath opened, releasing a bright shaft of light into the bedroom.

I saw that Steve and Bette had disappeared from the room as well, their images replaced by large Bruce Weber prints in thin black frames. The furniture had changed, too, everything matching black lacquer and chrome, including the bed, which was no longer a hard futon but a king-size platform with a fan-style headboard. Clothes littered the floor.

A dark-haired young man stepped out of the bathroom, naked, rubbing his nose and giggling. In the bathroom, I heard the steady stream of piss splashing down in the toilet bowl, echoing off tiled walls.

"Oh, hey," he sniffed. "You want to do a bump? We saved a line for you."

I shook my head. My perceptions were fucked up enough already.

The guy shrugged and walked toward the bed. He was as handsome as the models that adorned my walls, his smile bringing out the sharpness of his cheekbones. He had a slim, athletic build—the proverbial swimmer's body—that had been waxed smooth, save for the dark tufts of fur beneath his arms and at his crotch. His thick, circumcised cock hung to the left, curving up slightly at the head. His balls were drawn up slightly, bulging in the tight, clean-shaven sac.

"Maybe you want to do something else?" he asked mischievously, bringing up one of his legs and resting his knee on the edge of the bed. His eyes were glued to my crotch.

I stretched on the bed like a cat in a sunbeam. "Maybe." I fought the urge to ask his name.

The toilet flushed, and a moment later out stepped another naked young man, this one taller, skinnier, and blond. He was cute, though his face appeared permanently fixed in a bored expression, and when he smiled it looked more like a grimace.

"What'cha guys up to?" he asked, moving toward the bed, his cock—longer than his friend's, though not as thick—swinging gently as he strode. As he got closer, it became clear he wasn't a natural blond; not only was his pubic hair almost black, but what I thought was a shadow falling across his face was actually dark stubble. Dangling from his right ear was a small silver cross, above that, a thin silver hoop.

I suddenly remembered where I'd met them, if not their names: Backstreet. Of course! I'd dubbed them GQ and George Madonna, the dark-haired one decked out in an Armani knockoff, seemingly posing for imaginary photographers, and the bleached-blond doing his damnedest to look like the love child of George Michael and Madonna, replete with fishnet shirt and leather jacket. I thought they were silly at the time, until I noticed them staring up at me from the dance floor. Moments later, they joined me at my perch on the second floor.

And now—now they were rejoining me in my bed. GQ snuggled next to me, throwing his left leg over my left thigh. His index finger traced my upper lip. "I like the 'stache," he giggled. "Makes you look like Magnum."

His reference to my facial hair shook me. Until that moment, I had thought of myself looking the way I had with Russ: clean shaven and clean cut, my brown hair a little too long to brand me a square, but not long enough to be lumped in with the hippies.

"I'll take that as a compliment." I got confirmation in the form of a kiss from GQ, his dick swelling against my thigh as I pushed my tongue into his open mouth.

George Madonna sat on my right, idly playing with my cock, while his boyfriend kissed me. I gyrated my hips, thrusting against George Madonna's hand, while my right hand stroked his lower back. Next thing I knew, my hand was moving over the curves of his petite ass, G.M. now hunched over as he sucked my dick.

"Oh yes," I moaned into GQ's ear, adding that I thought his friend gave great head. GQ responded by kissing me even more ferociously. He was hard now, really grinding his cock against my leg.

At some point, GQ's rigid dong found its way to my mouth, about the same time G.M.'s mouth made its way to my balls. GQ moaned loudly, holding on to the headboard as he stuffed his fat, curved cock down my throat. I brought my knees up and spread them farther apart to give George Madonna easier access to my ass, should his mouth move lower. It didn't.

GQ was less subtle in his hinting. He pulled his cock from my mouth, turning so his back was to the headboard, and then lowered his ass over my face. I dipped my tongue between those firm globes of flesh, finding the tight ring buried there and working my way inside. GQ gasped and giggled, saying my mustache tickled. (I wondered if he imagined Magnum was eating his ass.) Then I felt the heat of George Madonna's body over mine. GQ's moans went up a few more decibels—and with good reason, as he was getting it from both ends: my tongue digging into his hole, G.M.'s tongue swirling around his curvy cock.

In the midst of his ecstatic cries, GQ said he wanted me to fuck him. George Madonna hopped off the bed then hopped back on with a condom and lube in hand. "Gotta play safely," he quipped before tearing open the condom packet. He had me wrapped and ready in seconds.

I remained on my back while GQ lowered himself onto my throbbing cock. "I wanna watch it go in," George Madonna said, his eyes glittering with cocaine-enhanced excitement.

Strange, I thought, how I'm the top, yet I feel totally passive, lying here while this guy I've known for all of five hours rides me like a rodeo cowboy, his dick, quivering like a tuning fork, dripping precome onto my belly. The thought evaporated as quickly as it formed, erased from my mind by the glorious sensations radiating through me as GQ squeezed the walls of his ass around my cock.

George Madonna inserted himself between GQ and me, moving in to suck his friend's cock. He lay across the bed on my left, his crotch just far enough out of mouth reach to deny us some sixty-nine action. I fingered his smooth butt instead.

GQ seized a fistful of G.M.'s bleached-blond locks, breathlessly announcing he was about to come. I saw George Madonna's head bob faster, eager, it seemed, to hasten his boyfriend's orgasm. GQ arched his back and made a croaking noise, like he had a scream stuck in his throat. From his rigid posture, I could tell he was shooting his load, G.M. happily drinking every last drop.

Well, not *every* last drop. When George Madonna was done, he sat up and turned around so he was facing me. A trickle of jizz glistened on his chin. He flashed me one of his grimace-like smiles and leaned down to give me a kiss and to give me a taste of GQ's tart spunk.

Our lips parted, and I was once again looking into the eyes that had been haunting me since . . . well, when, I couldn't be certain.

"Who are you?" The question came out a terrified whisper.

The old man's voice sounded so distant I wasn't sure if he spoke at all, yet I remember his words. "You already know."

I pushed him away and pushed GQ off of me. "Hey, you didn't even come," GQ protested as I jumped off the bed. As soon as my feet landed on the floor, I spun around to confront them, though about what I wasn't sure. Mostly, I just needed to confirm that the old man had been a hallucination, that he had disappeared as quickly as he appeared. I wanted to confirm that GQ and George Madonna were part of the physical world.

All I confirmed was that I was losing my fucking mind.

The old man was gone, but so were GQ and George Madonna. The clothes on the floor and even the condom on my cock had disappeared. All that was left was an empty bed.

A sickening tightness formed in my gut, as if my stomach were collapsing on itself. Icy needles formed beneath my skin and stabbed their way up from my arms to the back of my neck. I backed toward the bedroom door, my eyes remaining on the vacant bed, bracing myself for the possibility of something arising from the rumpled sheets. Once I reached the door, I darted out of the room and bolted down the darkened hallway. I kept running until I reached the end of the hall, passing into . . .

Daylight.

"Well, well, well," a male voice chortled. "*Someone* knows how to make an entrance."

I looked in the direction of the voice, finding an old man, but not *the* old man. In fact, this old man wasn't all that old, being at least a decade younger than the man who'd been haunting me. He was sitting on a pale gray sofa, thumbing through a copy of *Vanity Fair.* He was handsome, there was no denying that, even if he was older than the guys I usually went for. His body wasn't bad, either, from what I could tell: broad chest, muscular arms, and well-developed legs. He was still fuckable, for an old dude.

I smiled at him, playing along, like I had meant to barge into his living room butt naked. "Wait until you see the rest of the show."

He set down the magazine. I noticed it was an issue with Heath Ledger on the cover, the one where he's wearing an undershirt and exposing a teasing swath of bare belly. "I hope audience participation will be encouraged," said the man, rising from his seat. "Surprised you're able to do a show at all after last night. I'm glad, but surprised. You could barely stand up when we left Louis and Warner's party."

"Really? I don't remember." Though I didn't remember getting drunk at a party, I did remember where I was, and whom I was talking to: Fort Lauderdale, in the condo I shared with Dave.

"Just as well," Dave said, walking toward me. "Don't worry, I got you out of there before you did anything *too* embarrassing. You did throw up in their hydrangeas on the way to the car, but I don't think anyone saw that.

Except me, which was when I decided I would not take advantage of your weakened state when we got home."

I shook my head, blushing. "I really don't remember."

Dave pulled off his tank top. "That's why I'm taking advantage of you now; I want you to remember every minute."

Now shirtless, I could see more plainly how well Dave had weathered the years. Salt-and-pepper hair, matching the hair on his head, covered his trunk-like torso, and though his pecs sagged somewhat, they were still thick with muscle. Likewise, the definition of his abs had been erased by time, but his stomach, I was pleased to see, had not expanded. He could, in fact, still be described as a muscle daddy.

What he couldn't be described as was my type. I always preferred men my age or younger. Dave was similarly inclined. "I've always liked younger men," he'd quipped on our first date. He was fifty-seven then; I was in my mid-forties. When Heath Ledger appeared on that *Vanity Fair* cover, I was over the top of fifty.

I was even more shocked when I put my hands on his chest and saw the hair on my arms. "I'm going gray."

"What do you mean *going*, Santa?" Dave chuckled, fingering my evidently white goatee.

I kissed him to change the subject. It was a tender kiss, the type of kiss that kindled romantic feelings rather than sexual. But the kiss heated quickly, going from romantic to lustful in seconds. Dave, shorter than I, reached up and put his hands around my neck, digging in his fingers as he held me to his lips, pushing his tongue against mine.

My arms encircled him, holding him tight against me—so tight my stiffening cock struggled uncomfortably between our bodies. Dave reached down and took hold of my swelling organ, his eyes going from my dick to my eyes and back again. With his free hand, he took one of my wrists and, without saying a word, started walking backward, leading me to the sofa.

I stood before him while he shucked off his shorts. His huge cock jumped forward. I didn't consider myself a size queen, but I couldn't help but be impressed. I reached for it, hungry to put it in my mouth, but Dave pushed me onto the sofa.

"Not yet," he singsonged, kneeling between my legs.

I leaned back against the sofa cushions and moaned deeply, my body enveloped in pleasure as my cock was enveloped by Dave's experienced mouth. He took my cock all the way down his throat, held it, then slowly released it an inch at a time. I tried to watch him suck my dick—I *wanted* to watch, to see my cock disappear into his mouth—but then another wave of pleasure overcame me and I closed my eyes, riding it blindly.

Dave lifted my legs up from the floor. I took the hint, and brought them up to my chest, wincing as my knees made a noise that sounded like a rope about to snap. My cracking knees, however, were quickly drowned out by my ecstatic groans as Dave tucked into my ass.

"Oh-yes-oh-yes-oh-yes," I panted mindlessly, my body trembling as Dave's tongue tunneled into my asshole. He chewed delicately on the rubbery contours of my rosebud, biting just hard enough to make it twitch.

He stopped abruptly. "You've got a beautiful ass," he said, working two fingers into my hole.

"It's all yours," I sighed.

Dave removed his fingers and leaned into my parted

thighs, his shaft resting against my spread asscheeks. His cockhead pushed against my balls, drizzling them with precome. "It better be," he replied.

He fucked me then, needing little more than spit and his cock's juices to enter me. I grabbed on to the seat cushions and shut my eyes, enduring the uncomfortable tension of his entry. And then he was on top of me, his cock buried inside. The tension eased into pleasure.

We kissed sloppily, going after each other's mouths as if the other man's lips were prey. Dave squeezed my shoulders, his grip tightening as he fucked me in hard rhythmic thrusts. My hands traveled down his sweat-dampened back, then lower to the rise of his ass, caressing his buttocks while searching for his hairy hole. Before I could finger him, though, Dave picked up the pace, and I had to wrap my arms around his neck, holding on for dear life as he pounded my ass.

"I love you so much," Dave said, the words coming out in a throaty groan, while his balls slapped against my quivering butt.

My reply came out as an adenoidal grunt: "I love *ungh!*"

Dave was now slamming into me, putting his full weight behind every thrust. The sofa banging against the wall provided a backbeat for our sharp cries, deep moans, and whispered obscenities.

"You're so fuckin' hot," Dave hissed, gripping my cock. *Thump-thump-thump.*

"Ah . . . I'm so close," I moaned, trying to hold back the rising ecstasy by sheer force of will.

Thump-thump-thump.

Dave was pulling on my cock, jacking me off in time

to his thrusts. "C'mon, give me that load," he said, his mouth contorted in a strained rictus.

Thump-thump-thump.

I shut my eyes tight, not wanting to open them for fear of seeing the old man again, for fear that what I was experiencing wasn't happening. I kept my eyes closed for fear that when I opened them, it would all be over. As long as my eyes were closed, I could hold on to the sensations coursing through me, enjoy them regardless of whether I was dreaming or on drugs or going insane. As long as my eyes were closed, I was getting a hot fuck from a man who loved me and whom I loved in return. At this moment, it was real and it was the only reality that mattered.

Then that reality burst, exploding in thick white jets of come. "Oh, yeah, baby," Dave growled, pumping my cock with his fist.

My body jerked and twitched, each orgasmic tremor seemingly stronger than the last. Then, in one final shudder, I was limp, breathless and satiated, hearing nothing but my heartbeat.

Thump-thump-thump.

I slowly opened my eyes.

I was in bed. Alone. It was morning, the sun so bright that it seemed to punch its way through the slats of the window blinds.

Thump-thump-thump.

Someone was pounding on the front door. Equally frantic pressing of the doorbell followed the frantic knocking. A man's voice shouted: "C'mon, I know you're home. Open up."

I got out of bed and headed to the closet to get my bathrobe, shouting for my visitor to wait just a minute.

Next to the closet door was the dresser, and on top of the dresser were photos. There were four of them: one of me taken during a Gulf Coast vacation in the '70s, on display because it showed off my body in its prime, even if my hair made me cringe; another photo showed Dave, stretched out in a chaise lounge on the patio, asleep, his boner ill-concealed in his bright yellow Speedos. Another photo was of Dave and me, together, taken during a trip to Majorca to celebrate Dave's retirement, the two of us burnished by the sun and looking happy—and ignorant, Dave finding out six months later his days were numbered.

I heard glass breaking and, moments later, the back door opening. "Jim?" a male voice called. "Jim? Jim! Goddammit, Jim, answer me!"

I remained motionless, not even bothering to speak when my visitor—Mike from next door—rushed into the bedroom. My eyes were stuck on the fourth photo displayed on top of my dresser, a four-inch by six-inch snapshot of my sister and her two kids, who were now married with kids of their own. Standing among them, wearing a grin with which I was all too familiar, was an old man, trying in vain to hide the wrinkles on his face behind a snow-white beard.

"Shit, shit, shit!" cursed my neighbor.

I turned to see Mike at the bed, frantically trying to revive the old man who lay there. I wanted to tell Mike he was too late, but knew he couldn't hear me; no one could. So I stood there silently, staring at the old man on the bed, realizing I would never see his face again.

LOVE ON THE ROCKS

Rob Rosen

I'd been in the bar for a couple of hours. It was a slow night, a Wednesday. Work had been tough. I had a big problem that wasn't getting solved any time soon, so I needed to unwind, forget my troubles, get laid—not necessarily in that order. But the place had been relatively empty, slim pickings at best. In other words, when the lights were raised and they got ready to close up, I wearily downed my drink and went to the back to use the facilities before my drive home.

Guess I was in there longer than expected. "We're closed already," the bartender said when he noticed me returning. "Sorry."

"No sweat," I replied. "Just taking a leak." I headed out and noticed him staring at me in the reflection of the front window. I turned and smiled and nodded. He returned the smile with one of his own—a big toothy number that caused the skin around his eyes to crinkle. He had two huge dimples and laser-intense blue eyes. I hadn't noticed them before, the bar being dark up until that point. "Have a good night," I said, reaching for the handle.

"Still got about an hour to go. Gotta clean this mess up. It'll be tomorrow by the time I'm finished."

Seemed like he was chatting me up. Fine, I figured; I had nothing else to do. "Yeah?" I said. "Sounds lonely. Want some company?"

The smile widened. "Don't you have someplace better to be?"

"Better than this? Are you kidding?" The bar was a dump, but he was cuter than hell. I'd take my chances.

"Suit yourself," he said, motioning to the stool I'd been sitting at. "Your seat awaits you, sir."

I turned around and sat back down. He put a shot glass in front of me and poured. "Scotch. On the rocks." He poured himself one, too. "Name's Scott."

"Todd."

We shook on it, lingering a little longer, not wanting to break the human contact. "'Excuse me," he finally said, and ran to the back room. He returned a couple of minutes later. He'd changed into a pair of shorts and a tank top. "My cleaning gear," he said, by way of explanation.

"Nice," I said. It was as gross an understatement as was ever uttered. The tank revealed sinewy, muscled arms and a matting of chest hair that poked out over the neckline, that and a tuft of hair just above the top of the shorts, which were so snug that they barely left anything to the imagination. And, trust me, I had ample imagination to go around. Though, judging by the package inside those snug shorts of his, not nearly as ample as him. In any case, he noticed my staring and shot me a wicked grin.

He started cleaning the area behind the bar first. "All

the cute guys in here, and you're going home alone? How come?" He had his back toward me as he emptied the trash cans. All the better for me to see his hairy, muscled calves and even hairier thighs, not to mention the cutest little butt this side of the Mississippi. Heck, let's make it both sides and call it a day.

"I'm not all alone," I corrected. "And the cutest guy is right here." I pointed his way.

I downed my scotch. He poured me another. "Sweet-talking the bartender, huh? It'll get you far."

"Not sweet-talking; telling the truth." I took a sip. "And how far exactly will it, to quote, *get me?*"

He winked, his neck flushing crimson. "Go pull the blinds down and cover the pool table for me, and then we'll see just how far."

I did as I was told. A few minutes later, I returned to my seat. Scott had rewarded me by taking off the tank. "Gets hot in here," he said, with a smirk. The guy was hairy. Way hairy. And lean as hell. He had flat pecs and thick, rigid nipples, those washboard abs you usually only see in underwear ads, a six-pack with a seemingly extra set of cans. While he cleaned the bar, they tensed and trembled.

"How come I've never seen you in here before?" I asked, removing my shirt as well. He looked over in mock alarm. "What?" I said, with a grin. "You were right; it is hot in here."

He started unloading the dishwasher as he answered my question. Even his back was defined, with just a slight spread of fur above his nicely rounded ass. "Started here a week ago. Moved to the city two weeks ago. Thought this was as good a place as any. Gotta work nights until my career gets going."

"Career?"

He turned and smiled again. "Modeling. Did some in college. Thought I'd make it full-time." That explained the body. And the face. "And you?"

"I'll tell you later," I replied. "First . . . " I held my glass up and shook it. "Empty."

He sauntered back over and held the bottle above my glass. I grabbed his hand before he poured. He looked up and locked those crystal-clear eyes of his onto mine, which is when I got up off my stool and leaned in. The bottle was set back down on the bar.

"Hey, Scott," I said, nearly in a whisper, leaning in even farther. I felt the cold bar press against my stomach. He leaned in as well, until our eyes were mere inches apart.

"Yeah, Todd?" he said, which also came out in a whisper.

The eyes stayed open. Our lips touched. His were soft, like silk. Like cotton. Like heaven. They parted to allow our tongues to swirl, to tango. I sighed, just slightly. The eyes closed. We pressed harder, kissed firmer. He smelled like booze and sweat, with just a touch of deodorant and cologne. It was a heady mixture, to be sure. His sigh echoed my own. The kiss got soft again. Tender. The eyes, at last, re-opened.

I finished my sentence. "Got any Bailey's?"

He laughed, pulled away, then returned with the bottle and poured us both a shot, again on the rocks. "For you? Anything."

"Man, the staff here sure is accommodating. Never noticed it before. Guess I gotta start coming to this place more regularly." I took a sip. It was cold and sweet, with just a mild burn. I added, "*Anything*, huh?" and set the glass back down.

Again the red crept up his neck. "Wipe down the tables first, and then we'll see." He handed me a clean wet rag, and added a kiss for good measure. Nix that; make it *great* measure.

It was a small bar, with only six tall tables. Pretty much everyone stood around or leaned against the wall. It didn't take long to clean them off. Quickly done with the task at hand, I returned to my stool, took another sip of my drink, and watched him count the bills and close out the register.

When he was done, he looked up at me with that glorious smile. I motioned him back over with a wave of my index finger.

"Now, about that *anything*." First, I pointed to my nearly empty glass. Obediently, he filled it back up. Next, I pointed to his shorts. "Off," I said.

"What would the department of health say about that?" He grinned and played with the elastic band just below his waistline.

"I'm sure they'd give you passing marks. Now, off." My breath grew faster and my heart rate quickened, chest pounding all the while, crotch right along with it.

He acquiesced. Slowly. The shorts crept down, revealing a trimmed black bush, then an inch of the base of his cock, then two. Until only the head was hidden and, soon enough, not even that. I'd been holding my breath the whole time. When he kicked off the shorts, I finally exhaled. Now he was naked, save for his sneakers and socks. His cock dangled down and just slightly out. He had a semi-woodie. Even softish like it was, it was a good five inches, with balls that hung far lower.

"Better?" he asked.

"Almost." I indicated that he should turn around. He did. The ass was even hotter without the material covering it. It was hairy and firm, with two concave indentations on either side.

"Better?" he asked, again, only with more of an edge to his voice, a low rasp.

"Almost. Put a foot on the keg to your right." He did as I asked. "Now, lean forward and grab the edge of the counter." His butt was now pointed at me, as were those mammoth balls that swung down so low that they could've been in their own zip code.

"Better?" It was almost a whisper this time.

"Almost. Reach back and spread the cheeks."

With both hands, he reached around and spread the hairy cheeks apart. The hair trailed inward to reveal a hairy crack and a pink hole that winked out at me. With his index finger, he touched the chute, smoothed it, caressed it.

"Nice touch."

"Yeah, thought you'd like that. By the way, I have something for you."

"Yeah, what's that?" I asked, all the while unbuttoning my pants and sliding down my zipper. *Ziiip.*

"This," he replied, reaching back around to his front and pushing his now hard cock through his legs. He pressed it up so that the fat mushroom head could rub against the hole.

"Nice," I said. "Turn around. Let's see it."

He took his foot off the keg and turned around for me. The cock was even bigger this way. Seven inches, easy. And thick. It pointed up. The meaty tip glistened with an opalescent drop of precome.

"Slap it," I said as I yanked my pants down around my ankles, then my underwear, to reveal my own six, even thicker inches of meat.

He slapped it; it bounced down and then up, as did his hefty balls. Scott moaned. The sound of the slap and the moan filled the room and my ears like a symphony. My cock grew even thicker, wetter. I pulled it, gave it a couple of tugs, sucked the salty spooge off my fingers.

"Don't be stingy with that," he said, moving toward me. Walking around the bar, he noticed my state of almost-undress, not to mention the thick cock in my hand. "*Mmm.* For me?"

"Yep," I said, releasing the beast and guiding his hand to it.

"Best tip I got all night." Our lips met again, firmer, with more urgency this time. He pumped my cock with his fist. I returned the favor. The eyes stayed open, yet again. The blue was jarring, mesmerizing, enticing. It drew me in like a cold pool on a hot day.

"You taste good," I said.

"Yeah?" He grabbed the bottle of Bailey's off the bar and tilted it over his fat cock. The tan liquid dribbled down and over. "Have some."

"Don't mind if I do." I jumped off the stool and sank down to my knees. His crotch now smelled awesome, like Bailey's and sweat, funky and sweet. I licked the alcohol off, sucked the remainder, and sunk my mouth down and around his curved cock, until he buried it down my throat. I gagged, backed up an inch, then swallowed again. And again. I was hungry for it. I kept sucking and sucking, finally tasting his bittersweet precome instead of the booze.

I got down on the ground and lay on the cold, hard

cement floor. "Stand over me," I said, and he did. "Now, feed me those balls of yours."

Grabbing the stool for support, he squatted over my face, rubbing his balls around my forehead, my nose, and finally my mouth. I popped one in, sucked gently, pulled down. Stroking his wet cock, I popped the other ball in, rolled both around in my mouth, pulled down again, harder this time. He moaned, loudly. The guy clearly liked his balls pulled, and so I obliged and tugged even harder.

"Yeah, man," he groaned. "Now suck on this." He shifted his body over, rubbing his asshole over my face until my tongue found its way to the bull's-eye. Same smell. Funky. Musky. Sweaty. I grabbed for his asscheeks, spread 'em far apart, licked around the hairy hole and then in. Deep. Deeper still. Until I was tongue-fucking him, making out with his asshole like it was his warm, wet mouth. He wriggled and moaned even louder above my face.

"Got an idea," he said, with a snap of his fingers. I watched as he stood up, then hopped on the bar—luckily, it was wide—all before landing atop it with his rump. He then leaned back, lifted his legs out and up while grabbing the front of the bar for support, and added, "Happy hour. Drink up." He poured some more of the Bailey's down his crack.

I kicked my shoes off and got out of my pants and underwear, then hopped back on the stool and licked my drink off his asshole. "*Mmm*, booze and butt. Great mixture." Then I plowed back in again, lapping at his hole, biting his cheeks, licking those massive balls and sucking on them again. It was a Scott buffet, served cold and raw.

I slapped his asshole with two of my fingers, then spit on it before rubbing the same two fingers around and then inside. I glided them in, first the tips, then up to the knuckles, then to my palm. Two fingers in and up, in and up, in and up. With my other hand, I found that thick, curved cock and brought it back to my mouth. I devoured the head, then sucked it to the hilt, until my mouth and my fingers were in pistoning unison. His big, meaty balls bounced against my hand as I finger-fucked him and sucked his dick for all it was worth. Soon enough, I felt his prostate harden, and his balls started to bunch up.

"Not yet, my friend," I said, pulling out my fingers and setting his cock free. "Can you do a one-eighty on that thing?" He got my drift and turned himself around, so that now his head was at the front of the bar. He rested his legs, for now, letting them hang over the other end. "I missed those lips of yours."

"Yeah? Take 'em; they're yours."

I grabbed his head, held it in my hands as I sat at the bar, caressed his mane of hair, staring once again into those blue eyes of his. My mouth found his. I forgot to breathe, just sucked and licked and bit at him instead. My hand found his nipples. They were full, hard as rocks. I tweaked them, slapped them, pulled and tugged on them. Like his huge balls, they seemingly ached to be tortured.

"Oh man," he moaned, his mouth still locked to mine. His hands moved below the bar and found my swollen cock. He stroked it slow and rhythmically as I continued working his mouth and nipples. "So thick," I heard him mumble. "Gonna fill me up with that bad boy?"

I stopped kissing him at that moment, pulling away a few centimeters, locking eyes with him again. "Yeah?" I whispered. "You want that thick dick up inside you?"

"Yeah, Todd. Yeah," he whispered back. Hearing him

say my name like that caused my breath to catch in my throat.

"Think there's room on that bar for the two of us?"

"Only one way to find out," he replied, shifting himself horizontally, so that he was lying down on the bar now. I grabbed our drinks and the bottle of Bailey's and set them down on the ground. Then I hopped on the bar, first straddling Scott and then lying down on top of him.

"Hi, dude," I said, again face to glorious face with him.

"Hi yourself," he said, with that wide, fabulous grin of his. Our lips, like two magnets, drew together, meshed, became one, melted together, as did our bodies as they slipped and slid over each other on top of the bar.

One of my hands found a nipple. One of his found one of mine. We both groaned together, still kissing, still staring. Our cocks bumped and ground. His legs lifted and wrapped around my waist, pulling me closer, if that was even physically possible anymore.

"Look at the corner of the bar," he whispered into my ear before taking a lobe inside his mouth and gently biting down. I pulled away and looked over my shoulder. There was a jar of rubbers down there.

"Man, a whole jar? Is that a dare? Doesn't this place have to reopen at some point?"

He laughed. "Let's try one for now." So I did. I got on my knees, reached over, and found a gold foil with a pretty yellow rubber inside. I handed it to Scott. He slid it over my fat cock with a leer and a giggle.

"Fill me with it, man," he pled.

"Best offer I've had all day." Heck, let's say all year, maybe longer. I reached down between his hairy, muscled thighs and found that sweet hole of his again. Spitting on my fingers, I opened him up, getting him lubed, ready for my thicker than thick cock.

He lifted his legs up. I positioned my body between them, resting the head of my dick against his hole. I stared at him again, kissed him again. I gently pushed a millimeter inside, then two, three, then the whole fat tip."

Scott sucked in his breath as his head tilted back. It was rapture on a bar.

"Yeah," he said, in a long exhale. My cock slid in farther and farther, deeper and deeper, splitting him apart, filling his hole, at last reaching the hilt before stopping. It was like we were one now. I didn't know where he ended and I began. We were just one big mound of sticky, sweaty flesh grinding into the wood.

And then I slowly pulled out, all the way, and then pushed the head back in and slid all the way home again. I repeated this, pulling out, popping in, deep, then out, again and again and again. Harder each time. Until I was pounding his ass, and the bar was rocking and creaking. And the harder my cock slammed into his, the harder our mouths mashed together.

Soon enough, we were both moaning in ecstasy, loudly, filling the small bar with our raspy groans and grunts, all while my cock slammed, slammed, slammed against the back of his ass. And, man, how I came, bucking and rocking against that hairy, hard ass of his. He came, too, without either of us touching his cock, just from the friction of our bodies.

His come flew and spilled over our stomachs, our chests, our chins. As he exploded and I exploded, it felt as if there were just the two of us alone in the whole wide universe. Just me and him and my mouth and his mouth and his blue eyes and my brown ones, together as one atop that bar, which was now slick with our sweat and his gooey, sticky, aromatic come.

"*Mmm*," I heard in my ear as my cock softened, at long last, and I pulled out of him, collapsing on his body, all smiles and relaxed muscles and bliss.

We lay there like that, gathering our strength back, not saying anything, just kissing and staring.

"I need a drink," I finally said.

"Good place for it," he replied, with a laugh.

We pulled apart, our sweaty bodies making a slurping sound as we did so. We hopped off the bar. The cool ground shocked my bare feet. Scott filled a glass with ice and we shared a last blast of Bailey's together.

We cleaned our mess up. I helped him finish the rest of his closing-up duties, mostly in silence, with furtive glances every so often. When we finished, we got dressed. I put on his underwear, he put on mine, in a final intimate exchange.

"Ready?" he asked, grabbing the keys to the place.

"Suppose so," I said, looking back longingly at the jar of rubbers.

He laughed when he saw what I was staring at. "I don't have to be back here for ten hours or so."

Now it was my turn to laugh. "I gotta be at work in six."

"And that's funny why?" We exited the bar and he locked the door behind him. "Hey, you never did tell me what you did for a living."

With a knowing smile, I handed him my business card. "Two problems solved," I said.

He looked at me quizzically. "You're a magazine

editor?" A glimmer of understanding appeared behind his fantastically blue eyes.

"Yep," I said. "An editor whose cover model got arrested this morning, which is why I was at the bar to begin with, drowning my sorrows. I don't have a jar of rubbers on my desk, but if you're looking for work . . . "

"Two problems solved, right?"

"And after the shoot . . . "

"We shoot. Again."

"And again. And again. And, hey, I even got a bottle of Bailey's at home."

"On the rocks?" he asked, wrapping his arm in mine as I headed us to my car.

"On the rocks. On your cock. Up your ass. Yeah."

"Yeah."

We got in my car and drove into the day.

HEMOGLOBIN

Richard May

It began that summer in Valeska, my village back home on the plains of Udmurtia, then part of Imperial Russia. The night air was humid and still, so I left my shutters open, hoping for a breeze. After some time, I fell asleep, but woke abruptly, as if from a dream. A bat was at my neck, drinking my blood. I knew then that I'd soon be dead, since there was nothing against rabies in those days. I tried to pull the beast off of me, but its fangs were too deeply embedded.

I must have fainted from the blood loss. When I woke again, the bat had become a pale-skinned man with dark, wavy hair. He was naked and lying on top of me. His cock was engorged and so was mine. The stranger sneered, yanking my legs into the air before ramming his cock up my ass. I screamed, but no one seemed to hear me. He held my arms back while he sucked and fucked, riding me like a Vyatka mare.

The pain quickly became pleasure. I had wanted this

before, with boys and men. This, though, was my first time. The man sneered a second time when he saw I was willing, and he set my arms free. My hands caressed his ropy back muscles, the wide slopes of his shoulders, and his bulbous ass. At my touch, his fucking became more violent, like that of a wild creature. Suddenly, he came inside me, filling me with come, even as he further drained my blood. All this was done without a word between us.

Minutes later, he withdrew and reclined on his side, letting me observe him. His body was muscular and milky white in the moonlight. I began to jerk myself as he watched, expressionless, until I came in jolts, spurting into the night air.

"Good boy," he said sardonically in Russian. I was still breathing heavily. Slowly, before my eyes, he became a bat once more, hairy, dark, and winged. I watched with terrified eyes as the creature flew out the window and into the dark, across the light of the full moon.

The next morning I was sure the man must've been a dream or a delusion, even if the bat was not. There was, after all, the bite mark on my neck. My mother noticed. I said I must've scratched myself on brambles.

The symptoms took a few days to appear. My parents thought it was the flu; I hadn't told them about my night visitor. When the fever and headaches came, I left; I didn't want to hurt my family. I walked along the river, looking for a good place, but what place is better than another to kill oneself? I dove into the wide waters. When I breached the surface the first time, I fought the urge to save myself, and swam into the middle of the river where the current was cold and swift. I let myself be pulled along by it. For miles we traveled, the Cheptsa and I. I sank repeatedly, but always bobbed back to the surface. I could never stop myself from taking a breath. Finally, the current brought me to the shore, and I staggered out of the water, thinking how next to take my life. Someone spoke to me in Udmurt, my own language.

"The water does not want you," an old man on the bank above me said. I tried to shake the river from myself, like a dog. "Wait," he told me and trotted toward a gray hut not far from the little beach I stood upon, my chest heaving all the while.

He soon came running back with a blanket and heavy rags. I removed my clothing, then dried myself with the rags and wound the blanket around me. I saw the old man's interest while I was naked. He was not bad looking for an old man. His name, he told me, was Mardan.

"Are you hungry?" he asked, and, when I nodded, he took me in to a breakfast of steaming buckwheat. While I ate, he watched me intently. "You are about my size," he decided and brought me clothes to wear. When I dropped the blanket to put them on, I saw his desire rise.

Mardan let me rest that first day, but we slept together the second night. He had a strong body, and worked mine well before we slept. I had dreams, which the old man said were visions. He was a shaman, and decided during our first days together that I would make a good one, too. I agreed to be his apprentice for as long as the disease would let me.

Insomnia came and then hallucinations. I told Mardan about the bat who became a man. "Do you have a cure?" I asked.

He looked at me with old eyes. "There is only one cure, Kedra. Blood."

"No! I cannot do that!"

"You will, whether you want to or not."

"But you . . . you have been so kind . . . "

"I will prepare an amulet for myself," he said, his eyes nervous now.

"I have to leave."

"No," Mardan begged. "Stay. Perhaps we can find a way."

I knew he only said that because he loved my body, but I felt safe with Mardan, and the thought of finding a way, as he called it, rooted me in place.

In three nights, the hunger came. I attacked him, but his amulet kept my new fangs from his throat. I tried to rush out the door, but Mardan reached it first. He began a chant, which calmed me enough for him to bind me to the bed. He gagged my mouth.

I watched him cut his arm and let his blood drip into a bowl. It was the most beautiful color and smelled delicious. He removed the gag and poured a little of the rich red fluid into my mouth. I begged for more, until Mardan fed me the rest. I grew calm, my fangs retracting. There was some little blood left thickening in the bowl, but he refused to give it to me.

"We will see how long this dosage lasts," he explained, quite medical in his approach.

Each night, we expected the hunger to return, and it did, at the next full moon, but for three weeks I lived a normal life, within certain bounds. For example, I could not go out during the day unless I was completely covered. I became nocturnal, active when the sun set, tired when it rose. Mardan adjusted his schedule to overlap with mine.

The night the hunger returned, I told Mardan at the

first sign. He bound me to the bed and cut his other arm. I drank from the bowl gratefully and felt refreshed. The dosage was the same. Mardan plucked a tune on the krez until I fell asleep.

We continued like this for twelve years, Mardan teaching me his skills and knowledge as a shaman and medicating me at each full moon. We created a crème that allowed me to go about in daylight hours if I kept my eyes down. I did not age, but Mardan did, and he was already old to begin with. At last, he died. His friends and I sacrificed the rooster and buried Mardan in his grave. I retired to his hut to consider what to do next. I was without my lover, without my medication.

I needed blood only infrequently, but obtaining it in a small village would be noticed. *I* would be noticed. Besides, I still held hope I could find a cure, even though Mardan and I had used every chant he knew and every plant available, and nothing had kept the symptoms from returning. He'd concluded that we needed more knowledge, and said I would find it in a larger city. I had not acted on this conclusion while he was alive, but now I said good-bye to his friends, gave away his belongings, and went to Izhevsk, our capital, to study with the great shamans Mardan had listed for me while he was alive. They eagerly taught me all they knew, pleased with my level of interest and diligence.

I still needed my monthly *medicine*, of course, and I went hunting for it among the dregs of Izhevsk when the first headache began. I also craved sex, now that Mardan was gone. I fucked my donors in their hovels or against an alley wall. They were grateful that such a good-looking young man would notice them.

I was not greedy; I followed certain rules. I took as payment for the fuck only the dosage I required. I always drank the minimum necessary, hoping I wouldn't turn my sources into monsters like myself. I never returned to the same man, at least for blood. I grew more confident when there was no increase in the reported cases of my disease, and I encountered no other vampires as competition.

Eventually, my shaman teachers declared that they had taught me all they knew. They suggested I continue my studies with a Russian in Izhevsk: a doctor, they called him. They gave me references and new clothes. I applied at the doctor's home and office, and was accepted. When he asked me my name, I told him Vesya, the first of many new names I assumed.

"What is your family name?" he asked. I had none, but knew I must invent one. The doctor had a last name, Rogovsky.

"Valeska," I told him, taking the name of my village.

"Vesya Valeska," he repeated. It sounded good. I stared at his glasses and made a note to buy some of my own. I told the technician that my eyes were sensitive to the sun, which was the truth. The dark tinted glass he made was perfect.

Dr. Rogovsky had strange ways. He was not at all spiritual, and he used no chants. He did not talk very much with the afflicted, as Mardan had done. But he did do one miraculous thing: he used leeches to let blood from his customers. He explained that this would strengthen them, which made no sense to me. If drinking blood made me stronger, how could letting blood do the same for others? But I didn't question his method; it would have its benefits for me.

As his assistant, I had many menial jobs. One included disposing of the blood taken from the doctor's patients. I would hold the bowl as blood seeped into it, then remove it quickly from the room, since patients often faint at the sight of it. In the anteroom, I would drink it, if it was time. I gave thanks to the gods before each bowl.

Although I no longer drank from men, sex with them continued. My new partners were from higher levels of society. Middle-class and wealthy men came to see the doctor for their ailments. We noticed one another and arranged to meet. Their bodies were clean and beautiful. It was a very good time for me. I was healthy and had all the lovers and blood I wanted.

But it was a difficult time in Udmurtia. Crops had failed and plague had spread throughout the towns. Russians blamed the Jews, as they always did. Dr. Rogovsky was Jewish, so he made hasty plans to move to Moscow, where he had learned his medical skills. I asked to go with him. Under his tutelage, I would learn not just about blood but how the body works. And, of course, there would be my medicine.

Luckily, he agreed to take me with him. We packed his equipment and our belongings, and left one moonless night for Moscow. The city amazed me—so many tall buildings and such beautiful men. I think my cock stayed erect the first three days without pause.

Dr. Rogovsky said I should study at the university, his alma mater. He still had friends there. But my Russian wasn't very good and my basic medical knowledge was inadequate, so he spent two more years teaching me, with the goal of preparing me for medical school. I practiced my Russian, especially with the many men I met. My Udmurt red hair and pale skin were novelties in Moscow, though they had never been back home. Many Udmurts look like me. Russians are dark or blond. In Moscow, I was a rare commodity and in demand.

The men would say their names when we met. They looked confused when I told them mine. "I'm not Russian," I would explain. None of them had ever been to Udmurtia. My ethnic background seemed as exotic to them as my looks. At one time, I thought I would make my name more Russian, but too many people already knew me as Vesya.

I became more Dr. Rogovsky's associate than his assistant. I did research at the great medical libraries of Moscow, admitted by his name and credentials, and reported to him what I learned. He thought my interest in the blood system novel. I developed medicines and tried them with animals, and eventually, with his approval, on volunteers among his patients. We made many beneficial discoveries together. When I applied to medical school, my fame was already beginning. I was accepted without examination.

The school authorities allowed me to study with the best teachers, right away. Indeed, they treated me almost as a colleague. They were excited by my blood research and encouraged me to continue, as well as to study medicine in general, of course. This left me little time with Dr. Rogovsky, but I did continue clinic hours with him out of gratitude and because he was growing older. It was difficult for him to see his old patients, much less anyone new. I obtained more than enough blood at the university, but I was loyal to Dr. Rogovsky. He treated me almost as a son.

When he died suddenly—I diagnosed it as heart

attack—he left me his house and practice. I was a doctor myself by then, focusing on research medicine, but I gladly took over his practice. I was still looking for a cure for my disease and needed humans with blood disorders for my experiments.

People commented on how young I looked, so I took to adding white to my hair and applying special lotions to my face and hands that made me appear older. Still, I knew the ruse couldn't last, so I evaluated where next to live and applied for a position as an instructor at the great medical college in Heidelberg. The Germans were surprised when such a young man with such a strange name arrived from Russia.

I stayed at Heidelberg many years, now knowing to gradually age my hair and skin. I had sex with men as my older self if I knew them and as the ageless me if I did not. I continued my fruitless research until it was time to die and start a new life.

After Heidelberg, I moved to Paris. I lived through revolutions and counterrevolutions, never leaving because of the beauty of the city and her men. Paris was also a scientific center, and I could continue my research. I kept trying for a cure, testing each possibility on animals and then, if rabid symptoms were alleviated, on myself. But none of the medicines or vaccines ever helped my vampirism. I still needed blood every month during the new moon, but at least the dosage never increased. I always wanted more, but managed never to take it.

I discarded the practice of bloodletting in Paris. I espoused adding fresh blood, not subtracting it. I was the first one to call adding blood a transfusion. I was not given credit, but I was still the first.

I developed more sophisticated crèmes to protect my skin from the sun. This led to other discoveries, which aided sufferers of skin disease. I studied dermatology at the great Hôpital Saint-Louis. This bemused many of my colleagues. Why would a famous researcher and practitioner in blood disease be interested in dermatology? I decided to move on again, before the questions were answered—or worse.

I became adept at preparing my death. I aged myself and "died," substituting a cadaver for my body, always arranging for cremation. I left my practice to other men, having no natural heirs, and would quickly find my way as a new man to a new place.

New York was my next home. I appeared once again as a young man, and set up a practice on Park Avenue, among other fashionable doctors. My name was now Henri-Luc Chenault. I was a graduate of the Hôpital Saint-Louis, which was true. I had a dual practice in dermatology and hematology, and I still yearned for a cure for immortality.

Most of my patients wanted my services as a dermatologist. They were mainly middle-aged or elderly matrons with time and wealth who wanted to stay young forever, or at least to appear younger looking. I could have argued against eternal youth, but they would not have agreed. My own skin was my best advertisement. When people asked, I told them the truth: I used my own crèmes and stayed out of the sun.

In New York I found more men who looked like me— not vampiric, of course—but there were many redheads with pale skin and pale eyes like mine. Most often, they were Irish and working class. I enjoyed being naked with them, but I didn't expect to find a continuing relationship among them. I didn't expect to find it with anyone, in fact. I wanted love but worried about having it. Wouldn't my lover discover my secrets? So, I remained distant with the men I met.

There came a day, however, when there was an exception.

Jack Callaghan was Scottish, as well as a doctor. He had the thick, woolly red hair of the Scots, but, unlike my Irish encounters, was a professional. He had gone to medical school in Edinburgh, and was in New York for further studies at Lenox Hill Hospital on the Upper East Side. I lived nearby, as did the majority of my patients. I sometimes lectured at Lenox Hill on dermatology and blood diseases. I met Jack there at one of my classes.

"We have something in common," were the first words he said to me after we were introduced.

I blanched—though I was already as pale as one could get—but did my best to recover. "And what is that, Dr. Callaghan?" I asked, hoping he wouldn't hear the quaver in my voice. He pointed at my hair and his. "Oh," I said, greatly relieved. He suggested we go for coffee, and I agreed, taking care to don my tinted glasses before we exited the building.

"You wear glasses against the sun?"

"Yes, my eyes are sensitive."

"Mine too," he said. "Perhaps I should try dark lenses as well."

He wore eyeglasses to see. Behind them, I noticed that his eyes were green. They looked back at me calmly, and we shared the look of recognition. I stuffed my feelings back inside myself and promised to give him the name of the service who made my lenses.

We walked to a café near the hospital, on upper Madison. There, over his tea and my coffee, we talked about ourselves. "I've been to Paris many times," he said. "Your accent is strange." My heart skipped a beat. "Are you from Provence?" he asked.

I settled back in my chair, hoping he hadn't seen my alarm. "No, Nancy," I replied, as blandly as I could. "In the north, near Belgium."

"I've never been there," he said, smiling. "Is it nice?"

"Not especially," I answered, forcing a laugh. I steered him back to Paris. By our second cups, we had arranged a dinner, both knowing what would follow.

In Jack's bedroom I found that his body was as white and ethereal as the man's who had made me a monster. Was he like me in more ways than hair color? I lay down beside him and gave my neck to him. His lips grazed my skin. I waited for the fangs, but none came. I adjusted our positions and made love to his body, paying careful attention to his small, pink, pointed nipples, since he shivered so when my lips brushed over them. I raised his legs and entered him slowly, joyous to hear him gasp in pleasure. His legs clinched my back to hold me close. I leaned toward his face, toward his lips, toward his achingly inviting neck.

"What is it?" he asked, when I abruptly pulled away from him.

"I should not have stayed," I said, brushing my longish hair out of my eyes before sitting up.

"Why?" he asked, which I didn't answer. "Stay with me, Henri," he insisted seductively, his pale, muscular arms reaching up, his neck stretching.

My fangs ached to rip into his flesh. The moon would not be full for several days, but I wanted Jack's blood as much as I wanted his body. I wanted the life force of him inside me. I wanted my come inside him.

I forced myself to stand and dress. Jack sat up. "Is it something I did or said?" he asked, while I pulled on my trousers.

"No," I answered simply, afraid to say more.

He stopped me from doing up my trouser buttons, and pulled them and my underpants back down, taking my erection into his mouth before beginning to suck. I let him swallow my seed while I held him by his copper hair. When he asked again, I agreed to stay, my first full night with a man since those with Mardan.

In the morning, he drew apart the heavy curtains across the bedroom window. I yelped when the instant heat singed my body. "Oh, I'm so sorry," he yelped back, and hurriedly shut the drapes.

"So much sun so suddenly," I tried to joke. "Do you have a robe?" He showed me two. One reached to the floor, so I put it on. Jack slipped into the other.

We had coffee and tea, wearing his robes. He suggested breakfast nearby, but I demurred. "My patients," I explained, which was true. I promised to see him again for dinner. Afterward, I invited him to my home, which was better prepared for defense against the sun. Thereafter, we always spent our nights together at my house on Upper Fifth.

Within three months, I found myself in love. I didn't say the word to Jack, hoping he'd lose interest in me, but one night he said it first.

"I love you, Henri."

My heart sank. He waited through my silence and the ticking of the standing clock in the hallway.

"Don't you love me?" he asked at last.

"Yes," I replied, with a heavy sigh.

He sat up against the dark walnut headboard, folding his arms as he frowned. "You don't sound at all happy about it."

In truth, I wasn't. It meant I would have to die again. I lay prone on the bed, watching my lives parade before me in the midair of my bedroom.

Jack spoke into my silence. "Well, that's it then; I'm going home."

I didn't try to stop him, but did ask, "Will I still see you tomorrow?"

"No, I'm going home. To Scotland."

"When did you reach this decision?" I asked, surprised I didn't feel relieved.

"Just now," he replied. His green eyes stared at me without anger, without any emotion at all. "I've had an offer to join a practice. McLeod. In Edinburgh." I'd heard of him. Eminent. Growing older. Likely needing a sharp young doctor on the rise to bequeath his patients to. "I had thought to turn him down, but now . . . " He waited for me to say something. I wanted to. I longed ferociously to plead with him to stay, to love me, but that was impossible. I couldn't love anyone, for their sake and mine. The gods were giving me a gift I simply could not accept. I remained silent as he dressed and left, without a look back.

Jack left for Scotland a month later.

I returned to my old habits: teaching, caring for patients, seeing men only for sex. I tried, unsuccessfully, to forget Jack. I embraced my work with patients frenetically, accelerating my blood research. I wanted so much to be just a man, a man who could let himself be loved. I was getting closer. My fangs rarely emerged, once Jack was gone. I still needed fresh blood once a month, but had successfully decreased the dosage to half.

My time in New York grew short. Over the years, I had gradually grayed my hair and aged my skin cosmetically. I stooped slightly for effect, but my colleagues and their wives became suspicious, especially the wives, who knew cosmetics and the details of aging more intimately than their husbands. So, once again, I prepared my death. I began the rumor that I was ill, that it was a hopeless ailment. At last, I left my hat, coat, and suicide note on the Brooklyn Bridge in the middle of the night, when no one was near. I'd booked my passage on a freighter heading for Australia as a young man named Paul, looking for adventure.

In Sydney, I applied for medical school and was accepted. I began my life and research again, but this time with a greater sadness than before. I thought a great deal about Jack. He had become a world-renowned doctor and medical researcher himself. I began a foolish correspondence with him, as the new me, not the old. Of course, at first it seemed harmless, just hero worship for a great physician from a medical student in faraway Australia. But our words became more personal when we began speaking once a week by telephone.

The first time there was silence when I answered. Then, one word: "Henri?" My heart sank. I had been unbelievably foolish. I started to hang up, but then he shouted, "Paul! I'm sorry. Your voice reminds me of . . . oh, well, in any case, how are you?"

He said several times in succeeding conversations that

he would visit me, but I always put him off. Yes, I looked younger than him now, but I suspected he would know me in an instant, as he had known my voice. It was easy to dissuade him—the long distance and increasing trouble in Europe. The Germans had forced Austria into a union of German-speaking peoples and taken the Sudetenland. It was not a time to be traveling far from home.

When Japan bombed Pearl Harbor and Darwin, Australia and the United States both declared war. I had finished medical school and my residency. I volunteered to be an Australian Military Forces doctor.

We set up field hospitals throughout the East Indies. My fellow Aussies always marveled at my bravery. I retrieved the wounded fearlessly, running into action while gunfire blazed. They didn't know I couldn't die, at least not from ordinary bullets.

Somehow, Jack and I kept up an irregular correspondence throughout the war. He was too old and too important to fight, but he organized the home hospitals for those wounded in battle and aerial bombings. He became even more famous and beloved. I felt pride in his accomplishments, more than in my own.

After the war ended, Jack announced he was flying to Australia and could not be put off by any more reasons or excuses. I debated whether to disappear again or just not be in Sydney when Jack arrived, but I couldn't make myself do either. I'd joined a prestigious medical practice. I had my patients to think of. Besides, the more I thought of Jack, the more desperate I became to see him, so I made a deal with myself: one visit. Then, after his return to Scotland, I would prepare my own departure, but to where and as whom I didn't yet know.

I watched the BOAC plane land at Sydney Airport. It seemed so small to have come so far. Steps were rolled to it. The door opened. I stretched my neck to locate Jack, reminding myself that he was so much older now. I recognized him immediately, however. He still had copper hair, albeit with some white throughout the red. He was dressed for our summer, in a light suit, carrying a broad-brimmed hat. I wanted to run to him. I wanted to sing with happiness. But I did neither. I had never met Jack Callaghan before, at least to his eyes. I made myself walk deliberately to baggage claim, where we had agreed to meet.

His back was to me, but I knew whose back it was. I tapped him on the shoulder, and he turned around, smiling then not, exclaiming loudly, "Henri!" The people around us stared.

"Paul Evans," I told him in my Australian accent, holding my hand out to shake. He pulled me in close in a clamping hug.

"I can't believe it! I can't believe it!"

My fears had been realized—someone knew me—and, for the first time in nearly two hundred years, I gave up my pretense. I struggled, but my body betrayed me. I held Jack in my arms as willingly as he held me in his. I loved him. If he still loved me, there was only one thing left to do.

I drove us to my home, a two-story house with a basement laboratory. Once I'd closed the door on the outside world, Jack's arms went around me again. His lips kissed mine repeatedly and at length. I led the way upstairs to my bedroom.

As I undressed him, I saw that Jack's body had thickened a little, but he still moaned when I played with his tight, pink nipples and he still eagerly sucked my cock, preparing me to enter him, and, when I did, his eyes still danced with the same delight. My groans also seemed to come from the past, though farther back, from times with Mardan in my first safe place, so very far away. I thought of Mardan dying. Jack would die as well. Still, I pushed away my thoughts of history and pressed Jack's legs back as far as they would go. We were here now, the place I'd never wanted to be.

I pummeled his ass, as if I hadn't fucked anyone in the many intervening years. That was not true, of course. I was always young and beautiful, and men were always willing. I kissed along Jack's neck without fear; my fangs never emerged in those days, not anymore, not if I didn't want them to. Only my lips and tongue traced his veins. My hands went to his shoulders when my mouth reached his chest. He was still so handsome, all red and pink and glorious, but, yes, I could see the wrinkles and the aging skin. I felt the loss of all those years, as much as I felt Jack's body. He began to yell, interrupting my reverie.

"I'm coming, Henri! I'm coming!"

When he shot into the narrow space between us, I let my cock explode inside him. We roiled together, conjoined and coming. I stayed inside him afterward, reluctant to leave, now that I was there.

He frowned up at me. "You're alive," he said, his face showing his mind was reasserting control. "I heard . . . " he began. I started to pull out of him. "Don't! Please, don't. Never mind what I heard. But how?" I eased myself back inside him, still fully engorged, and began my story.

Of course, he didn't believe me, until I willed my fangs to emerge. There was then terror in his eyes. I retracted my fangs. His horror confirmed all my repeated fears throughout my living death. My mind commanded me to leave, to run, but my body refused to go.

Jack observed me all the while, a clinical habit I knew all too well. He asked various questions, all medical and scientific. I answered everything, hoping it wasn't too much to know. "It sounds as if it's become a manageable disease," he summarized, like he was making a diagnosis.

"Yes, manageable, forever. I will never die. Everyone else does."

"But I don't have to," he said mildly, his green eyes observing the reaction of my gray.

"You must be kidding!" I yelled, springing away from him. His benign look told me he wasn't. I tried to get out of bed; he pulled me back.

"No, Jack. I won't."

"We'll find a cure. We'll work on it together," he said, sounding so certain. "Look at the progress you've made. You've decreased the amount of blood you need. You have control of your fangs, ointments, glasses against the sun." It didn't seem like very much for two hundred years, but I automatically considered the possibility. My eyes roamed down Jack's body as I thought. We *could* be together. I wouldn't be alone anymore. I wouldn't have to be afraid of love.

But I couldn't. I couldn't infect him with my incurable disease and condemn him to immortality, which, of course, is what he had insinuated.

"No," I said, sadly but definitely. In response, he climbed out of bed and took up his clothes.

"We could be together forever," he said as he rummaged through the pockets of his slacks.

Forever. I had lived with forever and fought against it for centuries.

"I can't decide now," I told him. "And you shouldn't either. At the end of your visit, we'll talk again." But before then, I promised myself, I would already be gone.

"No," he said as simply as I had. He displayed a small revolver. "Silver bullets," he said, spinning the cylinder.

"Jack!"

"I already guessed. It was only logical," he said, with half a smile. "The blood research, the crèmes, your reaction to the sun. I traced you back. I made the connections between the men you had been." Then, he frowned. "But enough delay. You make me like you or I kill you; that's now your choice to make."

"You're insane!"

"Perhaps, but I can't let you leave again," he replied. He straightened his shoulders. "I'll kill you and then myself. But don't make me do this, Henri. Let me love you. Let yourself love me."

I considered my alternatives, hands clasped, though not in prayer. If I wanted to die, here was my opportunity. However, if I wanted to stop him, I easily could. I was far stronger than Jack, and faster. I looked at him, calculating. He was pointing the gun at me, his finger on the trigger. He loved me that much.

"All right," I said. "Put down the gun and come here."

"No, you come here." He indicated my path with the gun.

I stood, my cock erect. Quickly, Jack's was too. I walked into his arms, our erections twining. He stretched his neck for me, pointing the gun at my head. I let the old desire rise as my fangs emerged, slowly, so slowly, as if they were as unwilling to do this as I was. I gave him one more chance.

"Are you sure? Everyone you love and need will die."

"Except you," he said, pressing the gun against my temple.

I kissed his lips and then his neck. I touched his day's growth of beard with the tips of my fangs and pressed them into his pale, pale skin. At the first delicious taste of blood, I heard the gun land on the carpet. I tried to stop, but I couldn't. Blood has a taste that mortals cannot imagine. I drank while he moaned softly, as if he were enjoying it.

When he awakened the next morning, Jack asked if it had "worked." In answer, I opened the curtain a few inches. He immediately cried out in pain, shielding his eyes. I closed the gap and pulled him into my arms. What had I done? What had I done?

"Thank you," he said into my neck. I could feel his fangs. I let him take his medicine.

CONFERENCE CALL

Michael Roberts

I was sitting on Ron's cock when the phone rang.

I wouldn't have answered if it hadn't been my second number, the one I use for chat lines and contact ads.

We were on the sofa, and the phone was on the coffee table in front of us. Ron was wearing a condom, and therefore I was wearing his condom. We are utterly devoted to each other, but we try not to go to extremes. I have my contact ads, and he has his bar hops, so there is prudence in protection.

I had to lift slightly from Ron as I punched the button and took the handset. Just as I was going to speak, Ron punched me with his prick, shoved his cock back into me, and instead of saying hello, I squealed into the receiver.

"What?" said a masculine voice on the other end of the line.

"Sorry," I replied. I slapped at Ron's chest, and he grinned. "This is Dong Master Dave"—not my real name.

"I'm, ah . . . " responded my caller, "I'm Sexy Simon"— probably not his real name, either.

"Hi," I said. Starting these things was always awkward. "How're you doing?"

We exchanged a few more pleasantries. After a pause, Simon said, "So, um, what're you wearing?"

I could have said that I was wearing my boyfriend, but instead I said, "Nothing."

"Nothing? Really?"

"Really. Nothing. I've been waiting for you."

"You have?"

This might take a while to get going, I realized.

"You bet. I was hoping you'd call today, Simon, and I wanted to be ready for you." I raised my eyebrows and shook my head at Ron. He smiled, resting one hand on my naked leg, which I was resting on his naked lap. "So, what do you want to do?"

"I, ah, I ah . . . " I was about to say good-bye and hang up, but at last he said, "I want you to suck my cock."

"I'd like to do that," I said. "I love to suck cock."

"You do?"

"I sure do," I answered. The dialog was like a bad porno movie. "How big are you?"

"Five foot eight."

"No, I mean your cock."

"Oh. Sev—eight inches."

I flicked on the speakerphone. I slipped off Ron's dick, stood, walked to the end of the coffee table, and kneeled. Ron looked at me for a moment, then rose and moved behind me. As he did, his rigid prick bounded from side to side.

"Let me see your dick," I said to Simon. "Oh, that's a great dick."

"Just a sec," said Simon. "I'm still unzipping. There."

"That's a great dick," I repeated. "I can't wait to eat it."

"I can't wait to be your meal."

Ron spread my cheeks. He trailed his cock along my crack.

"I love your dick," I said to Ron, and Simon said, "I want it in your mouth now."

"Give it to me," I said.

"It's yours, baby," said Simon, and Ron pushed his prick up my ass.

As often as I've had Ron's cock riding me, it's never enough.

I sighed.

"You like it?" asked Simon.

"I love it," I said.

Ron began to fuck me.

I never know what Ron's going to do. Sometimes he's content with my sitting on his cock, raising and lowering myself at my own tempo; sometimes he screws me slowly with his long schlong for a long time, so long that I ache and almost want him to stop—almost; and sometimes he batters me, his speed and force so great that I'm sure he's going to pound me into the bed or propel me across the room.

"What're you doing?" asked Simon.

"I'm running my tongue around the top of your shaft and across the slit, teasing, tempting."

"That feels good."

"You taste good. Your flesh is warm. Warm and tasty."

"Take more of me."

"I'm gliding down your rod," I said. "You didn't tell me you're so thick. I can barely get you in my mouth."

"I want you to deep-throat me."

"It's going to be a while. Half of you is in. There's so much of you."

Ron pulled all of the way out, then drove back inside. My asshole had relaxed when he withdrew, and it jolted as he reentered me. He did that again. The third time, he waited for a bit, and when he shoved into me, he went all of the way. His crotch crashed against my butt, and I gasped.

"What's wrong?" asked Simon.

"I'm just trying to get some air," I said. "Your cock's so big, I can scarcely breathe."

"Inhale it all, baby," whispered Simon. "Take all of my big cock."

"I want all of you. There's just a ways to go. I'm almost there. Your dick fills my mouth. A bit more—more—I've got all of you, I've got all of your cock in my mouth, and my jaw's spread so wide, I think it's gonna break. If I stick out my tongue, I can reach your bush."

"Oh, wow!"

"That's the way I feel, too. I love pubic hair tickling my tongue."

Ron's nest was scratching my ass as he rubbed it against me and swiveled his dick, stirring me with his swizzle prick.

"Now I'm gonna suck you," I said to Simon. "I'm gonna give you a blow job that'll make your teeth curl. Here I go. I'm moving up and down your cock, your big thick cock, and I'm holding your balls, your big bursting balls, rolling them around while I suck your cock."

I grabbed my own moist erection. The coffee table had a glass top, and I watched through it as I jacked myself.

"I want you so much," I said as Ron went even faster,

sharper right and left. "I w-w-want your cock so m-m-much."

"You've got it, dude; you've got it."

"Give it to me!"

Ron gave it to me.

"I'm giving it to you," said Simon, his voice now rising.

Ron was fucking me raw. I felt every bit of his considerable length, his hefty girth. He spread my cheeks and went in farther, faster.

"Oh! Oh! Oh!" I exclaimed as Ron's dick dashed against my asshole.

"Tell me," gasped Simon. "Tell me—"

"Your prick is hitting my tonsils," I told him. "I can barely, I can barely—"

"I can barely hold back," said Simon. "I wanna come. I don't wanna come."

"I want you to come. I want you to shoot in my mouth. But I don't want you to come just yet. I want to suck you some more, a lot more."

"You've got me so hard."

"You've made me so hard."

I looked down through the glass top of the coffee table. My hand was racing along my rod. My stomach was twisting. I felt my nuts ascend into the base of my cock.

Ron's generous globes slapped my butt. When they didn't, I knew they too had risen. Ron was panting so fiercely that the temperature on the base of my neck shot up.

Ron's breath was hot, and his cock was hotter, blazing into my entrails.

"I can't," wheezed Simon. "I don't—I've got to—I'm gonna—"

"Me too," I whispered. Ron was fucking me with such intensity, I felt certain I was going to pass out.

"Give it," I whimpered.

"Take it," Simon cried.

Ron, of course, said nothing. He didn't need to; his cock spoke volumes. It was rearranging volumes, in fact, shearing me one way, then another, yet another. My insides were pretzeled.

"I can't," said Simon tightly. "I'm gonna—oh, dude. Argh—arrgh—argggh," he gargled—or something like that.

"It's too much! I can't take it all. Your jism's running down my chin. You're gonna drown me. You—"

There was a silence that indicated Simon had disconnected, then a dial tone.

And even though there was nothing in my mouth but teeth and tongue, I swallowed, and I could taste the come drizzling down my throat.

Ron put his head on my shoulder and plastered me one last time with his powerful prick and shouted and flowed fluently. As for me, I attacked my pulsing pud once, twice, three times more, and I shook, and "Urgh—urrgh—urgggh," I gurgled—or something like that—and I jetted all over the rug.

"If you'd like to make a call," said the speakerphone, "please hang up."

I hung up.

ABOUT THE AUTHORS

JONATHAN ASCHE's (jonathanasche.com) work has appeared in numerous anthologies, including *Best Gay Erotica of the Year, Volumes 1* and *2*. He is also the author of the erotic novels *Dyre, Moneyshots,* and *Mindjacker,* as well as the short-story collection *Kept Men.* He lives in Atlanta with his husband Tomé.

LOUIS FLINT CECI's poetry has been published in *Colorado North Review.* His short stories have appeared in *Diseased Pariah News, Trikone,* and *Jonathan,* and in the anthologies *Queer and Catholic* and *Gay City Volume 4.* His first novel was *Comfort Me.* In 2016, as publisher of Beautiful Dreamer Press, he edited *Not Just Another Pretty Face.*

DALE CHASE has written male erotica for eighteen years, with stories published in numerous magazines, anthologies, and collections. She has two erotic Western novels in print. Her latest book is *Hot Copy: Gay Erotica from the Magazine Era*, from Lethe Press. Chase lives near San Francisco.

When not daydreaming about plotlines and characters, **ANDRA DILL** (Twitter @aedill) works in the medical field to pay for her horse, dog, and cat. She writes, practices yoga, rewrites, reads voraciously, writes some more, and has been talked (tricked) into completing two half marathons.

LANDON DIXON's writing credits include stories in the magazines *Men, Freshmen, [2], Mandate, Torso,* and *Honcho*; stories in the anthologies *Ultimate Gay Erotica 2005/2007/2008, Best Gay Erotica 2009/2014,* plus many others; and the short-story collections *Hot Tales of Gay Lust 1, 2,* and *3.*

T. HITMAN is the nom-de-porn of a professional writer who once contributed monthly columns, features, and short fiction to *Men, Freshmen,* and *Unzipped* magazines.

RHIDIAN BRENIG JONES is settled back home in Wales after several years abroad. He lives with his husband, Michael, and French bulldogs, Coco and Cosette. He writes before work, when the three best things in his life are still asleep.

KENZIE MATHEWS lives in rural Alaska. Her erotica stories have appeared in *Lesbian Lust, Lesbian Cops, Rumpledsilksheets: Lesbian Fairy Tales, Lesbian Erotica: 2011, Lust in Time: Erotic Romance Throughout the*

Ages, and *Of Devils and Deviants*. One of her dark fantasy stories was included in *The Big Book of Bizarro*.

RICHARD MAY writes gay short stories about how men meet. His work has appeared in his collections *Ginger Snaps: Photos & Stories of Queer Redheads* and *Inhuman Beings*, his Kindle series *Gay All Year*, and numerous literary journals and anthologies. Rick also organizes the Word Week literary festival and an online book club.

M. MCFERREN is a queer, nonbinary nerd native to Texas and now in NYC. They enjoy hollering the love that once dared not speak its name, as well as good whiskey and horror films. They have contributed stories to numerous anthologies, and their first novel is *The Unmentionables*.

RICHARD MICHAELS has been featured in three previous Rob Rosen anthologies: *Best Gay Erotica 2015* and *Best Gay Erotica of the Year, Volumes 1* and *2*. He also had stories in *Special Forces* and the Beautiful Dreamers Press collection *Not Just Another Pretty Face*, as well as in several prominent gay magazines.

LEE MINXTON's erotic writing has appeared in *Clean Sheets*, *Forum (UK)*, the *Good Vibrations* webzine, the *Blowfish* catalog e-newsletter, and the anthologies *Big Man on Campus*, *Surprise*, and *Naughty Stories from A to Z, Volume 4*. Currently, she is working on an all-male novella.

GREGORY L. NORRIS (gregorylnorris.blogspot.com) writes and lives in the Outer Limits of New Hampshire with his husband, their small pride of rescue cats, and his emerald-eyed muse.

MICHAEL ROBERTS has published in four other Rob Rosen-edited anthologies: *Men of the Manor*, *Best Gay Erotica 2015*, *Best Gay Erotica 2016*, and *Lust in Time*. A dozen stories have appeared in collections from STARbooks Press and Alyson Books, and he has written licentiously for cruisingforsex.com and leading gay magazines.

KARL TAGGART lives in the suburbs east of San Francisco, remaining under the radar as he occasionally writes stories for anthologies. Taggart got his start writing for *Men* and *Freshmen* magazines. He likes horses, motorcycles, and hot men, and is presently contemplating new work featuring all of these.

Unbeknownst to her dissertation committee, **T. R. VERTEN** (Twitter @trepverten) was really a spy in the house of academia. A decade of bone-dry work on Realist representation turned out to be an aesthetic manifesto in disguise. Her erotica writing has appeared in anthologies from Cleis, New Smut Project, Republica, Burning Book, and Ravenous Romance.

ABOUT THE EDITOR

ROB ROSEN (therobrosen.com), award-winning author of the novels *Sparkle: The Queerest Book You'll Ever Love, Divas Las Vegas, Hot Lava, Southern Fried, Queerwolf, Vamp, Queens of the Apocalypse, Creature Comfort, Fate, Midlife Crisis*, and *Fierce*, and editor of the anthologies *Lust in Time, Men of the Manor, Best Gay Erotica 2015, and Best Gay Erotica of the Year, Volumes 1* and 2, has had short stories featured in more than two hundred anthologies.